THE DEATH OF ME

RACHEL LANGLEY

THE DEATH OF ME

In loving memory of my Grandma Anne.
Thank you for sharing my work wherever you went,
from the deserts of Arizona to the rivers of France.

We miss you so much.

CHAPTER 1
(LANEY)

"This one here, 2359, has become defective," I heard a woman say. I could tell she wasn't talking about me.

"Defective?" asked a second woman.

I kept my eyes closed, relaxed, as though I were asleep. I didn't want them to know that I was conscious and could hear every word.

"Defective, no good," a third woman—I assumed 2359—muttered repeatedly in a sing-song way, like a child learning a new word.

"She's lost her senses, and cannot function normally. Obviously," the first woman explained, annoyed. "Perhaps she was never fully-functioning, but hid it well." *Or perhaps y'all made her go crazy.* She ordered 2359 to be silent. There was a loud clap of skin hitting skin, and I realized 2359 had been slapped.

The first woman seemed like she was instructing the other one, as if this was a teaching hospital. But it wasn't a hospital. This wasn't a place where people came to get well. It was the science facility, where they performed experiments on us in order to find a cure for their ancient disease, a disease that some believed was caused by a curse. And to break that curse, I was supposed to marry the Antonian king. At least, that's what we'd been told. I shuddered internally.

I wanted to marry Hollister. *Hollister*. Where was he? We'd been together, finally back together, before the sleeping gas had overtaken us. Before I'd even taken a peek at the room, I'd known in my bones that we'd been separated again. I didn't have to look. I knew he wasn't there. 2359 was there—not him, not 327. I swallowed back my tears as I heard footsteps coming in my direction.

My body tensed up, ready to fight, but my wrists and ankles were bound with thick leather straps. Just before the women had entered the room, I'd regained consciousness and had tried to free myself, but the straps were too tight, burning my skin whenever I struggled against them. Relax. With clenched fists, they'd know I was awake. They were beside my bed now. I could feel their eyes watching me and strained to keep my muscles still and calm my breathing. I wanted to spy. I wanted to hear what they might say if they thought I wasn't listening, to gain any advantage in my current state of helplessness.

"What's her identity?" the second woman asked. Would she use my name, or had I already been assigned a number?

"She's 1," replied her superior, a note of disdain in her voice. I had been numbered, like my parents and Hollister and the rest of the *bodies*.

"But I thought all the bodies receive three or four-digit assignments," the second woman said.

"Because she's the one, Dr. Bassa assigned her the number 1. He thought it was creative." The disdain in her voice showed she clearly did not.

"This one was captured with 327, correct?" the young woman asked. *Hollister.*

"Yes," replied her superior.

"And will they both be removed for their actions?" Removed? Did she mean killed?

"We must wait for Whirl's instructions. Maybe not this one, but most likely 327."

My jaw and fists clenched at the same time, fear expanding in my stomach. *Hollister.* I needed to find him. Again. The women must have seen my reaction. I felt a sharp, hard pinch on the back of my arm, and my eyes flew open, glaring up at the first woman, the older woman. She wore khaki linen pants, a light green blouse and a white lab coat. She must have been one of the scientists, and she was the same woman I'd seen earlier, the one who had pulled the alarm and set the sleeping gas in motion. She glared back at me, such anger in her dark eyes.

"See?" she said to the younger woman beside her. "You must learn to read them. Otherwise, they will think they are more clever than you. She's been awake this whole time."

"She's been awake, she's been awake," sang 2359 from her bed. I turned my head to glance at her.

"Don't look at her," the scientist ordered, grabbing my chin, pressing her nails into my skin, and forcing me to stare at the ceiling. She had a hatred for me that seemed to come from somewhere I couldn't understand. I knew the Antonians didn't see us as human, but as bodies, that we were inferior to them. But there seemed to be something deeper to her actions, something personal.

"Let go of me!" I yelled, tossing my head vigorously back and forth to loosen her grip. The straps on my ankles and wrists severely hindered my movements, minimizing any ability to resist. She could do anything she wanted to me. It was a frightening, vulnerable, powerless thought.

She bent down, her face close to mine, her mouth at my ear. "You're only safe for now because I have orders not to harm you." Safe? This wasn't safe. *For now*. Those were the key words.

The young woman beside her seemed uncomfortable, her eyes averted to the floor. Did she realize what kind of job she'd signed up for? Assuming she'd chosen this. I wasn't sure many in Antonia were given a choice. Cautiously, she asked, "Should I take her blood now?"

"No," I said, but her superior said yes. I hated needles. Leela was the one who liked this kind of stuff, the one who wanted to be a doctor. *Leela*. Where was she? Had she escaped or did they also have her bound in a bed somewhere?

The scientist smiled cruelly at me and stepped back, allowing the younger woman to come forward. I examined her; she was dressed in a green scrub-like uniform, her dark hair pulled back from her face, her eyes intentionally avoiding mine. I glanced down at my arm and then quickly away, not wanting to watch her take my blood. It was the first time I'd noticed there was an IV in my hand. What were they pumping into me?

"Why do you need my blood?" I asked as the needle pricked my skin.

"So we can find out what makes you so *special*," said the scientist.

"There's *nothing* special about me." I rolled my eyes. "You're scientists. You don't really believe in the curse, do you?" She didn't say anything. It seemed like she didn't know for sure what she believed. Neither did I.

From the other side of the room, 2359 began singing, "The curse is real, the curse is real."

The scientist's jaw tightened. She had very little tolerance for 2359's defects. "Hurry up. Let's go," she ordered.

The woman in scrubs gathered her supplies and removed her gloves. Then they left. The door beeping—locking—behind them. I was alone with 2359 who immediately stopped singing and began laughing.

"So you're the one?" she asked. "You're not what they expected." She laughed, happy about it.

The woman appeared to be in her mid-thirties, with fiery red, tightly curled hair and fair skin. In Antonia, I imagined red hair must have been even more rare than blond. Her eyes were sharp, but unhinged, like maybe her words couldn't be trusted, but she smirked perpetually as if she had many secrets, but would only share a few.

"What were they expecting?" I asked.

"One of *them*. Not a *body*," she whispered, looking around to make sure no one overheard her. But there was nobody else around. Unless...perhaps they were observing us through the one-way mirror—the same way Hollister and I had observed Rick being used in the blood-swapping trial.

"Did you see them bring me in here?" I asked. "Did you see them do anything with a young man, my age, tall with blond hair?" Maybe she'd seen where they had taken Hollister. I could only hope he was somewhere nearby.

"A man?" Her eyes grew excited as she smiled. "That would be nice. Men aren't allowed in this area."

"What is this area?" I pressed for more information.

She was quiet for a long moment before her face became scrunched and her palms began rubbing her temples. "I don't know, I don't know, I don't know," she repeated, reverting back to a childish voice.

"It's okay. It's okay," I tried to soothe her.

"Too many questions," she spat at me, her adult voice returning, her face scowling at me.

I felt like I needed her. Even if she was crazy. Or *defective*, as they had called her. She was numbered like the rest of us. We were in the same situation. I apologized, "I'm sorry. I'm just trying to find a way out of here."

She rolled her eyes and firmly stated, "There is no way out." Just then, there came a beep at the door. Somebody was coming. She glanced at the door, then back at me, and she quickly whispered, "Don't trust anyone." Then she began humming the same tune from earlier.

The woman in green scrubs had returned, slipping silently through the door. She went to 2359 first. "Please don't," 2359 begged. "I'll be quiet. I promise. You don't have to." She was being injected with something. She soon stopped resisting, and the room became silent. What had she done? Did they not like her talking to me? Then why did they put us together in the same room?

I expected the woman to leave, but instead she came toward me, a syringe in her hand. I was next. "Please, you don't have to do this," I begged also. "You aren't like the others. I can tell. Please, don't."

She was already inserting the syringe into my IV.

"Don't worry," she said. "I'll take care of you."

Then, like 2359, my eyes grew heavy, and I was out.

CHAPTER 2
(LEELA)

With every step forward, my heart cried, "Go back!" I had left them there—my sister and Hollister. They'd come back for me—even though they shouldn't have—but I'd left them. Why? How? *Whirl's army was coming. They're still coming. We had to leave,* I reasoned with myself. But did we? Had there been no other way? Durham continued to order us onward. *This is life or death,* he kept saying as encouragement. But I wasn't encouraged. This may have been life for me, but death for my sister. And Hollister. And the children. I couldn't erase their faces from my mind.

Whirl's men were bearing down on us. They were quicker than I'd anticipated. But that was my naiveté. They were soldiers after all, even if they had spent the previous evening celebrating their victory with drink. It was morning, and they were ready for the hunt. We kept on at a fast pace, exhausted and sweating. I stayed near Curwen. He was weak, and I was the only one immune to the disease he'd been injected with. Whirl had sentenced him to death. Angry tears kept blurring my vision, and I blinked them away every time.

Where were we going? *To the mountains*, Durham had said. Why? Because I'd be safe there. But Antonia had taught me that safety isn't real. It's an illusion. Anything could happen at any moment. Like the soldiers who had almost caught up to us. An hour earlier we'd been distracted—they'd been arguing about which direction to travel, and I'd been begging to go back and rescue Laney, Hollister, and the children. Two soldiers had almost snuck up on us, but Greer's radio alerted us to their proximity. Then we'd tricked them. Three of us led them on, while Greer, Sheldon, and Mara waited to ambush them as they passed.

When the threat had been eliminated and they returned to us, Greer said quietly to me, "My orders are to keep you safe, but we will not stay with this group for much longer." He glanced around at the rest of them; he only saw traitors.

"There's nowhere else for us to go. You have no other options," I fired back.

"I will," he said more to himself, nodding his head in confidence, his dark skin shining beneath sweat and sunlight.

I shook my head at him and marched on. The sun continued to rise higher in the sky though I only caught brief glimpses of it through the dense canopy. The forest was leading us up the mountains. The purple mountains had been drawing me to them since the moment I'd first observed them from the second-story window in Curwen's house. They'd drawn me further still when I'd admired them, perfectly framed, in the massive floor-to-ceiling window in the grand hall of Gigandet's palace. Was it just that I'd always loved mountains, that I'd grown up with them always in view, or was there something different about these mountains, something waiting for us there?

Mara and Greer didn't share my eager anticipation, both of them more cautious and superstitious from the tales they had heard. Henley had said going to the mountains was strictly forbidden, that it wasn't safe. Mara had heard that the purple flowers there were poisonous. But then I remembered, in that dark dungeon beneath the palace, Mara had whispered about how she would sometimes imagine her parents living free in the mountains, having escaped during the rebellion. Were they free? For her sake, I hoped we'd find them there.

Durham strategically ordered Mara up front with him, knowing she would be tempted to approach Curwen despite warnings to stay away. They only knew that he'd been captured and was now wearing a surgical mask on his face. Surely, they had put it together without us needing to say the words. He was infected. I was the only barrier between the Antonians and the infected one. Periodically, I looked back to check on him. He seemed fatigued and short of breath, but was that because of the hike or were these symptoms of the disease? How quickly would it progress? How did it transfer—by air, by contact? I needed more information, but I couldn't ask questions. We kept our heads up, ears alert, and mouths silent, not willing to risk attracting anymore soldiers.

As though reading my mind, Sheldon switched on his radio to check the location of Whirl's guards. From the distance between us, it sounded like a bunch of static. But he announced loudly, "They've been ordered to pull back, to retreat to the science facility and wait for further instructions." I breathed a sigh of relief, but a small concerned voice wondered what kind of force they would return with. The six of us would be no match for the number of soldiers I'd heard marching on the second floor of the palace, their boot stomps pounding fear into my heart.

But they were gone, for now. Durham heard the news, but didn't stop.

"Can we break now?" I shouted ahead. "Curwen needs a rest."

"No, I don't," he whispered sharply to me.

Coming towards us, Sheldon said, "I'll help support him."

"No!" I protested, stepping between them. "Stay back."

Confusion passed over his face, then defiance, as he tried to push past me to help his brother, but I put my hands on his chest and held him back. "She's right. Stay back," Curwen finally said from behind me. "I'm fine. She's overreacting…and wasting time. Let's go." Cutting his eyes at me, he went around us, giving a large breadth between himself and Sheldon.

"Soon!" Durham called back to us. "You'll know when."

What did he mean? Had he been to the mountains before? He believed it would be safe there. He must have known something. These mountains were like mine back home, old mountains of rolling hills rather than steep slopes. We'd been ascending before I'd even realized since there was a gradual incline as the forest continued. I kept waiting for the trees to taper off, but they didn't. I waited for the purple flowers to appear, but they didn't. But suddenly, like Durham had said, I did know when we could rest. We all did.

About halfway to the top—I guessed it was halfway—the trees began to change, sporadically at first, and then altogether. Instead of a vibrant green, their leaves were a vivid, deep purple. Instead of the russet brown, their trunks and branches were gray. The ground was carpeted with light pink flowers that had fallen from the trees. It was more beautiful than the

Royal Empress trees at the palace—because it was wild and free, and it wasn't cared for by slaves. By my mother.

"We can rest here a while," Durham said. He dropped his backpack at the base of a tree, and gently leaned the rifle against it. The rifle that had been used to kill Anderson. Curwen had pulled the trigger--to save my life. I could have spared him from doing it. I could have shot Anderson myself. I'd had the perfect aim and opportunity. But he had been forced to do it. Or had he wanted to? To avenge Muriel's death? I could read nothing from Curwen's face other than exhaustion.

"After we rest here, then what?" Greer demanded. "What's your plan?"

"We're seeking refuge with the ones who live here," Durham said nonchalantly—the way he explained everything he knew would shock or surprise us. He said everything calm and steady, as if nothing were ever a big deal, never adding extra details. But his words grabbed all of our attention, all eyes on him, waiting for more.

"Who?" Greer asked, becoming frustrated. His eyes narrowed into suspicious slits. "Who lives here? Bodies? How do we find them?"

"We don't find them," Durham said. "They find us."

"You've been here before?" I asked him. None of the others had, at least none acted like they had.

"Only once. Years ago," he said. "But I've never been to their camp. Just to a drop-off location." What had he been dropping off? Did they have people who regularly dropped off supplies?

"So, we're going to wander around until a group of runaway bodies find us?" Greer asked.

If Durham ever became annoyed with Greer, he didn't show it. "We don't have to wander. Just stay put. And, they're not all bodies. Some of them are Antonians, the ones who escaped persecution during the rebellion. My ears perked up. I could see Mara's did too, her dark eyes meeting mine. That was her hope for her birth parents. Was Durham the one who had given her that idea? Did he know if her parents were in the mountains? Could he have reunited Mara with them, but had instead chosen to raise her as his own daughter?

Durham's response didn't leave Greer unfazed. He didn't want to work with bodies or rebels—it went against everything he stood for, all the laws and propriety he'd been taught; it went against the monarchy. But there couldn't be a monarchy without a monarch, and he didn't know if his king still lived. He walked a little further up the mountain, away from us, but still within sight, and planted himself beneath a tree.

The remaining five of us stood in a large circle, Curwen and I on one side, Durham, Sheldon and Mara on the other. In helping my family, what had become of theirs? The four of them examined, analyzed each other. Mara's shaved head, stitches across her scalp. Sheldon's bruised eye, stitches across his cheek. Curwen in a surgical mask, sentenced to death. Whirl had inflicted punishment on them all.

They wanted to know what had happened to Curwen. They eyed him expectantly, waiting for an explanation. They already knew, but they needed to hear the words. He exhaled deeply, the way he usually did when he was about to share something important, but he appeared weak, his hand gripping a low tree branch for support.

"Sit down," I ordered him. Then, turning to the others, I said, "They injected him with the disease. Sheldon, I need the emergency kit from your bag, please." I heard him unzipping it, but it was Durham who brought it to me as I knelt on the ground beside Curwen. I could feel Mara's eyes burning into me; she probably blamed me for everything. After all, he had said that Laney and I would be the death of him. I glanced up for a second to see tears running down Mara's face.

"Do you need anything else?" Sheldon asked, his voice full of concern.

"Y'all need to go farther away, so he can safely remove the mask." I couldn't bear any more of them getting infected. Curwen's forehead was burning up, the mask only making him hotter; he was sweating and shivering at the same time. They hesitated at first, but Durham demanded they join Greer up the hill, and they slowly retreated as I sifted through the emergency kit for some fever reducer. "You too, Durham," I told him.

He shook his head and refused even when Curwen insisted he leave. "He's my son. I'll stay." He remained several feet away.

"I'm sorry I couldn't do better," Curwen apologized, pulling the mask away from his face. "With everything. I should have done better."

"I could have helped. You should have come to me," Durham said. "But quit talking like you're going to die."

Curwen swallowed the pills I'd given him and looked at Durham with sad eyes. "We all know how this goes. Antonians aren't immune. There's no record of any who've survived."

"You're not going to die," Durham insisted firmly.

He sounded so sure. Was he simply in denial? Or did he know something about the disease, about a cure that he hadn't shared? Had he let all of the Antonian people suffer with the disease when he knew a way to cure it? Had he wanted it to spread so that the unrest would continue, so that he could gain more support for his resistance group? I still couldn't be sure what kind of man he was. He had rescued me, but was it only so he could use me for his own political purposes?

"Either way, I need to get back to Gigandet and marry him," I said. "That will break the curse and save you, right?"

"No," Curwen and Durham said simultaneously.

Before I could question them, Sheldon whistled for our attention, pointing where he wanted us to look. There were two figures coming out of the trees toward us. There was a woman, thick and strong, her long dark hair in braids, her skin bronzed. The man beside her had an average build with brown hair and a full beard, but he appeared physically strong as well. It was essential they be strong to live and survive in this remote place. They seemed to be around the same age as Durham, the same age as my own parents.

The man held a rifle in his hands. I glanced over to where Durham had set his gun. It was gone. How had they taken it without notice? We'd been too distracted, too off guard, too unprepared. Durham had been right —we didn't find them; they found us.

CHAPTER 3

(HOLLISTER)

"Hollister," a deep, country voice called.

"Would you stop?" came another man's voice. "He's not awake yet."

"We won't know when he's awake if we don't keep calling him," the first man replied.

I could hear them clearly. I knew who they were—men from my barrack—but they sounded far away. Blinking rapidly, trying to adjust to the complete darkness, I strained to see something. But it was only black, every direction I looked. Beneath me was a metal surface, cold and damp.

"Laney, are you here?" I whispered loudly. The sound echoed. Where was I? Where was she? How long had I been unconscious?

"Hollister!" both men said at the same time. Dale and Etienne. Dale had been a farmer in Georgia, and Etienne, a Canadian who had inherited his great uncle's vineyard in France. They, like me, were suited for working in the Antonian fields, so we'd been assigned to the same barrack.

"Where am I?" I asked. "Is Laney here? Have you seen her?" I tried to mask any panic.

"Laney?" Etienne asked, confused. I'd never told them about her. Whenever Rick would bring her up, I would silence him. Nobody needed to know my weakness. "No, no. They only brought you and lowered you into the pit."

The pit. I could stretch out my arms and touch both sides. The walls were metal too. How deep was it? I stood up. Surely my height would be an advantage. As I reached up, jumping several times, to see if I could find the ledge, I felt only more slippery metal.

"How'd you get here?" Dale asked. "What's happening out there? We ain't seen you in days."

Ignoring his questions, I asked some of my own. "How long have I been here? Where are y'all? You sound far away. And where is this pit?"

"I think we're in the basement of the science building…" Dale said.

"We're locked in a couple of cages," Etienne added. "The pit is in the center of the room. We only get light and glimpses of the room whenever they open the door. Or turn the bright spotlight on…"

"Where are the rest of the men?" I asked.

"Don't know," Dale said. "Rick was here, but they took him. Haven't seen the rest of 'em since the attack."

The attack they had staged without me. It wasn't supposed to be an attack, not at first. It was supposed to be a silent escape. Then, when we were somewhere safe, we would regroup and plan our attack. "Why didn't y'all wait for me?" I demanded.

"I tried to tell them to wait," Etienne said, a hint of apology in his voice.

But Dale was defensive. "For all we knew, you coulda been dead! Where were you?"

How could I explain it to them? I wasn't where I should have been. Leela had secured my freedom and passage home. But I should have been with the men. I had been enjoying comfort and good food while they had carried out the plan I'd created.

My prolonged silence prompted Etienne to repeat the question. "Hollister, where were you?"

"I was home," I said quickly, ashamed of the answer.

"Home?" Etienne spoke so softly, sounding even farther away.

"It's a complicated story, but the king sent me home, back through the lightning."

"Then what the heck are you doing here?" Dale nearly yelled. "Why would you ever come back?"

"It was the right thing to do. I couldn't leave y'all here."

"You're a darn fool," he said. I didn't need to see him to know that Dale was rolling his eyes hard; he wouldn't have thought twice about coming back to help any of us. That was him—honest, selfish, unapologetic. "Well, you're no good to us down in that pit, so you oughta try and get outta there before they come back."

"I don't think there's a way out."

Dale argued, "You're clever. You'll find a way." *I doubt it.* How could I climb slick metal?

"The guards will probably be back soon," Etienne warned.

I was used to hearing their voices in the dark. That's how it was at night in the barracks, unintentionally learning the men by their accents and word choice, their crude speech or lack of it. We had planned to stage our escape before the sun came up, so knowing their voices would have been an advantage as we made our way through the forest. But they'd gone ahead without me. Durham had said very little about the attack; it had been overshadowed by news of Leela still being alive.

"Guys, what happened with the attack?" I asked. "I heard some were killed."

"Yeah, some guards." Dale laughed. But I found no humor in death.

"That wasn't part of the plan," I said.

"So? We had to improvise," Dale countered, unfazed.

"It was almost as though they knew it was going to happen," Etienne explained. "I think one of our men may have told them." That didn't surprise me. Not everyone had been on board with the escape plan; it had been hard to know who to trust. Some of them had been in Antonia so long, they'd grown accustomed to slavery or didn't think there was anything left of their old lives to return to. They didn't have a Laney, or if they had, she'd long since moved on.

Where was Laney? Was she in another pit somewhere? Were they torturing her or performing tests on her? Had Whirl already taken her life? Or, if Gigandet somehow lived and conquered Whirl, would she be forced to marry him? Though that last thought was almost the hardest one to consider, it was the one I preferred. At least she'd be alive and kind-of free. *Just not with me.* Could we do better than that? I wasn't sure anymore.

Interrupting my thoughts, Dale said, "Uh, Hollister, I don't hear you trying to get outta there…"

"Dale, why don't you get out of your cage and then help me out of this pit?" I asked in frustration.

Dale chuckled. "These ain't no rinky-dink, lock-and-key jail cells. These here are thick steel bars only opened electronically by a control panel by the door."

Etienne added, "I could disable the lock mechanism if I had some kind of tool. But we have nothing."

I felt in my pockets. Had they taken it? Surprisingly, no. A poor oversight. I still had the transporter I'd grabbed from Gibson's box. Curwen said it was no good, that it couldn't be used for lightning travel. Maybe it could be used to get us out of here. It was old and metal, and after removing the back cover, I could feel several metal parts inside as well —could Etienne use any of them as tools?

Just then, the door beeped and opened. Some light cascaded in from the hallway, but it was still dark at the bottom of the pit. Two sets of heavy boots strode across the room; I could hear them in unison. Suddenly, a light —the spotlight Etienne had mentioned—shown above the pit, almost blinding me. I shoved the transporter back into my pocket with one hand and shielded my eyes with the other, squinting to see who had arrived. The pit was at least twelve feet deep.

Out of the silence came a screaming, crazed voice. "Where. Is. *She?*" he demanded. Even before I could see his face peering over the edge of the pit, I knew it was Whirl. But who was *she*—Laney or Leela?

"Who?" I asked.

"Don't play dumb." He sneered at me. "How did she escape?"

"I've been in this pit. How would I know?" It was hard not to push his buttons, just to see how crazy he could get, how pinched and ugly his face could become. I should have tread more lightly, had more fear. I should have taken the stories I'd heard about him more seriously. But I could only wonder: Who had escaped—Laney or Leela? Or both?

"Do you *want* to die today?" he threatened.

"Sir, he's supposed to be part of the trial," said a man I could not see, a man who must have been stupider than me. Whirl swung around, disappearing from my sight. There was a loud thud. "I'm sorry, sir," the man whimpered an apology.

"Get up!" Whirl yelled. "And prepare the pit." Prepare the pit? Those three words made my stomach drop. I heard the other man scurry to his feet. Whirl returned to peer over the ledge, walking around the pit, circling me before attack. He repeated, "Do you want to die today?"

I didn't *want* to, but I was willing. I'd told Laney I was willing to die for this cause, for the slaves to be free. But this wasn't the time or place. A quiet death in a pit, in a basement, would do nothing to help them. If I showed him respect, would he spare me for now? Everything within me despised him, and almost choking on the words, swallowing my disgust, I said, "No, sir. I do not want to die. But I can't tell you what I don't know."

He glared down at me for a moment, as if deciding what to do with me, and then his face became very calm before a smile pulled at the edges of his mouth. "Is the pit ready?" he asked the other man.

"Yes, sir," he replied quickly, eager to please, to avoid any more abuse.

Whirl nodded at him. "Then commence."

I was not eager to please him. I tried to show no emotion, no fear, even though I had no idea what was about to happen. First, there was a rumbling sound that caused a slight vibration beneath my feet. Then, from the top of the pit—there must have been small openings I couldn't see—icy cold water began pouring down on me. If they filled it enough, I could swim to the top and get out.

"He's telling you the truth!" I barely heard Etienne protest over the rush of water.

"Oh, I believe him," Whirl said loudly, smiling down at me. He believed me, but continued with the torture—or murder—just for fun. Just then, a cover began to slide across the opening of the pit, to close me in. It was clear like glass, but I was sure it was the hard, unbreakable plastic they'd used in other areas of the facility.

As the water continued to pour over me, my mind flooded with the memory of almost drowning in our pool as a child. My mother had gone inside to do something, and my father was passed out drunk in the lawn chair. The only thing that saved me was our dog barking, alerting my mother that something was wrong.

But there would be no one to save me this time. There was no dog to sound the alarm. There was only a wolf snarling down at me, his icy blue eyes content with his actions. The water was already up to my chest, so frigid my teeth chattered. I began to float in the water as it rose higher, wondering if Whirl would stop it at the last second, if this was his way of instilling fear in me. But I wasn't afraid of him. I was afraid of what would happen if I wasn't there to help the slaves…to help Laney and her family. Her mom was already gone. Who else would die before this was over?

Me, apparently. It would be over for me soon.

Though muffled, I could hear Etienne begging Whirl to turn off the water. He was braver than I'd first thought. Dale certainly wouldn't risk being the next one in the pit by saying anything. I didn't say anything either though. I should have been screaming, begging like Etienne, but I felt no urge to do so. It would be a waste of energy, a futile sound. I wouldn't go out that way, giving Whirl that kind of satisfaction.

Shivering, I kicked my feet slowly and moved my arms to stay above the surface. There were only a couple more feet before the water would be at the top, my air supply gone. Reaching up, my fingertips could touch the plastic cover. When I was a bit closer, I punched it just to see if, by any chance, it was breakable. It wasn't. Whirl laughed loud enough that I could hear him over the roar of water in my ears.

The water was to my chin. It seemed to be rising faster as the seconds ticked away, counting down to the end. My end. I leaned my head back so my face could remain above water. The spotlight was blinding; I couldn't see anything but the light. Just before the water submerged me completely, I took one final deep breath.

CHAPTER 4
(LEELA)

They approached cautiously, but with confidence—he more friendly, she more suspicious. What did they think about Sheldon, Mara, and Greer wearing guard uniforms? It was the same uniform that had once enslaved them, assuming they were *bodies* and not rebel Antonians. Durham hurried to meet them; he wanted to be the first one to make introductions, to paint a picture and manipulate our story. Would he tell them the truth? He had waved for us to come. I tried to help Curwen up, but he refused my arm and stood on his own, replacing the mask over his face. Sheldon, Mara, and Greer were also headed toward them.

Laura and James. Those were their names. "They're going to take us to their camp," Durham explained after introducing all of us.

"We're taking you to our medical station," Laura corrected him. Her accent was not Antonian; she had been a body. She seemed skeptical of us, on guard. "For treatment. Then you can be on your way."

"Treatment?" Mara and I asked simultaneously. Was there a treatment for the disease? Did they have a cure?

"Isn't that what y'all came for?" James asked. His accent was familiar; it sounded like home. "For this one?" he pointed at Curwen who was standing farther away.

"Is there a cure?" I asked with hope.

"No." James shook his head, confused by our reactions. "But it helps alleviate the symptoms and prolongs life. If that's not what you came for, then why did you come?"

Safety, an illusion.

Refuge, a place to rest.

Time, a moment to plan.

Help, a supply of resources.

But Durham intervened before any of us could speak. "That is what we came for. Curwen was injected with the disease less than twelve hours ago. I'd heard that there may be help for him here."

Was that true? If it was, why hadn't he told us that? Durham was so hard to understand, to grasp, to put in a category. Was he good and trustworthy, or was he not? I noticed Laura was scrutinizing me. I did my best to hide my questions and confusion about Durham's character, but my facial expressions usually gave my thoughts away.

Laura's eyes narrowed. "Okay, you and you," she pointed at me and Curwen. "Come with me. James can take the rest of you to our camp."

All at once, the four of them expelled groans and words of protest.

"We will not separate," Durham declared.

"Leela's not going anywhere without me," Greer said, taking a threatening step forward.

James shifted the gun under his arm, not aiming it at anyone, but just reminding us that he had it in his possession. Something told me he was skilled with the weapon. But I also knew Greer would not surrender without a fight. His only duty was to protect me. His duty was his life. That had been Gigandet's last command to him. *Perhaps his final command, if he died.*

Trying to quell the commotion, Sheldon explained, "We've only just been reunited, so you can understand it's difficult for us to be separated again."

"You'll be reunited again soon," Laura assured us. "When we're done at the medical station, we'll meet you at our camp. That's our offer. If it's not good enough, you can all leave, and go back where you came from."

I knew this wouldn't be good enough for Greer. The other three didn't like it, but seemed more willing to accept the offer if it meant Curwen would receive treatment. They loved him; Greer did not. Greer had moved to stand behind me, closer to Curwen than he had dared venture before. I knew I wasn't going anywhere without him. Curwen could have gone alone with Laura, but I wanted to support him and learn about the treatment. Gingerly, I asked Laura, "May Greer please come with us? He's been sworn to protect me."

This seemed to pique her interest. She studied us for a long moment, and then said, "He may come. But all his weapons remain with James."

Greer wanted to protest even this offer, but I shook my head at him, the way he had often shaken his head at me, instructing me on how to interact with Gigandet, when to speak, when to remain silent. These were my people now, non-Antonians, and he decided to listen to me, to follow my queues. He pulled the electric baton and the taser from his belt, and reluctantly handed them to James. "I'll take care of these and make sure you get them back," James told him.

As Curwen and I went to grab our packs, Durham followed us. He spoke softly, so no one else could hear. "Pay close attention to everything. And ask a lot of questions," he instructed. "I want to know as much as possible about this treatment. It may be useful to us."

I was taken aback. I wanted to know about the treatment too, but was that all he cared about? He was treating this like another intel mission, like the one he'd sent Curwen on to find me. Except this time Curwen could be dying. But he didn't appear fazed or bothered by his father's request. It seemed to be the nature of their relationship.

Laura led Curwen, Greer and me toward the west at a gradual incline, on a well-worn path we could have found, if we'd looked for it. James took the others in the opposite direction. I hated to see them—mostly Sheldon —go, but Curwen's medical treatment had to be first priority. If we could delay the progression of the disease, it would give me enough time to get back to the city to marry Gigandet, break the curse, and save his life. Even thinking it felt stupid, to believe in an ancient curse, a folklore passed down for generations. But when Anderson had held my head under the water, when I'd thought I was going to die, that's when I'd realized I did believe. Breaking the curse could save him. But was Gigandet still alive to marry?

The sun was high in the sky. It was midday. The purple-leaved trees offered some shade, and their pink flowers would occasionally float to the ground before me. I focused on them to ignore the burn in my legs. They reminded me of my mother. *I wish I could have saved her.* Curwen was fatigued, and I was exhausted after twenty-four non-stop, death-filled hours, but we kept a good pace trailing behind Laura. Greer brought up the rear.

After what seemed like half an hour, we were at a higher elevation, and Laura announced that we'd reached the medical station. It didn't look like much. There were only a couple large wall tents hidden among the trees. In the center was a fire pit; they had dug a hole in the ground and built a wall of rocks around the edge. An empty pot hung above it, and it had clearly not been used recently because it was full of leaves and debris. How often did they have to use the medical station?

Laura paused before one of the tents, gesturing for Curwen and I to enter, but she stopped Greer, suggesting he remain outside to reduce his chances of contracting the disease. "Also, could you please get a fire started?" she asked him. "I'll need to boil some water." He consented, but looked annoyed, perhaps still upset about his weapons being taken away. But, I had no doubt that he could do a lot of damage without them.

It was dark inside the tent, but Laura quickly tied back a couple of window flaps to let some light in. There was a rustically-built, well-worn cot to the left. She directed Curwen to rest there. He lowered himself gently; I could tell he was afraid he would break the cot and end up on the ground. The fabric seemed like it might give way at any moment as it groaned and creaked beneath his movements. He lay back and closed his eyes. I felt his forehead again, and was grateful to feel that his fever was nearly gone.

A bench lined the back wall, and I took a seat there. Laura lit a lantern in the corner, and then knelt in front of a large wooden box, almost like a travel trunk, except there were no hinges. The lid simply slid off—after she unlocked it. Inside, I glimpsed a variety of medical supplies—more face masks, syringes, bandages, some emergency kits—but Laura intentionally tried to block my view as she rustled around in the far corner. She grabbed what she needed—something small—and immediately returned the lid and padlock.

"How do you have medical supplies?" I asked, curious.

Laura hesitated, but then explained, "We have *friends* who bring us things sometimes. Though they haven't been able to bring us a transporter yet, we're still hoping for that." She laughed bitterly. They could have all gone home by now. I wondered if Curwen had a transporter with him, if we could offer it to them. But he gave me a sharp look; he knew what I was thinking, and his eyes said no, be quiet.

Instead, he asked, "Who are these *friends*?"

She shrugged. "We don't know their names. Or their faces, really. We communicate through notes. We write down our needs; they bring us what they can, when they can."

"Could they be part of the resistance?" I asked Curwen before I could stop myself. He cut his eyes at me, and Laura raised her eyebrows in curiosity. Then her eyes narrowed in suspicion.

"Why has a guard been assigned to protect a body?" Laura asked me, spitting out the word body like it tasted foul.

"I was never a body," I said, also having difficulty using that term. "I might have been if things had been different. It's a long story." And I wasn't sure how much I was supposed to tell her. Could she be trusted? I glanced at Curwen for direction, for any indication of how much we should share with Laura. I could tell he wanted to err on the side of caution, to only tell her what she needed to know. But I needed to know—was it okay to tell this woman that I had the mark? *Not now, not yet*, an internal voice whispered.

"We have time," she said. "You're the only non-Antonian among them. How'd that happen?"

Just be succinct. "My parents were struck and enslaved. Curwen brought my sister and I here to rescue them."

She needed to be told the whole truth. She needed to know that Whirl's army might come to her mountains, to her camp, to her people. But I needed to know more about her. "How long have you been here?" I asked. "Where were you struck from?" Her accent was different—American, but not southern.

"I've been here for almost thirty years. They took me from San Diego."

"You must have been young," Curwen said.

"I was sixteen. I escaped from them on my seventeenth birthday."

"Shouldn't that be illegal?" I asked, looking to Curwen for a response. She'd been just a kid. She'd spent her whole life in this place.

"Yes." Curwen said, disgusted. I was sure we were both remembering the children locked in the science facility, the ones from my hometown, the ones we needed to rescue.

"How did you escape?" I asked her.

She gave me a smirk. "You haven't answered my question. Why is a guard assigned to protect you?"

Curwen and I looked at each other. He wasn't going to answer. He was giving me the freedom to decide what I shared, for once not asking me to pretend anything. But I didn't know what to tell her. The mark on my neck —it was mine. For most of my life, it had meant nothing. For the last two weeks, it'd meant everything to everyone. What would it mean to Laura? Did she know about the curse? Surely, she did, if she was treating the disease.

I started to speak, not sure what would come out of my mouth, when Greer threw open the tent flap. "She's being protected because the king has requested it," he explained. He'd been listening. "She doesn't know why. I don't know why."

"Why would the king care about you?" she asked, more to herself than to us. "I know you're only telling half-truths. But I'll leave the subject alone…for now. Don't expect me to answer your questions though when you can't answer mine. Transparency builds trust."

Greer simply said, "The fire is ready."

"Good. Leela, please get the water going," she instructed. "There is a pot and water supply in the other tent. Leave Curwen to get a little sleep." I glanced at him to see if he was okay with me leaving. He nodded, then turned his head away and closed his eyes. My muscles felt like jello as I stood. We all needed rest and sleep.

Thankfully, there were more benches around the firepit. Once I had the pot filled with water, I sat down again, waiting for it to boil. *A watched pot never boils*, my mother used to say. I'd always argued with her. Of course, they do. Every time. In their own time, whether we have the patience to wait for it—that is the question.

"What are you thinking?" Greer asked, sitting across the fire from me.

"About my mother," I said. "Did you ever ask Gigandet if I could keep her ashes?"

He shook his head. "Never had a moment to discuss it. I'm sorry."

"I put her lock of hair inside the book in my room. I'm sure I'll never see that again now that Whirl has taken over the palace." My exhausted mind was wandering to all kinds of places, to both meaningful and meaningless things.

Laura had left to get something, but just then she walked back into the clearing. "What did you say?" she demanded.

"When?"

"Just now. About Whirl."

Greer shot me a warning glance, but I ignored him. "Whirl attacked last night," I told her. "We barely escaped with our lives."

"And Gigandet?" she asked.

Hesitantly, I admitted, "We don't know…"

But Greer quickly added, "He's fine…hiding out somewhere, waiting for the right moment."

Did he really believe that? Or was he still trying to convince himself that his sovereign was not dead? We had been in the same place. We'd heard the guns fire, seen the bullets fly, watched the blood stain white uniforms as it poured from fatal wounds. Gigandet himself had been hit in the last moments before he'd ordered us to go on without him. How could he have gotten away?

"You must tell me everything," Laura said, eager and concerned. What did it matter to her, if she lived in a secluded camp on this mountain? What did she know of Whirl? Did she fear him as I did?

"No, we mustn't," Greer spoke firmly.

"What happens down there affects us too," she pointed out. "If you're seeking refuge with us, we deserve information. And we will have it."

"And what happens up here affects us too, apparently," Greer argued, glaring at her. "You've got a treatment for this disease. It could help people *down there*, but you're just letting them die."

"It doesn't cure them!" she nearly yelled.

"But what is it?" I asked her. "Please tell us so we can help them." I could marry Gigandet—that would help them. One minute I doubted he was still alive; the next I couldn't help but hope.

Once again, Laura wouldn't tell us anything unless we told her what we knew. Transparency builds trust. It was a fair trade, but I didn't want to make any decisions until the group talked about what was best. Had the others reached the base camp yet? Were they being welcomed? What if they had walked into a bad situation? We wouldn't know until we arrived ourselves. Hopefully, it wouldn't be long, as soon as Curwen was able to move.

While we were busy staring each other down, the water began to boil over. Laura marched past me, grabbed the ladle, and spooned some of the hot liquid into a cup. Then she disappeared into Curwen's tent. Greer rose to his feet and snuck up on the side of the tent to peer through the open window flap. I wanted to sit still, but followed his example despite how hard it was to stand and walk. Laura was using the bench as a table. She opened a small tube—what she must have grabbed from the wooden box earlier— and emptied its contents into the hot water. Then she crushed something else—the thing she must have gone into the woods to get—and added it to the concoction.

She tapped Curwen on the shoulder until he roused. She didn't seem to want to get close to him even though she was immune to the sickness, so I went around and entered the tent. "Here," I said, reaching to take the cup from her. "I'll help him." She paused, and then handed it to me and left us.

"I don't need any help," Curwen said, sitting up, attempting to appear stronger than he felt.

"Well then, here, drink this." I gave him the cup, but his hands were shaking again. The fever was returning. I put my hands over his to keep the drink from spilling and guided it to his lips.

He nearly gagged. "What is in this?"

"I have no idea. She wouldn't tell us."

"We've got to find out." He was determined. "It's what Durham wanted."

"Forget what Durham wanted," I said, anger in my voice. "We're not here on his mission."

"My entire life has been about his mission. It's hard not to think about following his orders."

"About that…" I began. "Your orders were to find the one with the mark. For Durham and Gigandet. When you found me, what were your orders then? Who were you going to turn me into?"

"I couldn't…" he said. "I wanted to keep you out of it. Pretend I'd never found you."

"I know. But what were you supposed to do?"

His head hung in shame as he continued to choke down the liquid. "I don't know. I was supposed to report to them once I found you. Then they would tell me what to do."

"Who would you have obeyed?"

His almost-black eyes met mine. "I honestly don't know. Maybe neither."

He seemed at the end of himself, so I decided to stop questioning him. He had nothing else to offer just then. He had to become well again. I could make him well again.

"She says this is only a treatment—not a cure," I said what he already knew. "So as soon as we're able, I need to go back to the city. I need to see if Gigandet is alive, and I need to marry him so you can be healed." My jaw was set with determination, ready to argue if he wanted.

But instead, his face twisted in confusion. "What do you mean, Leela? You're not the one who has to marry Gigandet. Didn't Laney tell you? It's her, not you."

No. She didn't. I stared into his dark eyes in stunned silence. Laney had given me a rundown of everything that had happened since we'd been separated. But she hadn't told me that—the most important part. Every moment, every word passed through my head as I examined them. And then something else clicked. As I'd bargained for my life with Anderson, I'd told him that he needed me to break the curse. I could still feel his hot breath and cold voice in my ear as he said, "They don't need you."

I hadn't understood what his words meant.

But now it made sense.

They needed her.

And they had her.

CHAPTER 5
(LANEY)

I woke in a crowded place full of hushed voices and crying babies. It was a large space filled with rows and rows of beds. The far wall, a gray concrete cinder block wall, was lined with cots they must have brought in when they'd run out of beds. I was surrounded by women and children of all different ages. Some of them were hooked up to oxygen masks. Others of them were trying to comfort and quiet the children. Without needing to ask, I knew where I was. There were bold black letters across the double doors on both sides. They read: QUARANTINE. I'd been placed among the sick—but why? There was no longer an IV in my hand, and I wasn't restrained. As I raised my arm to examine my wrists where the leather straps had rubbed them raw, I noticed writing on my palm. Scrawled in black ink, it said: *You'll be safe here. I'll be back.*

Had the young woman from the science facility written it? Her last words to me had been that she would take care of me. It had sounded more like a threat, like in the movies when taking care of someone meant getting rid of them, killing them. But was she really trying to help me? Here I was, being hidden in plain sight. Could I be safe here? Was the quarantine area also in the science facility?

"Excuse me," I said to the old woman in the bed beside mine. She turned her head slightly to look at me. She was receiving oxygen in her nostrils. I asked her, "Where are we?"

Her face looked confused and annoyed as she raised a finger to point at the doors, at the word quarantine.

"I know that," I said. "But where is quarantine? What building are we in?" I didn't care if I sounded stupid. I needed to know where I was, how close or far I was from the science facility, from Hollister.

"The hospital," she mumbled, her voice weak and hoarse. The more I looked at her, the more familiar she seemed, like I had seen her before.

"Have we met before?" I asked her. She struggled to turn and look at me, so I placed my bare feet on the cold concrete floor and took a couple of steps toward her. Her eyes widened when she saw me fully, and then she smiled. It was her smile I remembered.

"State records office," she said softly. I smiled and nodded.

She had sat down beside me in the lobby of the records office when I'd gone there with Curwen to find out the location of Hollister and my parents, where they had been assigned to work. That had been only a few days ago, but she appeared to have deteriorated quickly; the sickness had brought her down fast. She reached for me, but had no strength to lift her arm, so I grabbed her hand and held it firmly. Her skin was smooth and soft like rose petals, like Muriel's had been. A sob caught in my throat as the memory of Muriel's death flashed through my mind—her murder— her body, the blood, Curwen's anguished cry.

The woman before me, her eyes glazed over with unshed tears, studied my face. She asked, "What's your name?"

"Laney. And yours?"

"Ora." Her eyes narrowed. "You're not sick, are you?"

Maybe I should have lied, but instead I shook my head.

"You need to get back in bed," came a stern voice from behind me. I turned to see a woman wearing scrubs, her hair in a tight bun, a clipboard in her hand. But she was different—she didn't wear a face mask; she wore a shock collar around her neck. She was a *body*, a slave. They were using her as a nurse to administer care to the patients because there was no risk of her contracting the disease. It was both brilliant and tragic at the same time.

"She's not sick," Ora told her, pointing at me. "She shouldn't be here." I glanced at Ora sharply, how quickly she had betrayed my confidence. I had thought there was an unspoken understanding between us. In the state records office, she had said I reminded her of her sister; she'd wondered if we shared some family history. She'd seemed trustworthy. Then she added, "She'll get infected if she stays here." She was looking out for my well-being, not betraying me.

"You're not sick?" the nurse asked, suspicious. "You were admitted an hour ago by a medical professional. Whether you are sick or not, you've now been exposed and must stay here. Please get in your bed, now."

I hesitated, not wanting to obey, to get back in the bed and pretend to be ill. I didn't even know the symptoms of the disease. How could I fake it? Suddenly, there were shouts from the far corner, a woman crying, "Help! He's not breathing! He's not breathing!" She was holding a small child in her arms.

Scanning the room, there were no other nurses or doctors around. The nurse rushed in their direction. I followed closely behind, picking my way through the crowded room, a maze of women, children and beds. Everyone was trying to get a glimpse of the commotion as the nurse pushed her way through, making a path for me.

"Let me see him," the nurse ordered as she approached and tried to take the child from his mother's arms.

But the mother recoiled, turning her body away so that the child was out of reach. "I'll not have a *body* touch my son!" she spit out in disgust. "Where are the doctors?"

"They won't be here for another hour," the nurse replied, her face stoic. She wasn't going to force her care on the child. She was going to let the mother deal with the consequences of her own decisions. But I couldn't stand by idly.

"Give him to me," I insisted, stepping forward. "I know CPR." It was the only thing I knew to do.

Before she could refuse, I wrestled him from her arms. His body was stiff, and as I looked down at his ashen face—his thick, dark eyelashes catching my attention—it was clear he wasn't just not breathing. He was dead. I checked his neck for a pulse, like Leela had taught me. Nothing. I felt his chest for a heartbeat. Nothing.

"How long has he been this way?" I demanded, anger rising in my chest. Had they not been paying attention? Why had he been on the cots when he should have been in one of the hospital beds, hooked up to monitors?

"I don't know," the mother cried defensively. "We were sleeping. You said you could do something. Do something!"

"There's nothing to do," the nurse said, now that she could see him clearly. "He's gone."

"No! He's not!" the mother protested. "You're lying!" She seemed like she might hit the nurse.

I stepped in between them, holding her son out to her. "She's telling the truth," I said softly. "There's nothing that can be done. I'm sorry." My anger dissolved into sadness as she took his little body from me, clutching the fabric of his clothes, wailing a mournful sound. It reminded me of the sounds that had come from deep within my own chest when I'd learned of my mother's death, except there was something more visceral in her cries. I had to walk away as she sunk to her knees, cradling and rocking her baby.

There were tears in all the women's eyes surrounding us. Many of them gripped their children tightly, shielding their faces from the scene transpiring in front of them. They all looked at me as I passed, some with compassion and understanding, others with wariness, wondering if there really was nothing we—I—could have done. These people weren't here to get well; they were here to die, locked in this room, guarded by soldiers, none of whom had moved from their places at the doors. It was inhumane. But how could I expect anything better from a society that enslaved us? Did Gigandet know of the conditions down here? Was this his doing? Would I marry such a man if it meant these people would never experience something like this again, if it meant they would stop dying from this sickness?

Hollister. Any thought of marrying Gigandet brought him to mind. I had to get out of there. I had to find him and Leela. I sat back down on the hospital bed assigned to me—one that should have been given to the little boy—and began to analyze the space more closely. Ora had fallen asleep, though how she had slept through the commotion and the woman's continued crying, I did not know. There was a set of double doors on the right and on the left. Both were guarded by two female guards who wore face masks to protect themselves. It seemed like they were now aware of my every move, because even though they had not budged to help the child in any way, they had watched me deliberately do so.

In the far corner, a few women surrounded the mother, attempting to comfort her. But I knew she would receive no comfort from them. They could only offer their presence, and that would have to be enough. The nurse had retreated to the opposite corner and picked up a red telephone, perhaps to report the boy's death. How many deaths had occurred so far? Curwen had never given many details. Maybe he didn't know. There were only women and young children here. I assumed they had a separate section for the men—was it nearby? Could the same woman who'd brought me here have brought Hollister there? *No. Why would they care about keeping him safe?* What had happened to Leela? Had they captured her too? I needed to get out of there, to figure out a new plan.

The nurse had said the doctors would arrive in an hour. Maybe I could sneak out then, if there was enough activity to distract the guards. Suddenly, the nurse was headed in my direction, her eyes locked with mine for a split second before she looked down at a clipboard. She stepped between my bed and Ora's, her back to me as she checked Ora's vital signs. The curtain between our beds was partially closed so that I could not see the old woman from my position. After a couple of minutes, the nurse closed the curtain completely, shutting Ora off from everyone. Then she turned to me.

"Just let me pretend to examine you," she spoke softly, reaching for my arm.

"What do you mean?" I asked, mimicking her volume.

"You're not Antonian," she said. "And you're not sick."

"How do you know?" I asked.

"Because these people do not call it CPR," she explained. "You should be a body. How are you free?"

I nearly laughed. "I'm not free. I was captured and brought here by someone from the science facility."

Her eyes went wide. "You've met the scientists?"

"Maybe one or two of them." I shrugged. "They don't exactly introduce themselves."

"You're a body like me, but you touched her son." She had a satisfied look on her face.

"And you didn't," I accused. "You were just going to let him die."

"He did die. He would have died no matter what. The disease had progressed more than when he was initially assessed." Her eyes were blank. How long had she been here? How much death had she seen that she'd grown cold and accustomed to it? When she saw the shock on my face, she explained, "I was a doctor, a surgeon, before they struck me. Now, they've stuck me down here in this basement to care for dying people, people I can't heal, people who don't want me to touch them. And if they don't want me to touch them, I won't."

"Why aren't the Antonian doctors doing more? Why didn't they come?" I demanded.

"Besides the fact that they fear getting sick, they've also been ordered not to."

My eyes narrowed. "By who?"

"Who do you think?" she asked. "The man who's taken over the government. He secretly took over the hospital months ago. He wants a higher death toll; it makes Gigandet look worse and him look better."

It seemed like Whirl had weaseled himself into every area of Antonian society. He had gained access and power with the army, the scientists, the hospital…and who else?

"Can you help me get out of here?" I asked her, desperately pleading. She didn't answer for a long moment as if she were deciding whether she'd risk it or already planning a way to make it happen.

"You'll get to be free, while I'm stuck in this shock collar," she said. She didn't sound resentful, but sad. "I've heard that if you can get to the mountains, there are bodies who can help you. It won't be easy though."

"Bodies in the mountains?" I asked.

"Yes. Ones who escaped before you."

"Does that mean you're going to help me escape?" I asked, feeling hopeful. One of the guards coughed loudly and abruptly through her face mask and cut her eyes at us. She must not have liked the nurse spending so much time with one patient, especially one who didn't appear ill. "What is your name?" I whispered.

"I'm 567," she said, wrapping a blood pressure cuff around my arm. "I have been for five years. Before that, I was Natalie or Dr. Stark. I'll tell you the plan, but don't show any emotion or draw attention to us." She waited for me to agree before continuing. "The woman in the bed next to you has died."

I struggled to hide my surprise. "You mean Ora?"

"If that was her name, then yes. I will report it to the morgue. They will come to pick up her body as well as the little boy. You can hide under Ora's transport cart. When I take them to get the boy, you climb onto the bottom shelf of the cart. The sheet should cover you. I'll time it so that the guards will be changing shifts."

It sounded like a big risk, but my only option. Unless I wanted to stay until the woman in the green scrubs returned for me. The writing on my palm was beginning to fade. *I'll be back*, she'd written. Was it supposed to be a comfort or a threat? I wouldn't wait to find out. Before Natalie could leave, I grabbed her hand, and promised, "You'll be free soon too." She simply rolled her eyes in doubt and closed my curtain so that I could see nothing.

About half an hour later, she passed by and I heard her say, "Five minutes."

Then everything went according to plan. Two men arrived with transport carts. They transferred Ora to one of them, and then Natalie led them away to get the boy. I waited thirty seconds, listening first and then peeking between the curtains to see. The mother had begun wailing again, protesting and pleading for them not to take her son from her. I hated that she was experiencing such pain, but the noise and the distraction worked for my good. Ora's body cart was between our beds. Getting down on the concrete floor, I then crawled onto the cart's cold metal surface and lay flat, feeling confined in close quarters with the dead woman only inches above me. The white sheet hung almost to the floor on all sides, concealing me perfectly. All I could do was lay still, taking deep breaths and listening to the pounding of my own heart in my ears. This cart was not meant to carry the living, but the dead.

After what seemed like forever, the two men and Natalie were standing nearby, discussing the situation. Though their voices were muffled at times because I assumed they were wearing face masks, I gathered that the mother had put up a good fight, and they decided to come back later for the boy. It was against protocol, but neither of the men felt right taking the child away yet. "Okay," Natalie agreed. "Well, please take this one, so we can free up a bed."

And with that, we began to move, slowly at first as though they didn't realize how much power to put behind it—probably because Ora weighed nothing, and they didn't know they had two bodies on board. They paused when we made it to the exit door. I heard the familiar beep of an access card being scanned. Then the door clicked open, and we passed through, but then stopped again as the door shut behind us. Then there was an overhead voice, "Sterilization process will begin now."

Natalie hadn't mentioned this part. Suddenly gusts of air were blowing everywhere, the sheet rising and falling, my fear rising with it that they might see me. But they weren't paying attention. Again, after what seemed like forever, the voice announced that sterilization was complete, and it sounded like the outer doors opened. We were moving again.

"Did you hear that *body*?" one of the men said. "Acting like she has authority over us."

"I know," the other one agreed. "They need to stop assigning them to positions in the city. Let them stay outside."

My fists and jaw were clenched. Another door was opening. I could tell we had left the corridor and entered a dimly lit room. Then another door opened, and the cart was rolled into what seemed to be an even smaller room. It was cold and dark, only the light from the previous room cast a glow.

One of the men said, "Did you see news about the royal wedding?"

"Yeah," the other replied. "We should head over there after our shift."

Royal wedding? What did they mean? Had Leela been captured too? Was she still being forced to marry Gigandet? My heart pounded in my chest. Then the men shut the door. I was alone. With Ora. How many other bodies were in the room? I remained a minute, listening as the men left the other room, waiting for silence. When all I could hear was my own breathing, I slid out as quietly as possible, almost tumbling to the floor.

"Who's there?" came a female voice on my right. I froze in place, but my eyes glanced in that direction and could make out the faint silhouette of someone crouched in the corner. She turned a flashlight on and shone it in my face. Then she gasped. "Leela? What are you doing here?" she asked. "I thought you were dead!" Her voice cracked like she might cry.

She thought I was Leela. She didn't know that Leela was no longer blond, that we looked different for the first time in our lives. Should I pretend to be my twin? My brain scanned through all the details Leela had shared about her time at the palace. She'd only mentioned two women— which one was this? One had gone into the grand hall, determined to be with Gigandet, and possibly met her death. The other had disappeared and been nowhere in sight. I'd take my bets on the second one. "Are you Henley?" I asked.

"Yes, I am," she said as she stood up and came closer. She was wearing a mask over her mouth and nose. We were face-to-face; the light shining in from the small window in the door illuminated her features. She examined me for a long moment, then said, "But you're not Leela."

"How could you tell so easily, in the dark?" I asked. It had often taken people years to tell us apart.

"Because you're looking at me as if for the first time. And Leela would have had a different reaction to seeing me here, especially after what happened in the grand hall," she said.

"Yes. She said you disappeared before the wedding ceremony. Weren't you supposed to stay with her at all times?" I accused. "She wasn't sure if you were dead."

"Where's Leela now?" she asked. "It's Laney, right? Why are you here?"

"I don't know where she is. We got separated in the science facility."

Her eyes grew wide. "What were you doing there?"

"Trying to save some people. Why did you leave the grand hall?" I demanded.

"It almost sounds like you wanted me to stay there and get shot." She glared at me. "Your sister didn't need me. I went to Elodie's house to comfort her while Gigandet married another woman."

I hesitated for a moment. "But Elodie wasn't at home…"

"How do you know that? Do you know where she is? I've been searching for her. That's why I came to the morgue, thinking her body might be here…I snuck to the palace after the massacre and saw them clearing away bodies. Hers wasn't among them."

"Was Gigandet's?" I asked. Was he alive? Could I still marry him to break the curse, to help the sick heal? She shook her head. "Elodie went to Gigandet in the grand hall," I explained. "If she's not here, then Whirl probably has her."

47

Her face fell. "I assumed as much. I found a note in her house instructing her to go to the palace kitchen. It was signed with a 'D.' Do you know who that is?"

Leela had presumed it was Durham, but we'd never had a chance to ask him. For a moment, I debated whether to tell her, but then said, "It could be Durham—a man who has been helping us." I guess you could call it help, even if it was just for his own agenda.

"*Helping*?" she asked. "He led Elodie into a death trap."

"From what Leela told me, Elodie made her own choice," I countered, not that I really cared what kind she thought of Durham.

She shook her head. Then, she was silent for a moment before saying, "I wonder what that man meant when he talked about the royal wedding." *Did you hear the news about the royal wedding*? That's what one of the transport men had said.

"I think we need to get out of here to find out." I felt ready for a fight, though I hadn't had nearly enough sleep.

"*You* can't go out there," she said. "They'll recognize you immediately."

I shook my head. "I did not just break out of quarantine where people are dying to stay here with more dead bodies. I have to get back to Hollister, and figure out where Leela is so we can get to her too. Do you know the tunnels well? If we can get outside the city, I can get us back to the science facility."

"I know them well enough. But I'm not leaving the city until we find Elodie."

"Hollister may not have much time…" I argued.

"I don't know, or care, who Hollister is. Elodie may not have much time either." She wouldn't budge, and I didn't think I could make much progress by myself.

We had no idea what was happening outside of the hospital basement. The living quarters had been sealed off the previous night. Were the people still under lockdown? What had they awoken to discover? Did they know Whirl had taken over the government? Something had to have been communicated to them—but what?

Henley shined the flashlight up and down my body. "Well, you can't go anywhere dressed like that." For the first time I actually took notice of my clothing—a pair of gray pants with a gray shirt, like scrubs. "They'll immediately know you're a hospital patient." She went to the corner and came back with a small bag. Rummaging around in it, the flashlight in one hand, she pulled out some clothes and gave them to me. But I caught a glimpse of what looked like a phone in the side pocket.

"You have a phone?" I demanded, gripping and turning the bag to get a closer look. "Why haven't you called anyone for help?"

She glared at me for a moment. "Because the only people I could call are either captured or dead."

She must not have known many people, staying secluded behind the palace walls. But I knew at least one person who could help. "We need to call Phaedra," I said.

"The woman from the bakery?" she asked, annoyed and doubtful.

I insisted, grabbing the phone. "She can help us!"

She ripped the phone back and turned her back to me, pressing some numbers. She called an operator and requested The Flour Shop Bakery, and then thrust the phone at me.

"Flour Shop," a voice said.

"Is Phaedra there?" I asked. "It's important that I speak with her."

Suddenly I heard Phaedra's voice. "Is this Laney?"

"Yes. Can you help us?"

"I did help you. I sent someone who brought you to a safe zone. And you left it," she accused, somewhat angry.

The woman who'd brought me to the quarantine area had been part of their group. "She didn't explain herself," I said in defense. But if she could get inside the science facility… "Can you send someone to help Hollister?"

"I'm working on that now. What do you need from me? You said *us*. Who's us?" she asked.

My heart was overwhelmed with relief that Hollister was receiving help, that he might be okay too. Before I could answer her, Henley grabbed the phone from me. Their conversation was so brief, I missed all of it as I thought about Hollister's safety. Henley hung up the phone and said, "She's sending someone to us."

CHAPTER 6
(HOLLISTER)

They had turned out the light, and I could see nothing but black again.

Just when I believed it was my end, that I was going to exhale my final breath, the water began to recede. It must have been on a timer. It was a gamble. If the prisoner could hold his breath long enough, he'd live. If not, they'd have to dispose of a body. My face flat at the surface, I gasped for a new breath as soon as there was air. The water drained much slower than it had rushed into the pit. I moved my arms to keep my head above water, and it seemed like twenty minutes until the water had decreased enough my feet could touch the bottom, and I could stand.

When the water was just around my ankles, Etienne asked, in his faraway voice, "Hollister, are you alive?"

My head pounded, and my teeth chattered. I clenched my jaw to no avail. "Yes," I replied as loudly as I could.

"Oh, good! Good," he said. "Why didn't you just answer his questions?"

Was Etienne deaf? I *had* answered his questions.

Too wet, cold and exhausted to bother with a response, I sat down and propped against the metal side. My eyes wouldn't stay open. I began to drift into a fitful sleep, my head jerking every so often, my body shivering. Antonia had taught me what it truly meant to be tired and weak; nothing in my previous life could compare. The first time I'd been in the science facility—so they could run tests and take samples from me—they had taken so much of my blood I had been certain they were draining me to death. Draining? Drowning? Gunshot wound? How would I die? Which of us would live? Dale, of course. He cared more about his own survival than anyone I'd ever met. He'd make sure it happened.

Sometime later, in the middle of dozing off, something tickled my face. I brushed it away with the back of my hand. Then it was back, brushing against my cheek.

"Hey, you. Wake up," I heard a faint voice saying. "Wake up, Hollister."

There was light again. I blinked my eyes open, focusing on the thing that was touching my face, trying to make sense of what it was as it swung slowly back and forth. *A rope.* Weakly wrapping my fingers around it, I leaned my head back to look up. A face was peering over the edge of the pit, staring down at me expectantly. "Grab it, make sure it's secure, and I'll pull you out," the man said.

"Who are you?" I asked.

"Why does that matter?" I heard Dale say in the background. "He's helping you out. Ask questions later."

"Phaedra sent me," the stranger said.

Phaedra, the woman I'd met just hours ago. She hadn't known me, but she'd hugged me. She'd been delighted to hear that we had news about her sister. She'd wept when we'd told them about Muriel's death. Where was Durham that Phaedra was now calling the shots? Had something happened to him and the rest of the group?

"And Laney?" I asked. Had Phaedra sent someone for Laney too? If I knew Laney was okay, I could be free to focus on helping the others.

"Last I heard, she's fine," the man said.

"Is she here in the science facility?" I asked.

"No, she was transported out this morning. Although, I'm not sure it's much safer outside."

"What do you mean?" I demanded. What was happening out there?

"Look," the man said, annoyed, "we don't have much time. We need to go now. Would you grab the rope, please?"

I stood slowly, desiring to have a sense of urgency, but my flesh was weak, my body worn. I took a deep breath to muster as much strength as possible and wrapped the rope around my arm, gripping it tightly with both hands. I tugged to let him know I was ready. Phaedra knew my size; hopefully she'd sent someone strong enough to lift me. My wet clothes weighed me down even more. As he pulled, raising me a few feet from the ground, I attempted to use my feet to climb the wall, but they slipped, the surface too slick for any traction.

Midway, he stopped pulling, like he was out of energy or something. I heard him take a deep breath and ask, "Can you help?" He wasn't talking to me. Dale mumbled something in response, and then a second later, I began to rise again. I assumed both of them were working together somehow. They pulled me just enough until my chest and arms were over the edge. Then I dragged myself out of the pit. I lay there on my stomach on the hard concrete floor, taking deep breaths and still fighting to keep my eyes open.

"Are you okay?" the man asked.

I rolled over and stared up at him, examining him closely. He wore one of the black guard uniforms. He had a medium build and medium height with the same dark hair and dark eyes, like most Antonians. "I'm great," I said sarcastically. "What's your name?"

"I'm not allowed to say."

"Why not?" Dale demanded.

"Can't risk any of you revealing my identity. It would jeopardize the cause. The less you know, the less you can tell," he said matter-of-factly. Then, looking down at me, he asked, "Do you have enough energy to walk? I have a change of clothes for you and some food. But we need to leave now."

"Okay," I said, sitting up. "Then help me get these guys out of their cells."

I glanced around at the room that I had earlier only been able to imagine. Etienne and Dale were on opposite walls in separate cells. And Dale had been right—they weren't rinky-dink cages. The bars were thick, strong, unbreakable. The man had tied the rope around one of the bars of Dale's cell, which is how he'd helped pull me out. Most of the rope was piled at his feet.

The man picked up a bag near the door and approached me. "Here are some clothes, something to eat and drink. Hurry and change, so we can get out of here. The cameras in the hallway won't be disabled for much longer."

"Aren't you going to release these men as well?" I asked, gesturing to Etienne and Dale.

He shook his head. "My instructions were only to free *you*."

"I'm not leaving here without them," I said.

Dale slapped the metal bars with the palm of his hand. "Yeah, you ain't leaving me in here."

"I'm sorry," the man apologized. "Even if I wanted to, I don't have authorization for these cells. If I tried to use my keycard, it would be rejected and alert the guards that an attempt had been made."

I pushed him aside and approached Etienne. "You said earlier that you could maybe get them open if you had a tool." I pulled the transporter from my pocket and removed the back plate. "Would any of these metal pieces help?"

He stuck his hands between the bars to grab it from me. "This could work." He turned his back to me and went down on his knees, getting straight to work.

I turned back to the man. "Can you at least tell me what happened to Leela and Durham and the rest of the group? Did anyone get injured...or killed?"

"No," the man said. "They headed into the mountains to get away from the guards."

"Where the escaped slaves live?" I asked.

"*Supposedly* where they live." He seemed to doubt that bodies had ever gotten away, or if they had, that they had survived. "I can't risk being caught on the cameras. I'm leaving now, whether you come or not."

"Not 'til they're free." I stood firm.

"Well, here's the bag. You'll also find a map inside that can lead you out of the facility, if you don't get recaptured first." He stared me down, hoping I'd change my mind. When I said nothing, he sighed and reached for something in his pocket. "Here's an access card. It will open the exit doors."

"Thank you. Thank you for everything," I said, grabbing the card from him and shaking his hand.

Embarrassed by my gratitude, he said, "It was simply the mission."

"Maybe for you, but it's our lives."

As he was closing the door behind him, he said, "I'll contact them and see if they can keep the cameras disabled for another thirty minutes. That's all I can do."

"Great," Dale said. "Why'd you let him leave? He's the only person who can help us leave."

"He couldn't help us."

"More like wouldn't." He rolled his eyes and slapped the metal bars again.

Ignoring him, I turned to the other prisoner. "Etienne, what do you need? How can I help?"

"Change your clothes. Eat something. Look around for some kind of weapons we can use. I know they have that cabinet back there with all kinds of torture devices. Just give me a few more minutes."

How did he know what was in the gray, metal cabinet on the back wall? They'd said Rick had been here. Had he been subjected to the torture while they had witnessed it? I did as Etienne instructed, changing out of the wet clothes into dry ones, my body temperature beginning to return to normal. Thankfully, Phaedra knew what would fit.

Wrapped in a cloth, I found some fresh, still warm bread that was obviously from Phaedra's bakery. I broke off a piece and handed it to Dale. He grunted his gratitude. Etienne was too busy to eat. "You need to go ahead and find some weapons," he repeated. "Someone could come in that door at any moment. You need to be ready to take them down."

I didn't feel strong enough to take anyone down. I chomped on the bread as I walked around the pit, looking down into it to see how deep it really was. I had thought at least twelve feet, but now it appeared more like sixteen. Had anyone ever actually died in there—or had we all just come close?

The cabinet wasn't locked. The door screeched as I opened it. There were several electric batons and stun guns, as well as other basic tools like pliers and saws. I could only imagine what those may have been used for. Grabbing the batons and stun guns, I said, "Jackpot." Just then, there was a sound from behind me, and I spun around to see the bars on Etienne's cell retracting into the floor and ceiling. He'd done it.

"Well, I'll be a monkey's uncle," I heard Dale say. "Hey, where're you going?" he asked when Etienne didn't walk directly to Dale's cell. Etienne ignored him as he headed towards me, or rather towards the cabinet. He wanted to see what was available for himself. Shuffling around in one of the drawers I hadn't yet opened, he pulled out a couple of screwdrivers. He ripped off a piece of bread before sitting on the floor beside Dale's cell.

While he worked, I packed some of the weapons into the bag along with a couple of flashlights, and then studied the map the man had given us. We were on the basement level. He'd drawn a red line leading us down a couple hallways, up some stairs to an exterior exit. We would end up outside. But did I want to end up outside? Not only were my men here somewhere, but we now knew the children were here too. Laney and I had heard the scientist recording his notes. The children were being monitored and observed to determine which of them would be used in their trials and which of them would be placed for adoption with Antonian families. Would those families know that those children weren't from here? I couldn't let it happen. But what was the plan? If I successfully found them and released them, where could I take them? Where would they be safe until I could figure out a way to transport them home? Perhaps it was best to leave them where they were and focus on defeating the threat. *Whirl.*

It was much simpler for Etienne to work from outside the cell, so he had the mechanism disabled quicker this time. Dale was a free man. Part of me doubted if that was a good thing. "Give me one of those batons," Dale demanded as soon as he stepped out of the cell. If I had it in me to fight him, I would have suggested he just take a taser, something with less voltage. I'd never feel right about arming someone with his temperament, all impulse and no self-control. But he reached in the bag and took it. Etienne and I glanced at each other, silently communicating our distaste for Dale. Why'd we have to be stuck with him out of all the men from our group? There were so many better options than him.

"Okay, ready to go?" I asked them both.

Just then, there was a beeping sound as someone slid their access card through the keypad. Someone was coming. Dale was in the perfect position to hide behind the door, the electric baton in hand. Etienne and I hid in dark corners opposite each other. *Please let it be only one person.* It was. A male guard entered, carrying a tray of food. Before the door had completely shut behind him, Dale was on him, sticking him in the side with the baton. From the volume of it, he must have set the voltage as high as it would go because the man convulsed and fell to the ground, stunned, the tray crashing as well, food and liquid scattering across the floor.

Etienne and I both approached to examine the man. He was barely conscious, dazed and unmoving. "What are we going to do with him?" Etienne asked.

"Leave 'im," Dale said. "Let's go."

Etienne shook his head. "If we leave him, he'll alert others."

"Drop 'im in the pit then," Dale said as he bent to grab the man under his arms and started dragging him towards the center of the room, towards the deep hole.

I stepped between him and the pit. "We can't just drop him in. That could seriously injure him."

Dale turned and glared at me like I was stupid. "Do I look like I care?" he asked.

"We'll lower him down with the rope," Etienne suggested. "Like they did with you."

Dale let out a sound that was a cross between a sigh and a groan. "Y'all can do that if you want to waste your time."

They'd done it for me. It was the least I could do. I took hold of the rope, and Etienne helped me tie it around the man's chest underneath his arms. We slid the man's legs over the edge of the pit, his feet dangling. "Wait, wait," Dale said. He walked up to the man and snatched the access card from around his neck. "This might come in handy." He smiled at us like he wanted applause for his quick thinking, but I just gave him a blank stare until he moved away.

"Ready, Etienne?" I asked. He was behind me, holding the rope, as I slid the man's body completely over the edge. Then I stood up and took hold of the rope as well, and we slowly let the man descend into the depths of the cold, damp, dark pit. Knowing what it was like, I didn't want to put him there. But the cells were disabled, and this was faster than trying to get them working again. *He won't be there long*, I told myself. *They'll come and get him soon.* When it was clear he'd reached the bottom, we dropped the remaining rope down with him.

"Hollister," Etienne said. "Where's Dale?"

I glanced around the room. The bag was still there. But the map I'd left on top of it was gone. And so was Dale.

CHAPTER 7
(LANEY)

In previous conversations with Phaedra, it had always seemed like she didn't know much about Durham's business or the actions of the resistance, but she was clearly in command when he was away. Was he just away though? What had happened to the rest of the group when Hollister and I were captured? Had they been captured too? Had they escaped? Were they dead? Maybe Phaedra knew. I should have asked. But I could only focus on what I knew—that Hollister was in the science facility, that the doctor from this morning had said he would most likely be *removed*.

While we waited for whoever Phaedra was sending to our location, Henley stayed in the corner of the small, dark room, as far from the dead bodies as she could to keep from being further exposed to the sickness. After some time, the outer door opened, and we heard two male voices; they sounded the same as the ones who'd brought me there thirty minutes earlier. "Go hide," Henley ordered in a whisper. I went to the opposite corner, crouching down behind a counter.

The door opened, and they roughly, without respect, pushed in another sheet-covered cart, not entering the room themselves. Before they shut the door though, we heard one of them say, "Can you believe he's finally going to marry her after all these years?" The door closed. Their voices trailed off. *After all these years…* They must have been talking about…

"Elodie," Henley whispered, finishing my thought. This time she didn't choke back her tears.

I stood slowly, walked over to the cart that had just arrived, and could tell from the tiny shape beneath the sheet that it was the little boy from that morning, the one who couldn't be saved. With gentleness, I shifted the cart into position beside Ora's body. These two died because Gigandet had never married the right person, the one who could break the curse. Now he was going to marry the wrong person and more people would die, including his bride.

"Gigandet would never marry Elodie," Henley stated with confidence. "He wouldn't put her life at risk. He's supposed to marry Leela."

"No," I said. Then I hesitated to continue, before admitting, "He's supposed to marry me."

"What do you mean?"

I hadn't told anyone in Antonia what Gibson had explained to us—not even Leela. Because I hadn't wanted to believe it, to marry Gigandet. I still didn't want to marry him, but after seeing the dead and the dying, I had begun to better understand Hollister's words—there was something greater than us to fight for. I wasn't completely there yet, willing to give up, to sacrifice a life with him, but I could at least be honest about the situation we found ourselves in.

"Apparently the curse has been misinterpreted," I explained. "It can only be broken by the *match*—that'd be me—of the one who has the mark —Leela."

In the faint light I could see her eyes become confused and then skeptical. "Who told you this?" she asked.

"A man named Gibson. An ex-Antonian living in my dimension."

She seemed doubtful. "That's an interesting theory. But are you willing to risk everything for it? You could die if it's wrong."

"And Leela could die if it's right," I countered.

Just then there was a knock on the door. A figure stood outside, blocking the light from the small window. I crouched in the corner next to Henley as the door slowly creaked open. "Laney?" a male voice said. "Phaedra sent me."

Henley and I glanced at each other before I asked, "What's your name?"

"Jace," he said, still not entering. Jace was the man who had helped Leela escape from the palace during Whirl's attack. She'd mentioned his name only briefly on our walk to the science facility the night before.

"Yes, Henley and I are here," I confirmed, standing and taking a step forward.

He opened the door a little wider. "I'm not coming in; I don't have a face mask. But here." He kicked a bag across the floor. "There's a wig and hat in there for you to wear, as well as a change of clothes."

He stepped away from the door, allowing light to flow through the window again. I grabbed the bag and began shuffling through it. Phaedra must have packed it; it contained everything I needed. The wig was black, shoulder length, and wavy, with a straight bang, which would cover my light eyebrows. "Why do I need a wig?" I asked. "If we're just staying in the tunnels…"

"For extra precaution," Jace said. "Whirl has put Leela's picture out to all the guards. They're looking for both of you."

Henley stood up with her small backpack and slid through the crack in the door. "I'm Henley," I heard her introduce herself as I began changing quickly.

"You're the other one who was supposed to be with Leela's group last night," he replied. "They all feared you were dead."

"What is this we've heard about a royal wedding?" she asked him, not wasting any time.

"Whirl is forcing Gigandet to marry Elodie. It will take place on the palace steps within the next hour and be broadcast to all the civilians, who are still under lockdown." He was much better than Durham or Curwen at giving details. I imagined if one of them had been there, it would have taken twenty questions just to get that small amount of information. My new clothes were on—brown cotton pants and a cream-colored shirt. I pinned my hair up, but then struggled to get the wig situated correctly.

"Where are they keeping Elodie?" Henley demanded.

"In the palace, of course," he said. "Preparing her for the ceremony."

"Take us to her, now," she half ordered, half pleaded.

I opened the door and observed them both in the fluorescent light of the morgue. He was almost six-foot with a medium build and younger than I'd expected. His hair was dark, but shaved close to his scalp, almost as if he'd just graduated from military boot camp. Henley had black braided hair and olive skin, but half of her face was still covered with the mask.

The room looked exactly as I would expect a morgue to look—a few body carts, empty thankfully, and the freezers along the back wall. The floor was a glossy, finished concrete, unlike the rough concrete in the quarantine area—easier to clean. This must have been where Leela had seen my mother. There were black numbers above the freezers. Which one had held my mother's body? Leela hadn't told me that.

"Take us to the palace," Henley repeated, interrupting my thoughts.

"We are not going to the palace," I said. "We're going to Hollister."

"We're going to Elodie," she argued, staring me down.

"Actually," Jace said, "I've been instructed to bring you both to the resistance headquarters."

Henley glared at him and then at me. "You two can go wherever you please. I'm going to the palace."

"You'll be captured or killed," Jace warned her.

I could tell there was some fear in her, as there should have been. She didn't want to go alone. Jace, in his black guard's uniform, was armed with a gun, though I wasn't sure he knew how to use it. Leela had said he hadn't liked the rifle she'd acquired the night before. There was fear in Henley, but also determination.

"*You're* the one who's supposed to marry him!" she nearly spit the words at me. "You can't let her go through with it."

Jace glanced at me suspiciously, clearly confused by her statement.

"*I'm not* going to marry him," I declared. But was I? Would I do it for the sake of many lives? I could feel my wall, my resistance, slowly—very slowly—crumbling. I could still feel the lifeless little boy in my arms, his dead weight causing my heart to care, to beat faster for their people.

"You don't have to. But we must keep Elodie from going through with it. We need to get her out of there," she begged. "Hollister has people helping him. Elodie has no one." I could see the tears were about to spill over the brim of her amber eyes. She was right. Phaedra was sending someone to Hollister; she was working on a plan of escape for him.

My resolve was dissolving. Hollister and Leela would have chosen to help Elodie. "Okay," I agreed. "But if it looks impossible or we get into trouble, we're leaving immediately."

"Those aren't the instructions I received," Jace said. "I saw Elodie last night. She was determined to get to Gigandet despite all the bullets, despite the fact that she was putting the rest of us at risk. She won't come with us."

"We're going to try anyway," Henley said. "She'll listen to me." I didn't argue though I could tell Jace wanted me to. He did not want to go back to the palace, and I couldn't blame him after what Leela had described to me —Whirl's army, the gunshots, the blood, the dead men.

"Let's go and get it over with," I said to him. He glared at me in a way that reminded me of Corey, the way a younger brother looks when he completely disagrees but knows he has no choice, the way Corey looked when we wouldn't let him come to Antonia with us.

Jace's hands came towards me, gripping the wig and straightening it on my head. He grabbed the hat from my hand and put it on me. "I'm not trying to die today," he said without emotion.

"I don't think any of us are," I said. "Any word on the rest of my group? Do you know where my sister is?"

"Durham told Phaedra that if he couldn't return to her, if he didn't get captured or killed, he would take them into the mountains.

"The mountains?" Henley asked, her eyes widening in fear. "They'll die."

Jace rolled his eyes. "No, they won't." He turned away from us and began messing with the dial on his radio. It was mostly static until a voice came through clearly.

"How much longer?" said one man.

"Hair and makeup are running late due to the lockdown," replied a female voice.

"So how much longer?" the first man repeated, annoyed.

"At least half an hour," the female answered.

"Whirl won't like that."

"Then he can end the lockdown," the woman said just before clicking off. She was bold and didn't sound like she respected Whirl. Perhaps he didn't have the loyalty of every guard.

Jace turned back to us. "Okay, that will be our cover. I'm bringing you two to do Elodie's hair and makeup. But we don't have any time to waste. Let's go and get this over with," he said, mimicking my words. He went to the door, opened it, and peered out, looking down the dimly lit hallway in both directions. "It's clear. Come on."

Henley and I, with our bags slung over our shoulders, followed him out and to the right. At the end of the hall there was an exit door. I glanced back over my shoulder and saw a camera in the far corner at the other end of the corridor, but I breathed a sigh of relief when it wasn't pointed in our direction. Jace opened the exit door that led into the underground tunnel system. Lanterns were hung along the stone walls, perhaps every twenty or thirty feet, in both directions.

"I've never seen them lit up," Henley said, somewhat amazed.

"Whirl ordered the guards to light the lanterns," Jace explained. "Makes it easier to find people. . . like us."

"We need to go to the staircase," Henley said to him. "Do you know the way?"

"That's the same way Whirl's army entered the palace," he said. "Yes, I know the way."

He shut the door to the hospital basement. As soon as he did, Henley removed her face mask and took a deep breath. The tunnels weren't so frightening in the light. The night before when we'd been waiting outside the city wall for Leela to emerge from the tunnel, she'd been walking out of a cool, dark abyss, barely visible until she'd gotten close to the opening, to the starry night sky. But with the lanterns lit, it reminded me of a medieval castle.

"Can you both run at a slow and steady pace?" he asked us. "We need to get there before the real hair and makeup team shows up." We agreed, and he took off at an easy speed, more like jogging than running.

The ground was hard-packed dirt beneath my feet. The shoes Phaedra had sent for me—I'd been barefoot before—fit well, were comfortable and good for running. The closer we came—although I really didn't even know how close we were because I didn't know how far it was—but the closer we got, the more we moved toward danger, the more my stomach twisted into knots. Why had I let Henley convince me to go? She could have gone by herself. She knew the tunnels and the palace. She'd known enough to hide from the guards the night before; she could have snuck in to Elodie by herself. Instantly, I felt guilty even thinking those thoughts. *You would want someone to help you*, I heard Leela reason in my mind.

Suddenly another passageway appeared on our right, and we took the turn. "Almost there," Henley said. I'd never been good with direction; I relied on Leela or Hollister for that. But if one turn was all it took, I was certain I could find my way out of there when the time came.

"There will be guards as we approach the entrance. They wouldn't leave it unmanned," Jace said. "So, let me do the talking, keep your head down, but act like you're supposed to be there."

Was I *supposed* to be there? Was I *supposed* to marry Gigandet instead? I knew what he meant—to act like the hair or makeup artist, like my presence had been requested. But even that made me shiver, made me want to run the other way. We had no real supplies in our bags; if they searched them, we'd be found out immediately. We weren't there to make Elodie look pretty, but to help her escape, assuming she wanted to.

I could see them now, little black figures in the distance, two of them. I glanced down at the gun in the holster on Jace's belt, mentally imagining how quickly I could grab it. Leela had said he'd wanted nothing to do with the rifle she'd taken from the dead doctor. When had he been assigned the handgun, and did he keep it loaded? We slowed to a fast walk, not wanting to alarm the guards as we approached. But they ordered us to stop some distance away, drew their guns, and demanded to know our identities.

"I'm Hewlo," Jace said calmly. "I've brought the hair and makeup team to prepare the bride."

"Why did you come through this way?" one of them asked roughly.

"Because the protesting crowds with the lockdown were slowing us down, and I know Whirl is anxious to get on with the show," Jace explained.

"Come closer," the second guard ordered us, putting his gun away, but still keeping his hand on it. Had the real hair and makeup team already arrived? Would they accept our story? He wanted to examine us. We walked closer, but I kept my head down as I'd be instructed, the hat shielding my eyes even more.

But the first guard interrupted. "There's no time to waste. Go on up. And hurry." He stepped aside, and I could see the tall, narrow flight of stairs going up, up, up. The guard seemed to examine my face for a moment. *Look down,* I ordered myself. Jace did as the guard had commanded, leading us quickly up the stairs, sometimes taking them two at a time. I struggled halfway, out of breath, asking him to slow down a bit. He did, but barely. Henley pressed me onward from behind. We had to get to Elodie first.

Finally at the top, there was a large, heavy door with a smooth, metal latch. Jace turned it and pushed the door open, pulling back a curtain draped over it from the inside. I could see the floor was a plush, cherry red carpet, the color carpet that could be found in almost every church I'd ever been to. But this was not a holy place. People had been murdered here. The color did not bring peace, but dread, making me think of the blood that had been spilled the night before. How much more blood would be shed before this was over?

Once the door was shut behind us, Henley took the lead, taking us down the hallway a short distance, then turning left down a main hallway. She stopped in front of two beautifully carved double doors on the right. There was one guard stationed there as well. He almost put a hand on her shoulder to stop her, but she stared him down, daring him to touch her. Jace jumped in to explain. "Hair and makeup team," he said, nodding at the guard like they were old friends. The man stepped back and allowed Henley to open the door. Getting in had been easy. They were desperate to get Elodie prepared for the wedding, desperate not to upset Whirl, so they'd asked no questions. Would getting out be just as easy when we'd be escaping with their bride? Both of them—Elodie and me.

We entered the room, closing the door behind us. The floor was a breathtaking mosaic tile. There was a sitting area and fireplace on the left, a dining table and chairs in the center, and open french doors on the right. I didn't see or hear anyone. "Elodie," Henley called out.

Immediately she appeared in the doorway, in a white wedding gown. It was stained with blood. "Henley!" she said, her voice sweet. "What are you doing here?" She didn't look at me or Jace.

"Are you okay?" Henley cried, running up to her, checking her for injuries.

"Yes," Elodie assured her, stepping back. "This is the dress Leela was wearing. This isn't my blood. I don't know whose it is. . ."

From what Leela had told me about the ceremony from the previous evening, the blood belonged to Elodie's uncle. *Best not to tell her that.*

"Where'd you get the dress?" Jace demanded.

Elodie shrugged. "They brought it to me."

His eyes narrowed. "That means they found the rest area. I'll have to let them know we can't use it anymore," he said more to himself than to us.

Elodie was average height and slender, with honey-colored straight, silky hair. Her hair and makeup appeared to be complete already; she'd been working on it herself, it seemed. As I examined her, she finally turned her eyes on me. "Hi, Laney," she said after a moment. I nearly gasped.

How had she recognized me in disguise and known that I wasn't Leela? *She's highly observant, and it's very annoying,* Leela had told me. "Again, what are you all doing here?" she repeated.

"We're here to get you out," Henley explained, clearly confused by Elodie's response to our arrival.

Elodie shook her head and also shared in the confusion. "Why would I leave?" she asked, taking another step back. "I'm finally going to marry Gigandet."

Why had we risked coming here? This woman didn't want saving. Jace had been right.

"No, you're not!" Henley nearly yelled. "You'll die."

"Shh," Jace cautioned, checking the door to see if the guard had heard.

"Yes, I am," Elodie said firmly, nodding with a soft smile on her face, like a mother trying to convince a child. "It will be as it should always have been."

My first thought was *she's crazy,* but then came *you'd do the same for Hollister.*

"No." Henley was in tears. "Come with us please," she implored. "We can save Gigandet, find a cure, and then you can marry him."

"We don't have time for this," Jace warned.

"*You* can leave," Henley told him.

Just then, the door opened, and the one guard entered. It was his turn to look confused. "Are you ready?" he asked. "It's time to go down."

"Yes," Elodie said, her head held high as she took a step forward.

"No, no!" Henley protested. "This," she pointed at me and then grabbed my wrist, "is the one who's supposed to marry Gigandet! She's the one you're looking for!" The guard's eyes went wide with surprise, then narrowed in suspicion, as he reached for the gun in his belt.

I yanked my arm away and shoved her across the room in fury. Glaring at her, my eyes burned with tears of betrayal. At the same time, Jace knocked the guard unconscious. I hadn't seen it, but the electric baton was still tight in his grip. This time he grabbed my arm. "We have to go now!" he ordered.

Elodie rushed to the hall and looked both ways for us. "I'll take care of things here," she said, throwing a hard look at Henley. "Go to the left. There's a door to the courtyard at the end of that hall. The passcode is 4809628." We didn't hesitate to follow her instructions, running across the red carpet back the way we'd come, except taking a left instead of a right, repeating the passcode over and over. Anger still rose in my chest as we left Henley behind too.

Like Elodie had said, there was a glass door at the end of the hall on the right, unguarded but requiring the passcode she'd given us. It beeped open. It felt like I hadn't seen the sun in days, and the Antonian sun was fierce and high in the sky, but the towering palace cast a shadow and shade upon us as we moved across a balcony of white stones toward a brick staircase. It led down to a pathway that was identical to the one we had walked the night Gigandet had sent us home. Except we were on the opposite side of the palace. A white brick wall was on one side, the palace wall on the other. We could go left, to the rear, to the courtyard. But Jace pulled me to the right, his hand still holding my wrist. We shuffled along, remaining close to the palace wall. Up ahead, I could see a gate, and many moving bodies beyond the gate.

"What's happening?" I asked. "What's the plan?"

He stopped for a moment and looked back at me, thinking. "You can probably pass for my sister with the dark, wavy wig. If anyone asks, you wanted to see the ceremony, so I snuck you in. They're gathering a crowd to watch it. You'll blend in." Would I? I'd not seen myself in a mirror. Was this disguise believable? I would still keep my head down as much as possible.

At the gate, he tried the same passcode, and it beeped unlocked. Again, it seemed too easy. Surely, at any moment we would be found out. We would be captured, taken to prison, perhaps publicly executed. I tried not to imagine a million different scenarios of what could happen. Instead, I focused on my breathing, trying to calm myself before he opened the gate to chaos. "Wait for these two guards to pass, then we need to slip through quickly and blend into the crowd," Jace said. I simply nodded.

Their black-clothed figures passed, and Jace instantly stood, opened the gate a crack and passed through, pulling me through after him. We stood against the white wall beneath the shade of a tree, taking everything in. There were so many people and so much noise; I felt like I was back in the Antonian working quarters with Curwen, my first morning in this dimension, except everything here was all white, like in the living quarters. White pavers formed the wide avenue, trees lining each side. To our right was the entrance to the palace, the terrace decorated and prepared for the wedding ceremony. Facing the terrace was a large crowd of people. It was difficult to read the expressions on their faces. Were they frightened or excited or confused? Did they understand that the government had been usurped? Did they support this new ruler?

From our left, a group of civilians were being led toward us, a few guards bringing up the rear. One of them spotted me, and immediately shouted for me to get in line. I glanced at Jace. "What do I do?" I whispered.

"She's with me, sir," Jace responded after a moment of hesitation.

"No matter, we need more civilians," the guard said. "Get her in line!"

I clenched my fists to keep my hands from trembling. Is this what he wanted me to do? We certainly couldn't fight our way out of it. And we couldn't draw more attention to ourselves. There were guards everywhere, a crowd of perhaps four hundred civilians, as well as cameras. Jace sighed and gave me the slightest nod.

I joined the group and fell into step with the other civilians. Blood was pumping so hard through my veins that I could feel it throbbing in my temples. A lady walking beside me appeared uneasy. "What's happening?" I whispered to her.

She seemed startled to be spoken to, but said, "The royal wedding. They said we'll be the witnesses."

CHAPTER 8
(LEELA)

"Are you sure?" I asked Curwen, sitting on the ground beside his cot.

"Who told you this?" Because Laney certainly hadn't told me I didn't have to marry Gigandet. "Why wouldn't she have told me?"

Curwen shrugged. "She's your sister. You'd know better than me why she would keep it secret. Gibson told us."

"Laney mentioned a Gibson. She said he gave you a transporter so you could get back here. But who is he?" I asked.

"He's Durham's cousin," he said. "More than twenty-five years ago, he was the one who led the resistance. Then he went undercover with the bodies for some mission, and he changed. He became different."

"Slavery will do that to you," I said bitterly, rolling my eyes, thinking of my mother. She'd been different, a person I hadn't recognized who also hadn't recognized me.

Ignoring me, Curwen continued. "Well, he had to leave Antonia so he wouldn't be captured and executed. That's when the resistance went further underground, and Durham took over. Gibson is a strange man though. We found him in North Carolina, living near Phaedra's sister, Haleh."

Phaedra and Haleh, twin sisters who had been separated for more than two decades, living in alternate dimensions, neither knowing anything about the other. Would Laney and I end up that way? At that moment, I felt so much anger and betrayal toward her that I *almost* didn't care. I asked, "Well, how does Gibson know that Laney is the one who's supposed to marry the king? You said he's strange. Maybe he's wrong. . .or lying."

"He had a new interpretation for the curse. He said he learned it from an Ancient One."

At mention of the Ancient One, I thought of Mara and her quest to find the last living Ancient One. She believed he would have a way to cure the disease that didn't require me to marry Gigandet. Well, he did. Laney was the way.

I began, "We met a woman at the black market—"

"You went to the black market?" Curwen interrupted, displeased.

"Yes." Then frowning, I explained, "Gigandet sent all your books there to be sold. I wish I could have bought them back for you. I kept one of them, but it's still at the palace."

He was quiet for a long moment, clearly upset that his collection of books from my dimension had been confiscated and sold. Then, putting it to the back of his mind, he asked, "But why were you at the black market?"

"Mara wanted to find an Ancient One. We met a woman who said he had been captured a few years ago and was probably at the science facility. Did you see him there?" I was hopeful.

Curwen shook his head. "I saw as much as you saw."

We stared into each other's eyes. I was sure we were both remembering the children from my home town who were locked away behind the glass window, sleeping in row after row of bunkbeds. I could have named them all. If Curwen seemed so disgusted by a teenage Laura being struck, I could only imagine how he felt about those children, all under the age of twelve. It was against Antonian law to take minors from our dimension. We had to get back to them.

There was so much we *had* to do. Cure the disease. Rescue the children. Save the men from Hollister's barrack. Defeat Whirl. Free the slaves. Get home to dad, Corey, and Annabelle. My exhausted brain couldn't begin to know where to start. I leaned on the cot, closing my eyes and resting my head on my crossed arms. Curwen's hand rested on my head, his fingers playing with my newly-dyed brown hair for a few minutes until I fell asleep.

I woke to the sound of Laura unlocking the trunk and sliding it open again. She was removing some supplies and tucking them away in her bag. She saw me watching and whispered, "Just bringing some stuff with us, so we won't have to keep returning here daily." How long did she expect we'd be visiting with them? I was anxious to form a plan and head back to the city. The flap to the tent was tied back, and I could see Greer's legs stretched out. He was sitting just outside, leaning against the tent. "He fell asleep too," Laura said.

"What time is it?" I asked. "How long have we been sleeping?" My legs and arms were tingly and cramped from being in one position.

"Around six, I'd say. You've been out for a couple of hours at least. We need to get going soon, unless we want to walk the trails at night," she said.

"Which I don't recommend. I'm sure your group is ready to have you back."

I glanced at Curwen who was still sleeping. "You think he's ready to move?"

"Only one way to find out." She stood and approached the head of the cot. Bending over, she placed her hand on Curwen's forehead. "He feels good." Then she nudged his shoulder to rouse him. At first, he pushed her hand away and turned toward the canvas wall, but she shook him harder until his eyes blinked open.

"What is it?" he asked, his voice groggy.

"How are you feeling?" I asked.

He paused for a moment to assess himself. "Better, I think. I feel tired, but normal."

"You seem normal," Laura said. "Any fever you had is gone. Do you feel strong enough to walk to camp?"

He nodded and sat up. I stood and stepped back so he could have space to put his feet on the ground. "When do we leave?" he asked.

"Let's head out in ten," Laura said as she brushed past me and exited the tent.

"Is there anything to eat?" Curwen asked. Laura hadn't offered anything.

"I have some stuff in my bag," I said. "Let me grab it."

I started to leave the tent when Greer's broad chest blocked my way. He'd woken up too. He was wearing a surgical mask across his nose and mouth.

"Here's your backpack," Greer said, handing it to me. He shot a glance behind him where Laura had gone. "Someone was trying to snoop through it earlier."

We were strangers coming into her territory. I understood. I'd want to know as much about us as possible, especially when we weren't very forthcoming with information. I had done the same thing to Curwen when he had entered my home, searching his bag until I'd found a fake driver's license. Immediately, I had confronted him, believing he'd lied to us. That day felt so long ago, though it had only been a week or so.

"It's okay," Curwen said. "Leela knows all about snooping through bags, right?" He smiled, teasing me.

I rolled my eyes. "That's right, Andrew," I said, using the name from his fake ID. He smirked.

What could Laura have expected to find? The bag contained only the few supplies we'd been able to pack from the underground rest area. *And the map*. I'd also taken the map of the tunnel system beneath the city. I was certain it would be useful to us in some way. But had she found it before Greer caught her spying? I quickly took inventory of all the items in my bag. The map was still there, safe in the zippered side pocket. My sigh of relief alerted both guys to ask me what it was, but, afraid that Laura might be listening, I said nothing, shook my head at them, and began doling out packs of crackers and cookies.

Ten minutes later we hit the trail again, but Laura didn't take us back the same way we'd come. It seemed like we were going around the other side of the mountain. I wasn't sure if that was because it was a quicker route or because she wanted to confuse us, to keep us from ever being able to find our way back to their camp. But I still made mental notes of landmarks along the way, something my father had taught me to always do. The purple-leaved trees thinned out some as we reached higher elevations, but it was still lush with green shrubs and grass. The incline became less steep as well.

When we reached the highest ridge of one of the smaller peaks, Curwen stopped to observe the dark clouds and hazy horizon in the distance, taking a second to stare in the direction of his home. "It must be raining in the city."

I paused beside him. "Antonia crying for the loss of its king, maybe."

"What do you mean *loss*?" Greer demanded from behind us. "He's *not* dead."

"I didn't mean that. I just meant the loss of the monarchy," I explained softly, apologetically.

"Antonia wouldn't be crying about that," Laura said bitterly. "Let's keep going."

Gigandet had been only a kid when Laura had been struck. Did she hold him responsible? What had she meant? Were there more Antonians than I realized who were unhappy with their government? Would they actually welcome the change of power Whirl was bringing? I caught up with her and asked, "Do you think they'd prefer Whirl over Gigandet?"

"I think they'd prefer leaders of their own choosing."

"But would they?" I asked. "*You* would prefer that because you're American. But would *they*?"

She turned her face so that her eyes met mine. "Am I American?" she asked rhetorically. Then she picked up the pace, making it clear she didn't want to talk and the conversation was over. *Was she American*? The question repeated in my head—not searching for an answer, but letting itself sink deeper into my soul as I imagined what it must have been like to be her. *Displacement.* Where did she belong? How did or could she identify herself? What did her family believe had happened to her? Did they think she'd been a runaway teenager? Did they think she was dead? Or did they still have hope she was alive somewhere? She was somewhere they would never imagine. I still had moments of questioning whether this place was real.

Curwen fell into step beside me. I asked, "Curwen, do you think the people want to elect their leaders?"

"That's been the goal of the resistance for as long as I've been alive, to have a more representative government."

"The resistance wants that, but do the majority of the Antonian people? How many of them belong to your group?"

Curwen shrugged. "I don't know. I'm not even sure how I feel about it. To me, Gigandet's done fine since coming to the throne."

"Exactly," Greer said from behind us, the surgical mask muffling his voice a little. "So, why'd you go and betray him?"

"I didn't," Curwen argued, throwing a look back at him.

"Your mission was to find Leela for him," Greer countered. "You found her, and then didn't tell him."

I turned around so fast and stopped him in his path. "Because he was protecting me, trying to allow me to live a normal life," I said firmly, only inches from his face. "Something you care nothing about. Why don't *you* just go back to Antonia? You don't need *me* anyway."

"What is that supposed to mean?" he asked.

"Leela," Curwen said, grabbing my arm. He shook his head slightly, warning me, and then looked toward Laura who was observing the situation. She didn't need to know the truth about me. Not yet, anyway.

I took a breath and then glared at Greer. "Just don't say another critical word to Curwen."

Then I turned and continued on the path, not making eye contact with Laura as I approached, and she didn't say a word to me, but got back in the lead. No, I didn't understand all of Curwen's motives or reasons for doing what he'd done, but I did believe he had wanted to keep me out of the Antonian story. He'd found me, and I think he would have left me alone in that small Tennessee town, never telling us the truth, if he hadn't wanted to get our parents back for us. He knew what it was like to be orphaned, and he hadn't wanted any of us to stay that way, especially Corey and Annabelle. That much I understood. And now he was paying for it with his life, like he'd joked he would. He didn't need to hear Greer's accusations. Tears of frustration blurred my vision, but I blinked them away before anyone could see. *I* couldn't save Curwen. Laney would have to, but she would never marry Gigandet.

"How much farther?" I asked Laura. I just wanted to sleep and be done with the day.

"Another mile," she said.

It was less than a mile. I could hear voices before I saw anyone. But as we approached the final ridge, I could see Sheldon waiting for us at the top, keeping lookout. He stood and walked toward us; we stopped when we reached each other. Laura continued on. "Everything okay?" he asked. It felt like he was taking his time examining my face. Could he tell I'd been crying?

"It's fine," I said, forcing a slight smile. "She gave him a treatment. We rested for a while and then headed here."

Greer was still a ways behind, Curwen had finally caught up to me. He pulled the mask that had been tied around his neck over his nose and mouth, so he wouldn't expose Sheldon. *If that's how the disease is transferred.* We needed to know more. "How are you feeling?" Sheldon asked him. He was concerned for his brother. Worry pulled down the corners of his mouth.

"Exhausted, but otherwise fine," he said. "That treatment really seemed to help."

"We're all tired," I said. "How much longer 'till we can sleep?"

"About half an hour until nightfall. Let's get something to eat first," Sheldon said. Then he stepped between us, sticking one arm under my right arm and one under Curwen's left arm, supporting us the rest of the way up the hill. I began to protest his physical contact with Curwen, but he wouldn't listen, and instead kept dragging us up the mountain. "You've gotta see this place," he said with excitement.

At the top, the view did take my breath away. Their camp was nestled in a small valley between two peaks, close enough to the river that I could see the clear blue of it and hear the rushing water. I'd expected them to have built more permanent, solid dwellings, but there were just tents, some large, some small. I spied a few hammocks swinging beneath the shade of the purple-leaved trees. There was a group washing clothes downriver, and another group fishing upriver. Smoke rose from several campfires, and the smell of something good to eat drifted to us on an intermittent breeze. Laura had waited at the top for us.

"How many people do you have here?" I asked her.

"Just over 250, including the children," Laura said. Children. They had children. I could hear some of them in the distance, laughing and playing with squeals of delight. They'd had successful pregnancies and births. Did they have a doctor in the community? These weren't children who'd been struck—not like the ones from my town at the science facility—they had been born free in these mountains. They were the children of parents from another dimension. When they grew up, where would they feel they belonged? They wouldn't be wanted in Antonia. And would they ever adjust well to life anywhere else?

250. That was more than the population of my home town. Had they just done well multiplying, or did they get new runaways often? Remembering how impossible it had been to help my mother escape— we'd failed, she'd died—I couldn't help wondering how any of them had arrived there without being caught. Laura directed us down the grassy slope towards a couple of tents that were separate from the rest of the community, bordered by dense trees on one side.

When we reached our campsite, Mara came rushing up to me. Before I could say a word, she leaned in and said low, in my ear, "There's an AO here." Then she pulled back to examine the reaction on my face. Could this AO be the answer to everything we needed to know? Did he have another way to cure the disease? If he did, these people would have the cure and not just a treatment. Was he the same AO who'd told Gibson, decades ago, about the alternate curse interpretation, that Laney, not I, was supposed to marry Gigandet? Maybe he'd been wrong.

"Have you spoken with him?" I asked, attempting to disguise the hope in my voice.

"No." She shook her head. "They say he's sick and isn't allowed many visitors. He's the same one the scientists had, the one that girl from the black market told us about, but somehow he escaped and has been with

these people for a while now." She'd called them people, not bodies.
Perhaps there was hope for all the Antonians to see us as people, not slaves,
not less than.

"So, you all are to remain here at this spot," Laura said, annoyed.
"Obviously some of you have been wandering through the camp, but we
don't permit that—not until you've all been introduced and voted on. We'll
try to arrange that in the morning. I'm sure everyone's anxious to know
about you."

"They were," Mara said with an attitude. "That's why I went and
introduced myself."

Laura was unfazed. "You're all welcome to stay if you abide by our
guidelines. Otherwise, you can leave. Now where's Durham?" He and
James were approaching as she asked the question.

Laura needed only to raise her eyebrow at James for him to start
explaining. "I just took him with me to fill their pot with stew." He hung the
pot above our fire pit, the fire already burning. The heat from it felt kind of
nice. The climate here was cooler than in the city, and there was a light
wind that wound its way between the peaks. Durham placed a set of bowls
and spoons on one of the benches that encircled the fire pit.

"Thank you," Sheldon said with a smile. "We appreciate your
hospitality."

James returned a smile and said, "Well, you're quite welcome."

His accent was southern. "Where are you from?" I asked him.

"West Virginia," he said. "What about you?"

"Tennessee."

"Well, welcome to our home away from home."

We all thanked them again. Laura warned us again to remain in our area, and then they left us for the night. We dished up some stew and sat on the benches around the fire as the sun finally went down below the horizon. Curwen sat beside me, trying to maintain his distance from the rest of them. Mara sat across the flames. She kept tossing mean looks my way until I couldn't take it anymore. "Do you have something to say?" I asked her.

"Yeah. This is all your fault," Mara accused. "None of this would have happened if you would have never come here."

"Mara," Sheldon said sharply. "Something was going to happen eventually."

"Yeah, something with our group and the monarchy. Not Whirl infecting Curwen as punishment. He never would have been exiled. He wouldn't have had to sneak back and get captured."

"I would have been brought here either way," I spit back at her. "Because it's what your father wanted." I threw a look at Durham who was remaining silent.

"No, Mara," Curwen spoke up. "Whirl hated me long before Leela entered the story. He's just been looking for a reason to hurt me. I'm surprised he didn't do this sooner."

"Why did he hate you?" I asked. I'd thought I'd detected some tension between them that night in the meadow behind the palace, the night Gigandet struck them all home, and I'd remained behind.

"He felt threatened by my relationship with Gigandet. He knew Gigandet trusted me, but had little regard for him."

"But it wasn't real," I said. "Gigandet trusted you, but it wasn't real."

His face was pained for a split second. "It was real, Leela. My intentions toward Gigandet were never malicious. I did—do—think of him as a friend."

"But…you were just trying to gain information for Durham." I didn't want to argue, but I wanted to understand. How could he claim someone as a friend while intentionally deceiving him?

He sighed, tired, and tired of this conversation. "I knew what I was doing was for his good, for the good of Antonia. It wasn't to harm him."

"The only one who's been harmed here is Curwen," Mara said.

"And my mother and Gigandet and me and Sheldon and you. Perhaps Laney and Hollister. And who knows what happened to Elodie. Or Henley. And how many guards did we see get shot down last night? Curwen is not the only one dying. So many lives have been affected, don't act like yours is the only one." I was glaring at her, out of breath and angry.

She was about to respond when Durham said, "Okay, that's enough." He paused for a moment, then asked, "Leela and Greer, would you please give us a few minutes? We need to have a family meeting."

Greer glanced around at all of them with suspicion. He had remained silent. I hadn't expected him to come to my defense. He'd not spoken a word to me since I'd confronted him earlier. His only concern was to obey Gigandet and keep me alive. He didn't care what my life was like, how I felt, what I thought, as long as I was still living. He set his empty bowl down, then stood and walked away into the trees. I saw his flashlight turn on, the orb bouncing through the underbrush.

I just sat there, stubborn and done with secrets.

Sheldon could tell I wasn't going to move. He said, "I don't mind if Leela stays," and gave a small me close-mouthed smile, the flames illuminating his light green eyes.

Curwen quickly followed with, "I don't either."

Mara scowled. "It's not up to you."

"What is this meeting about?" Curwen asked Durham.

"You," he said.

Curwen nodded, like he'd already known it was about him. "Well, then she can stay."

I looked at Durham, daring him to force the issue. Finally, he sighed and said, "Fine."

Mara simply glared at me. She would probably never be my friend or treat me with lasting kindness. I wanted to stay. I wanted to know what he had to say about Curwen.

"Are we gonna talk about how long I have to live?" Curwen joked.

Mara said, "That's not funny."

"We're going to talk about the fact that you're not going to die," Durham said. What did he mean? What did he have planned?

Curwen looked at him inquisitively. "Do you know something I don't know?"

"You're not Antonian. Your body is already fighting off the disease, which is why you felt horrible earlier, but you'll be fine." Once again Durham said everything without feeling, as if he hadn't just revealed a life-changing secret about Curwen's origins, his identity.

Stunned and speechless, I just sat there, waiting for Curwen's reaction. So many emotions ran across his face.

First, relief. He wasn't going to die.

Second, anger. He'd been deceived.

Third, confusion. Who was he, really?

After a long silence, all he could utter was, "How?"

"Your mother was a body," Durham said. I internally cringed every time he used that word—*body*. Curwen's mother had been enslaved. Like my mother.

"But it's illegal for a pregnant woman to be struck," Curwen protested, clearly upset at the thought of it.

Durham nodded. "They didn't know she was pregnant at the time. It was too early…but rather than send her back, some scientists secretly decided to keep you, to perform experiments on you. They'd never had access to a non-Antonian infant."

"How did I end up with you?" Curwen sounded like Durham now—speaking methodically without emotion, gathering the facts.

"Gibson," Durham explained. "He was undercover as a body then. He heard some guards talking about it and got word to me, so that after your birth, we could smuggle you out. I brought you home with me."

"What happened to my mother?"

"I'm not sure. She may have died in childbirth. I could never find any record of her."

We all sat in stunned silence. From Curwen's tightened jaw, I knew he was angry. And what was Mara thinking? She must have been reevaluating all the thoughts and opinions she had about non-Antonians. And Sheldon, well I knew he would be completely accepting because as he'd said before *people are people no matter where they're from.*

And Durham, he didn't apologize for anything. Not for keeping it a secret for this long. Not for letting all of us believe Curwen was going to die. Not for letting Curwen get a treatment that he clearly didn't need just for the sake of learning more about it. No, he never apologized. He just suggested we all go get some sleep.

And me, well, I didn't know what to say to Curwen about his mother. Before dozing off, all I could think was: he's like me.

CHAPTER 9
(HOLLISTER)

Etienne cracked the door, and we stuck our heads out, looking in both directions down the dimly lit, concrete hallway. Dale was nowhere in sight. He must have run right, reached the end and then turned left—the shorter distance and the direction the map had indicated our exit. Were we going to follow him? Did Etienne want to leave like Dale, or was he still willing to help with the mission? The guard in the pit was beginning to make loud noises, shouting for help. I quickly pulled Etienne back and shut the door, hoping that would block out the sounds from anyone who might be nearby. Perhaps they wouldn't even take notice. Maybe they would think it was just another prisoner being tortured and pay no attention at all.

"What do you want to do?" I asked Etienne. "It's your choice if you want to go with Dale. I know our men and the children from my town are in this facility."

"Do we try to get them now, or leave and come back for them?" he asked. Then he smiled at my astonished face. "You really think I'd go with Dale? I'd rather eat nails. But he has the map."

"I memorized most of it, at least the way out of here," I assured him.

He nodded. "We can explore a little and then decide what to do."

"Here," I said, handing him a black sheet I'd found in the closet. No telling what they might have used it for. "Tear this into smaller pieces. We can cover the cameras with it, so even when they come back on, they'll still be blacked out."

As he ripped the sheet, he cut his eyes toward the pit where the man would not stop yelling. "We should have stuffed some of this in his mouth. Somebody's gonna hear him."

I leaned over the pit. The man glared up at me, his mouth closed for a second. I threatened, "Be quiet or I'm gonna fill this thing with water."

"You don't have the authority to do that," he said defiantly, underestimating us.

I held the access card up so he could see it. I was certain it didn't give me the authority to fill the pit with water since it didn't even have the necessary clearance to unlock the cells. But the guard didn't know what the card allowed. He felt for the card around his neck and realized it was gone, looking up at me with a hint of fear in his eyes. Apparently, his card held more authority than the one in my hand, and Dale had taken it with him-- but the man didn't know that.

"You're not going to get very far," was his last statement before he went silent.

Etienne was ready to go, the bag slung across his shoulder. I breathed deep before we opened the door again, praying I would have enough strength and energy if we came up against a fight. We went to the right. Although we were going to explore a bit, I still wanted us to be near the exit if we needed a quick escape. There were a few other doors down the length of the corridor that looked exactly like the one we'd just come out of, green and metal. There were numbers spray painted above them. Our room of torture had been number five. But we didn't hear any sounds coming from the other rooms, no screaming or shouting, no one coming in or out. At the end of the hallway, I draped a piece of the cloth over the camera.

"What is that?" Etienne asked, his face scrunched in disgust.

I hadn't noticed it at first. I'd never had a good sense of smell. But there was a stench, and it seemed to be coming from behind door number ten, the last door on the left. "Do we really want to find out?" I asked, hesitant to open the door. I already knew what the odor was—blood and decay.

Etienne seemed to know too. "We need to know who," he said softly, his hand on the door handle.

I nodded and slid the card through the slot. It beeped, and he turned the handle and pushed it open slowly. Immediately, we pulled our shirts up over our noses. It was dark inside, so I felt around on the wall for the switch and flipped it. The light cast a yellow glow across the room. There wasn't a pit here. A few cells like the ones Etienne and Dale had been in lined the wall on the right. Along the back wall lay the bodies. Four of them.

Standing just inside the doorway, without approaching them, I already knew who one of them was by the bright orange-red color of his hair. Calum, a young man from Scotland who'd just wanted to go home so he could care for his grandparents. Blood stains were splattered against the gray cinder block wall behind them. Etienne walked closer, his curiosity, his need to know, overpowering the awful smell. How long had they been dead? Had they been killed immediately after capture or sometime later when perhaps they didn't give the guards the answers they had wanted? Or, had they just been used for target practice by men who'd never used guns before?

Etienne had been to war. He'd seen men die and come upon dead bodies. Now it was my turn. I walked closer. Their bodies were beginning to bloat. Miguel, Adam, and Xavier were the other three.

"They've just left their bodies here like this," Etienne said in anger.

"Because they're *bodies*." I blinked back tears. After a moment of thought, I asked, "How many guards did y'all kill during the attempted escape?"

"Four." His eyes met mine. "This was payback."

I nodded. I should have been there. I could have stopped them from attacking the guards. Maybe these men wouldn't be dead. Maybe we would have actually escaped instead of being imprisoned in this place. "Let's go," I said. "There's nothing we can do for them now. Maybe if we make it out alive and defeat Whirl, we can give them a proper burial."

"If they don't dispose of the bodies first," Etienne said with disgust. Then he made the sign of the cross over each of the dead men while reciting something in French.

We looked both ways again and listened for any sounds before entering the hall and shutting the door behind us. I was sure there would never be anything that would shut out the sight or the smell from my mind. At the end of the hall, I pointed to the left and said, "That's the way to the exit."

He needed to know in case we got split up. "Let's go right and see what's down here."

In the new hall, the concrete floor was finished, smooth and glossy, like it had recently been renovated. The walls were no longer gray, but white, and the doors were not the green metal, but a nice, slick chrome. They reminded me of my mother. They were like the refrigerator she'd insisted we buy when I was a teenager. She hadn't wanted the black or white, but the shiny silver that showed every fingerprint and smudge. How had my mother reacted to the news that I was missing? It was a question I'd wondered many times since we'd been struck. I hadn't seen her in a year. She was remarried. She lived in another state. She had stepchildren. She'd be okay without me. Those were the things I told myself to make me feel better.

"Here, cover that camera," Etienne said, handing me a piece of cloth. Tall enough that I didn't need to jump, I snuck up underneath it, so I wouldn't be seen on screen, and placed the black fabric. Etienne would have had a hard time doing it on his own. We proceeded cautiously, weapons in hand.

The doors in this corridor had labels, and when we came to the third one on the right, I stopped in my tracks. The sign said *Trial 765, Blood Swapping*. It was vaguely familiar, like I'd seen it before. "We need to go in here," I said, pointing at the door. "This is what they were doing to Rick last night—blood swapping."

"You saw him?" Etienne asked.

"Yeah. He was in an observation lab upstairs. That's how they caught us."

"You keep saying *us*," Etienne said. "Who's *us*? You and this Laney person you keep asking about?"

"Yeah, they trapped us and gassed us 'til we passed out." I answered him without giving him the information he really wanted—who Laney was.

I hoped he wouldn't press, but he did. "Who is she?" he asked, curious but respectful.

"The woman I'd like to marry if we can all get out of this place alive."

"But you've never mentioned her…"

"Because I didn't want anyone to know what, or who, to use as leverage against me."

He was quiet for a moment, and then nodded and said, "That was smart. Dale would have made comments relentlessly like he did with the other guys." He took a breath. "Well, we can't defeat our enemy if we don't know our enemy. Might as well take a look, see what other kinds of horrors they've developed for us."

I slid the access card through the slot on the keypad. There was a beep, and a small green light lit up. Cracking the door, we both peeked inside. It looked somewhat like a hospital room. The floor was white tile, and the lights were dim. On the left side, the far side, the room was closed off by a blue curtain. I could see the wheels of a bed beneath it. We opened the door further and slipped inside. To the right of the door were a few counters with laboratory stations set up. That side of the room was dark.

But right in front of us was a large observation window, like the one I'd looked through with Laney when we had found Rick. The light was on inside the room, so we could see what was in it. There weren't any people. Instead, there were several rows of empty isolette beds. It was like peering through the glass of a hospital nursery, except there weren't any babies here…yet. This was clearly a new section of the facility being prepared for something new.

"What are they planning?" I asked with dread.

From behind the curtain a man cleared his throat, startling us. Then he said, sarcastically, "I'm going to guess it has something to do with babies."

I knew that voice. Charging across the room, I threw the curtain back. It was Rick. He smiled at me and nodded at Etienne. He was strapped to the bed with leather cuffs, an IV in his hand. It appeared to be just regular saline they were dripping into his veins, but who could be sure what they would put into our bodies for their experiments?

"Why do they have you in this room, with the baby stuff?" Etienne asked.

Rick shrugged. "Seems like they are still working on the other areas and this was the best space available." He turned to me and asked, "Where's Laney? Is she okay? I saw them carry you both away."

"They said she's fine. She's no longer here."

"Who's they?" he asked.

"A resistance group that's been helping us," I said as I unbuckled the leather straps on his wrists. Etienne worked on the ankle straps. "How are you feeling?"

"I'm okay. Just tired," Rick said. "You know how it feels."

"How would I know what blood swapping feels like?"

"Um…I heard them talking about how you were the first one they tried it on. And how you were taken away by Gigandet's orders, which messed up their initial phase. So, they started over with me."

"If I was, I don't remember it," I said. That must have been what they had done to me that night they took me from the barracks. "They injected me with something. I don't remember what happened after that. But if so, then yes, I know how you feel. You could sleep for days, but we've got to get moving."

"Where are we going? What's the plan?" he asked.

Etienne and I looked at each other, both unsure of the answer. "There's not really a plan at the moment," I said. I filled him in on what had happened since I'd seen him the night before—the pit, Whirl, the near-drowning, the undercover guard from the resistance, Dale leaving us, and finding the four dead men.

He sighed deeply, and then said, "Well, let's get out of here." He pulled the IV from his hand and swung his legs over the edge of the bed, his feet hitting the floor. He had socks but no shoes, and he was wearing something similar to hospital scrubs, in a light green color. "They don't have that many weapons," he explained. "Most of the guards in the facility are unarmed. I heard them complaining that one of the gun shipments was stolen."

So that's what Durham had been talking about the night before—he'd purchased the guns from the black market before Whirl could get to them. I could only imagine what the price must have been. Where was he stashing them? Did Phaedra know? Did she have them? Could we use them? The resistance seemed to be everywhere, and we needed them. It was time to accept we couldn't do this by ourselves. "I think our best option is to get to the resistance," I said. "They'll help us."

"You could have gone with them an hour ago," Etienne said. "But chose not to."

"We had different goals. He wouldn't free you too. And if I'd gone, we wouldn't be here with Rick."

"But you think our goals will be the same now?" Rick asked.

"I think we all want to defeat Whirl. That's goal number one."

They nodded in agreement.

I peeked out the door to make sure we were safe to move. Then back in the hallway, we traveled in the opposite direction toward the exit the guard had marked on the map for me in red ink. It was at the end of the hallway, but not far. Soon we came to a staircase on our right; it should lead us to the surface, to ground level. If I was correct, we would exit into the daylight. I went up the long flight of stairs first, the other two behind me.

At the top, I slid the keycard through the slot, and when it beeped, I turned the lever and gently lifted the hatch door a sliver. It exited to the woods; I could see tall trees with full, green coverage. To the right the sun was setting, a golden yellow glow between the trees. But to my left, maybe ten feet away, there was another body. It was Dale. I gasped and almost fell backwards, but Etienne grabbed my elbow to steady me.

"What is it?" he asked.

"Dale. He's been shot." They were just leaving bodies everywhere. A warning to us.

"Is he still alive?" he asked.

I shook my head. "No. He's gone."

I could tell because he'd landed on his stomach, his chin resting on the ground, the gunshot straight through his forehead. It was like he'd been running back to the hatch, trying to escape the fire. We couldn't go that way. We'd end up like him. It was clear that at least the guards patrolling the perimeter of the facility were now armed. In Dale's hand something white waved on a slight breeze. It was the map. I closed the hatch and sat down on one of the steps. Trying to erase the image of Dale's body, I focused on the map, what I could remember of it. There had been something more drawn on it; this hadn't been the end of the hallway. There'd been more red ink. But where had it led?

"I've got to get the map," I finally said.

"You can't go out there," Rick argued. "You'll get yourself killed. I'm not explaining that to Laney. I'll go."

I stood up and looked at him like he was crazy. "No, you won't. I'm not explaining that to Angie."

His eyes went wide, filled with hope. He'd been wondering about his wife and baby since we'd been here, whether they'd been struck and brought to this horrible place. It was the first thing I should have told him. "Are you saying…?" he started.

I smiled wide and nodded, grabbing his shoulders. "Yes, they're okay. Laney saw them after everything happened. They were even listed in the paper as the only ones not missing. They didn't get struck. They're okay." It was his turn to slump down on the stairs. He sobbed with his face in his hands.

After a moment, Etienne said, "All right. That means I'm going. Nobody will miss me if I die."

Before we could stop him or formulate a plan, he was already halfway out the hatch, his belly on the ground. We rushed to the top of the stairs to look out. Rick took one side, and I took the other, keeping our eyes alert for any movement among the trees. It was clear. Etienne quickly army crawled the ten feet, snatched the map out of Dale's curled fingers, and rushed back to us. We grabbed his arms and pulled him inside face-first. He was out of breath simply from the adrenaline. He handed the map to me and then sat down.

The red ink I hadn't paid attention to the first time now made sense. I pushed past Rick and went to the bottom of the stairs. There was a door across from the staircase; it was labeled maintenance. Opening it, the other two watching in curiosity, I found what would be expected—some brooms and mops and other supplies. But pushing them aside, in the rear, I could see a lever on the floor, another hatch leading down instead of up, to the tunnel system.

I turned the lever and lifted the hatch door. "This leads to the underground tunnel system. They've marked a meeting area, a secret room, not too far down here," I said. "Maybe we can stay there for the night and figure out what to do next." I didn't think I could keep going much longer without sleep.

Rick shrugged, as was his habit, and said, "Let's go."

CHAPTER 10
(LANEY)

The royal wedding. They said we'll be the witnesses. Witnesses. Whirl wanted people to witness his terror, to spread the news of it from their mouths. The cameras weren't enough to broadcast it over the screens in the living quarters. He wanted living people to share his evil deeds. I'd only seen him once, and I hadn't paid any attention. The night I'd been reunited with Hollister, Whirl had been the one to bring him to us in the meadow behind the palace. I hadn't paid attention to anyone but Hollister. There was only a vague sketch in my mind of what Whirl looked like. He was supposed to be the thing of nightmares—Hollister, Leela, Curwen, and even Gibson had spoken of him with fear in their voices—but I had only a faint image of him.

We reached the crowd in front of the terrace. Behind us cameras were set up, pointed toward the entrance of the palace, ready to capture everything. The cameramen ordered us to press closer together, to make the crowd appear fuller. I glanced around to find Jace. He'd been assigned a spot near the palace wall, in line with other guards, definitely too far away from me. I made eye contact with him. Or at least I thought our eyes met. From so far away it was hard to discern if he was looking at me or beyond me. There was a slight breeze, and a blanket of dark clouds was moving in our direction. I'd never noticed a cloud in the Antonian sky before then.

I asked a woman beside me, "Do you know what's going on here?"

She seemed confused by my question. "Yes. The royal wedding."

"Yes. But do you know Gigandet is no longer in control of the government?"

"Yes." She still appeared confused. "Did you not see the broadcast? The army has taken over." She didn't seem upset by this.

"Do you know how?" I asked.

"Peaceably. Gigandet surrendered. He's going to marry Elodie and go live in exile."

I shook my head at her. "No. There was a bloody massacre. Many people were shot and killed."

"That's a lie," she said, disgusted with me.

"Why do they have guns then?" I asked. "What do they need them for? It's illegal to bring them here."

The woman hesitated, and then in denial she said, "You should be ashamed for spreading such lies." She gave me a harsh look and then moved away, putting a few people between us.

If Whirl wanted them to believe the tale he'd spun, why was he going to send Elodie out in a bloody wedding gown? How did his mind work? It seemed like nobody knew. I tried to read the crowd around me. Some seemed calm, like the woman I'd spoken to. Some expressed excited chatter amongst themselves. They'd never seen a royal wedding before. It was a once in a lifetime event. But there were a few, like the first woman I'd talked to, that seemed uneasy. There was a tension in their body language. Were they the ones who knew the truth? Were they members of the resistance group led by Durham?

Before I could talk to any of them, the giant front doors of the palace began to slowly creak open. A hush went over the crowd, everyone's eyes fixed on the terrace with anticipation. Whirl exited the palace first, his head high and his steps purposeful. I knew it was him immediately, tall and slim with sharp, cold features and hair that was graying and growing thin. His black uniform was freshly pressed. He stepped up to the microphone and prepared to address the Antonian people.

"Good afternoon," he began in a raspy, deep voice. "I apologize that the hour is later than planned, but thank you all for coming here to be our witnesses today." *They didn't have a choice.* "As I have already announced, Gigandet has abdicated his role as king, and I will now oversee the state of affairs in Antonia, elected and supported by the guard as your new leader."

Whirl paused as if waiting for applause or shouts of jubilation, but it was simply silent. The army may have elected him, but these people hadn't. Then a lone cheer went up from the other side of the audience. And then another. And then another. Gradually there was a trickling applause across the crowd, some enthusiastic, but others appearing to do what was expected of them. Why were they applauding this man? *They don't know what he's done. Tell them.* But I couldn't get my mouth to open. Fear glued my lips together. I wanted to shout the truth. But nothing. I wouldn't be heard. I'd be killed. Almost on queue with my thoughts, a guard from behind nudged me with the butt of his rifle, ordering me to clap. I couldn't get my lips to part, and it took every effort to command my hands together.

The applause continued until Whirl raised his hands, signaling that he was going to speak again. Hush fell over the crowd again. "I have graciously given Gigandet the option to live in exile the rest of his days. He will marry Elodie, and the two of them will never be seen in Antonia again. Enjoy this ceremony because it is the last you will see of them," he said, smiling. He was trying to appear kind, but it was menacing. Didn't they hear the threat in his words? Did they really think the royal couple would live happily ever after somewhere? Surely, he would execute them once he was finished with them. Didn't they care about the spreading disease? Without the king, the curse could not be broken.

These people are just scared, I told myself. *Like you are. They're surrounded by armed guards. They've never seen guns before in their lives. They're scared for their lives. They don't really support him.* They just couldn't. There was nothing we could do to fight back…unless. Unless I was willing to remove my disguise and go up there, announce to all of Antonia that I could save their people by marrying Gigandet instead. But my feet were cemented to the white-hot concrete. I had no doubt that Whirl would kill me on the spot, shoot me down before I even reached the top of the terrace steps. What good purpose would my death serve?

Just then, the doors began to open again. Two guards escorted Gigandet out, one on each side of him. He was alive, but looked like he might pass out at any moment. His face was ashen, and he limped forward slowly. Leela had told me he'd been shot in the leg. We had to leave him behind, she'd said, almost in tears. *He'd ordered us to.* He may have been an oblivious ruler who hadn't seen the danger and threats around him, but he'd kept my sister safe for the sake of his people. Now his people stood watching as Whirl destroyed every bit of him. I tried again to move my feet forward, but they were planted, growing roots through the concrete. Jace also caught my eye—this time I knew he was looking at me—and he shook his head, as if he knew what I was considering.

The dethroned king stood before us as we all waited for his bride to appear. Would Henley come with her? How had Elodie explained what had happened to her guard? Did they know I'd been there, so close they could have caught me? Were they searching for me at that very moment? I shuddered at the thought, scanning the area to see if anyone had their attention focused on me. Only Jace, from what I could tell. I released my captured breath.

It was time. The doors were opening a third time. There was no music to announce the bride's arrival. If there had been, it should have been a death march. She paused in the open doorway with a bouquet of crushed flowers in her hands. Even though I'd just left her presence, it was as if I was seeing her for the first time. Slender and graceful, plain yet beautiful. Unlike Gigandet's pained expression, she was actually smiling wide, joyful to marry the man she loved. Because of Hollister, I understood her feelings, but it also seemed like complete madness. Was she mad to be so singularly focused? It would mean the death of her. I realized *she doesn't care.*

It took a moment for the witnesses to take in the scene. The dark red stains on the corset and skirt of her gown. I could sense some apprehension spreading among them. The woman from before looked back at me, her eyes wide and questioning. I simply nodded at her with a stoic expression. Maybe now she'd believe there *had* been a bloody massacre. Elodie took her place opposite Gigandet. She gave him a smile of encouragement, but there was only dread in his eyes. They clearly had not talked about this. Whirl was punishing Gigandet in the worst way possible.

Whirl smirked wickedly; he was enjoying it so much, his eyes bouncing back and forth between the two of them. It seemed like slow motion as a slight breeze lifted her hair and lightning lit up the sky, and then two seconds later—I counted—a roll of thunder rumbled. The scene was set perfectly. This day deserved rain. "Let's begin," Whirl said, his voice reverberating through the loudspeakers. "Gigandet, repeat after me. Elodie, I choose you to be my wife, to be bound to you for the rest of our days, until death parts us." Whirl put emphasis on the last part, happy that their days would be numbered and the parting would come sooner than later.

Gigandet hesitated. Then he said strongly, "I do not choose this. I'll not condemn Elodie to certain death."

A gasp rippled through the crowd. I couldn't tell what they were most shocked by. His refusal and disobedience—which I silently applauded—or that they hadn't seemed to consider the consequences of the marriage before that point. She didn't have the mark. She wasn't the match of the one with the mark. If the curse fell upon Gigandet, she would die. While I observed the crowd, I almost missed the look of fury that crossed Whirl's face. He seemed to almost choke on his anger as he tried to compose himself enough to speak. He glared at the groom and asked, "Would you like to try that again?"

Gigandet shook his head. "No."

Elodie was crying. In an almost inaudible whisper, she begged, "Please, just do it."

But he continued to shake his head. Maybe the last thing he would ever do.

Whirl's patience was gone though; he didn't have much of it. They'd set up microphones and loudspeakers because he didn't want any word to be missed. But he hadn't expected this. He hadn't expected Gigandet to refuse to say his vows. "You don't want to condemn her to certain death?" he yelled. "This is certain death!" As he said it, he swiftly pulled the hand gun from his belt and pressed the muzzle to Elodie's head.

Gigandet raised his hands and shouted, "No! Stop!" but his words were drowned out by the cries and screams that exploded throughout the crowd. Several, especially those near the front, crouched low, covering their heads. *It might be better for her to die this way.* I instantly regretted the thought. If she could live now, maybe we could save her later if she got sick.

She was as still as a statue. But then, her eyes on Gigandet's, she said through tears, "Just marry me. It's okay. It's okay. We'll be together." Some of the Antonians around me had begun to cry as well. *Just do it. Marry her. Don't let him kill her here, in front of everyone.* I'd already watched Muriel die the previous night from a gunshot to the head. I couldn't do it again. I'd never get my soul washed clean of the memories.

Without realizing it, I'd started pleading softly to myself, "Marry her. Marry her. Marry her."

Suddenly, the people immediately around me began to say it too. When they started, I stopped, watching in amazement as more and more of them joined, their voices coming together in unison, growing louder into a roaring chant. It went on for at least a minute. Gigandet kept his eyes on his bride. He never glanced at the crowd.

And then he said, "I will." I couldn't hear it over the chanting, but saw his lips mouth the words. Instantly, Whirl returned the gun to its holster, and there was silence once again.

Whirl ordered those who were still crouched to stand and face forward. Although frightened—or because they were frightened—they obeyed instantly. Whirl said the vows, and this time Gigandet repeated them. Elodie did too. The ceremony concluded without any more threats or guns drawn. The bride and groom held hands and turned to face us, Elodie smiling, Gigandet expressionless. I tried to imagine myself in their situation. Would I be so happy to marry Hollister if it meant I would probably contract the disease and die soon after? Hollister would never have said the vows. He would have fought Whirl, lunged at him, wrestled the gun from him, maybe even have killed him. If the guards didn't kill Hollister first. *Whirl makes sure there's no good outcome.*

The crowd didn't seem to know how to respond to the newlyweds. Perhaps they were finally seeing the truth of this new situation, new government, new leader. We were all grateful Elodie hadn't been killed in front of us, that Gigandet had submitted to the chants and decided to marry her. Had any of them ever heard a gunshot before? Maybe the ones who had traveled to my dimension many, many years ago. The people were silent. Whirl didn't like it. He wanted cheers and adoration for his cruelly concocted plan, and he demanded it by saying, "Let's all clap for the bride and groom!"

It was a slow trickle of applause until the guards all around us began ordering us to clap louder. We did. How much would fear control us? How far would we let it take us? I had to include myself with the Antonian people. I wanted to say *them*, but it was *us*. *We* were all standing idly by, all obeying the commands being fed to us. Of all of us, I had the greatest chance of changing what had just happened, if I had gone forward, if I had told the Antonian people that I could break the curse, that I could save them from any further sickness. Perhaps they would have rallied around and insisted he marry *me*. Instead, I'd started the chant for him to marry *her*. Had I subconsciously done it on purpose? Now, neither I nor Leela could marry him. He had a wife. *Until she dies.*

I shook the thought away, suppressing any guilt that tried to tug at me. We no longer had a purpose in Antonia. We could go home. No, I was wrong. Hollister had a purpose. He wouldn't leave until the slaves were freed. And Leela, would she leave? Probably not without helping the sick people. The sick people. Just two hours ago, I'd cared about helping them too. I'd held a dead child in my arms. I'd been smuggled to the morgue with a dead woman's body. How had my desire to fight gone away so quickly? *You're weak and apathetic and scared.*

I was near tears—tears of frustration and shame—when Whirl's voice cut through my thoughts. Gigandet and Elodie were being escorted back inside the palace. Perhaps the last time any of us would see them. Whirl said, "The guards will escort all of you back to your homes. Over the next few days and weeks, you will be informed about our new leadership structure and laws." At that moment, there was another flash of lightning and then the dark clouds opened up. Whirl hustled inside, leaving us in the rain.

There was lots of movement as everyone pushed and shoved, ready to be away from this place, and I scanned the area for Jace. He was walking farther away. It looked like he tried to say something to his superior, but he was ordered back in line with a group of guards who were entering the palace. I was on my own. The very thought nearly made me pass out, my stomach falling. "Come on!" a guard shouted. "Get moving." I glanced at him, and then forced my feet to move, uprooting them from the concrete, one in front of the other.

I heard one guard say to another, "We need to take them through the working quarter gates. The crowd is too large to contain at the main gate." There was a crowd in the living quarter, at the main gate, the one that had been locked the previous night when Curwen, Hollister, and I couldn't get through. The woman on the walkie earlier had said that there were protests. What exactly were they protesting if they didn't know the truth? The lockdown? The change in government? The wedding, knowing it would mean the curse wouldn't be broken? I prayed that they would fight back. In all the ways I had failed to do so during the ceremony. In all the ways I was incapable of doing so.

What did I do now? Where was I supposed to go? I didn't know my way around the living quarters, which all looked the same and didn't have any street signs or directions. How could I find Phaedra's house? I was alone, but not alone, crushed by bodies on all sides. I was separated from anyone I could trust to help me, shuffling through the herd of scared people who'd probably never witnessed any violence in their lives. Yes, they were witnesses, as Whirl had wanted them to be. The wedding had been broadcast in the living quarters, but these witnesses had been there. They could go home and tell their families and friends about their firsthand experiences and instill the fear in them too.

We'd made it through the meeting quarters, past the fountains, and had just entered the working quarters. It was dead, so unlike my first morning there. None of the businesses were open. Nobody had been allowed to work. The dirt kicked up beneath our feet, the only place within the city walls that didn't have stone tiles. The walls were no longer white after years of being stained with the red clay dirt. Curwen had said the living quarter was to remain clean. But the working quarter, not so much.

Suddenly, someone grabbed my arm. It was the woman who'd called me a liar. "How did you know it wasn't peaceful?" she asked.

"Because my sister was there."

"But—" she began to say something when a guard shoved her and ordered her to be silent. I moved away from her this time, pushing forward, squeezing myself through toward the front. We were approaching a gate to the living quarters. The State Records building was on the corner, so I knew it was the same gate Curwen had brought me through before. Could I find my way to his house from there? Was it even his house anymore, since he'd been exiled and all his possessions confiscated?

At the gate, the guard at the front said, "Go directly home. Nowhere else." He didn't want the crowd to grow at the main gate, but I was pretty sure none of us wanted to stay in the rain any longer. Most of us were soaked through, and even with the Antonian heat, I had chills. The gate beeped and people began to file through one after the other. When I went through, I had to act like I knew where I was going. But where? I kept my head down as I passed the guard and went to the right; I knew that direction was away from the main gate. I didn't want to encounter the mob or any other guards.

I walked a bit and then took a left down a narrower, empty corridor. I didn't want people to pay any attention to the aimless, homeless, sopping wet girl. But then I noticed my only glimmer of hope, a red flower in a window. It represented a safe house for those in the resistance. Just a few days ago I was paraded through the living quarters, under arrest, I had surveyed every red flower we had passed, wondering if the people inside would really help me if they knew I wasn't Antonian. Now, it was my only option to knock on that door.

I waited for someone to pass by before I approached. I didn't know what or who I'd find inside that house, but I couldn't stay outside all night, waiting for a patrol to capture and question me. I knocked and then waited. I could hear shuffling inside, but nobody was coming to the door. So, I knocked again, this time harder. Nothing. As I was about to knock a third time, the door opened.

"Can I help you?" a large, burly man asked, annoyed. I gasped when I saw him. "Do I know you?" he asked.

"Clive," I said. "We met at the State Records office a few days ago. I came in with Curwen."

He shook his head. "He came in with a blond."

"This is a wig." Did it really look that believable? "Anyway, I saw the red flower in the window, and I have nowhere else to go. Can you help me?"

His eyes narrowed to examine my face more closely in the dimming light of evening, and then said, "Come in. Quickly!" I stepped inside. He looked both ways, up and down the street, to make sure I wasn't seen before closing and locking the door behind us. "How is it you want me to help you?"

He wasn't happy with my arrival. I tried to ignore the tone in his voice. I tried to ignore the fact that his home had the same floor plan as Muriel's. Stairs to the right, living room to the left, kitchen in the rear, wide corridor down the center. I was standing in the exact spot where she had been shot. The blood. The fear. Curwen's scream. The murderer, a man named Anderson. Breathing deeply, I attempted to push the memory down, deep enough that it could be buried. It kept fighting for the surface though; it wanted to breathe too.

"Hello?" Clive interrupted my thoughts, pulling me back. "What do you want from me? You're soaking wet." What he meant was *you're getting my floor wet*. "Were you at the protest?"

"No." I shook my head. "I was a witness at the wedding." His eyes went wide. "They just brought us back to the living quarter."

"So then, why don't you go home?" he asked, desiring to be rid of me. "You shouldn't be out tonight."

Just then I heard a cough from the kitchen. A man. We weren't alone. Without being invited, I walked down the corridor and looked into the room. Two men were seated at Clive's round dining table, and a woman stood between them. They all stared back at me, silent.

"As you can see," Clive said, even more annoyed with me now, "I have company. So, why don't you go home?"

Now is the time. I had wondered how these people, the ones who belonged to the underground resistance, would treat me if they knew my real identity. Could they be trusted? Would they help me? Time to find out. Firmly, I said, "I am not Antonian. I do not have a home here. I do not know my way around. So, please be kind enough to call Phaedra for me, and find out where she wants me to go." At that moment, I surrendered any thoughts or plans of my own. Phaedra would certainly be upset with me for not once, but twice, ignoring her instructions.

The men stared at me, stunned. But the woman ordered, "Clive, call Phaedra."

"Right, right," he said, shaking himself out of shock. "I've just never talked to a free body before."

"I'm not a *body*," I said, my eyes fierce. "I never have been, and I never will be."

The woman's face was hard and determined like mine as she took a step forward. "No, you never will be."

CHAPTER 11
(LEELA)

There was a large, strong hand on the back of my head, a heavy weight on my body, pressing my face below the surface of the water. My eyes focused on the blue mosaic tiles on the bottom of the fountain, as I tried to ignore the burning in my lungs. Hold on. Hold on a little longer. "They don't need you," his voice whispered, cold in my ear. I thrashed awake, gasping for air. It happened several times that night, the nightmare. But it wasn't really a nightmare. It had actually happened. It was a memory. It was something I was sure I would remember even if I reached old age and began to forget everything else.

As exhausted as I'd been, I couldn't sleep, tossing and turning in between the bad dreams, my mind too consumed with our situation. I couldn't shake the feeling that we were completely unprepared for what was to come. I couldn't shake the dread that we'd all end up dead. What was the plan, and was Durham the one making it? Would we continue allowing him to make the decisions? Was he the one who got to gamble with our lives in order to achieve his goals? Too many questions, not enough answers.

I rose early in the morning and reclined in one of the hammocks with my legs hanging over the side. Mara had been sleeping hard when I'd left the tent, and fresh air called to me. Curwen and Greer were nowhere to be seen; both of them had slept outside in the hammocks, but they were gone when I came out. So, I swayed alone in the shade of the purple-leaved trees, drifting in and out of consciousness, remembering family camping trips, attempting to replace these new, horrible memories with the old, good ones, so that maybe I could sleep again. It didn't work. Gunshots, blood, water, and the mosaic tiles kept overpowering the s'mores and campfires and fishing.

When I opened my eyes, Sheldon was standing in front of me, his green eyes bright. He smiled broadly, but I detected a small wince, the action causing pain either because of the cut on his cheek or bruised eye. I scooted over in the hammock so he could sit beside me.

We were quiet for a little while, just listening to the sounds of nature, but eventually he asked, "What are you thinking about?"

I don't know why I wanted to tell him, but I wanted him to know. "So. . ." I began, "I'm not the one who's supposed to marry Gigandet."

His head turned quickly toward me, his eyes sharp. "What do you mean?"

"They interpreted the curse wrong. It's supposed to be Laney. She's my match."

He was silent for a long moment. "Who told you this? When did you find out?" It seemed like he wanted to be relieved, but at the same time was hesitant to believe. He'd always know the curse to be one way.

"Curwen told me yesterday. It's what Gibson told them when they got the transporter from him."

"But Laney didn't tell us that." He looked confused.

"I know." Anger began welling up inside of me again. I breathed deep and blew it away. "I don't know why she wouldn't have told me, why she wouldn't have…"

"She did come back to stop you from marrying him…" Sheldon was giving her the benefit of the doubt. "Maybe she just didn't want to believe that she had to marry him."

"Nobody's making her do that! But she could have at least told me I didn't have to." After a pause and a breath, I said, "I'm sorry. I just feel like I don't know her at all sometimes."

He nodded. "I don't think I know my family at all either. I can't believe Curwen's not Antonian. He's about as Antonian as they come."

"Does that change things for you?" Did it bother him that his brother was like me?

"No, of course not," he was quick to say. "He's my brother. I don't care where he's from. But he might."

"I hope not." I blinked back tears. Where was Curwen? What was he thinking about himself? Suddenly, I felt a panic and wanted to go find him, to see if he was okay. "Have you seen him this morning?" I asked, sitting up and putting my feet on the ground.

"No. He's probably gone off to be alone somewhere. He does that sometimes."

I nodded. Yes, I'd learned that about him before we had ever come to Antonia, before we even knew this place existed. He'd been gone all day in the pouring rain, and I had feared that he'd left us, that we would never know what had happened to our parents or how to find them. But then he'd returned just after dinner, soaking wet, dripping water across the hardwood floors, declaring that he wanted to tell us a story, a story that would reveal to us the truth of Antonia. He'd gone off on his own to decide whether to obey Antonian law or do what was humanly right, to wrestle with loyalty and morality. What was he wrestling with now? And what conclusion would he come to?

Not only had Curwen just learned that he wasn't who he'd thought he was, but he'd killed someone for me. We hadn't discussed it. I don't know if either of us knew what to say, if we had fully processed anything that had happened in the last two weeks, let alone twenty-four hours. I was sure he was wrestling with that as well. He'd taken a life to save one—mine. And I hadn't said thank you. The urgency to find him grew as I stood.

"Where are you going?" Sheldon asked.

But before I could respond, Laura called to us. She had approached quietly and stood beside the fire pit in the center of our campsite, waiting for us to come to her. I grabbed Sheldon's hand and helped pull him up out of the hammock. Mara popped her head out of the tent just as we arrived. "What's going on?" she asked, still half-asleep.

"It's time for all of you to be introduced to the council," Laura said. "The other three are already waiting."

"You have a council?" Sheldon asked.

She nodded. "We have to have some kind of leadership to govern these people.

"Are they an easy people to govern?" he asked.

She smirked. "Why? Do you want the job?"

He just laughed and shook his head. By this time Mara had thrown herself together and emerged from the tent.

I was the only one who'd followed the rules and hadn't wandered through their camp. Laura led us up river and up hill, around a curve in one of the mountain peaks. From that spot we could see down the mountain, in a slight valley, row after row of tents. There must have been a hundred. There were a few wooden huts as well, more permanent housing. Smoke rose from their morning fires. I wanted to go down to them, to walk through, meet the people and hear their stories. How long had each of them lived and survived in the mountains? Long enough to start and raise families. I couldn't help thinking again about the children who'd been born here when their parents had been foreigners, brought here to be slaves.

But Laura didn't take us down to their camp. She kept going uphill, towards the summit. Curwen, Greer, and Durham were standing beside a tree, waiting like Laura had said. They couldn't have been together that morning. I couldn't imagine any of them wanted to be in each other's company, especially by the way they stood far apart, not speaking, as we approached.

At the top of the mountain, there was a circle of large stones. On the stones sat eight people—five men and three women. James was one of the men. Beside him sat one of the oldest men I'd ever seen. *Could he be the Ancient One?* Mara and I exchanged a quick look; she was wondering the same thing. There were plenty of stone seats left for us to join them, and Laura instructed us to sit. She remained standing and began by saying, "We've called this meeting today because we have visitors, and it has become clear that something has happened in Antonia to bring them here.

We need to hear their story and find out what they want from us." Then she sat down on a stone beside James.

An older woman spoke up. "I thought they just needed treatment for that one," she said, pointing at Curwen.

Laura shook her head. "When I offered him the treatment this morning, he informed me that he is not Antonian, and therefore has a natural immunity to the disease. He has not demonstrated any of the symptoms, other than a slight fever yesterday, which we know is typical in those who have just been exposed."

It was hard to observe the facial expressions of every single person during this exchange, but from Durham's, I could tell he wasn't aware that Curwen had told Laura the truth about his origins.

Another man spoke with accusation. "So, it was a trick to get access to our camp?"

All of our group suddenly appeared panicked, worried that they would think we had evil intentions. At the same time, Curwen and Durham both said, "No."

They looked at each other, almost as if they were daring each other, fighting over who would continue to explain the situation. Would Curwen speak the truth, or would he let his father take the lead, perhaps spinning another tale? Instead, Sheldon jumped in. "No, it was not a trick. We came into the mountains because we needed to escape from guards who were after us. We just needed to get away. And, until last night, most of us did believe Curwen was Antonian and needed treatment."

"Why were guards after you?" the same man asked. "Three of you are wearing guard uniforms." His eyes traveled from Sheldon to Mara to Greer. He was right to be suspicious. They needed to know the full truth, the potential danger that could be coming to their community. *What happens down there affects us too*, Laura had said. She was right.

"I have the mark," I said before anyone else could utter a word. "I was going to marry Gigandet, but Whirl and his army attacked the palace during the ceremony. They have guns, and they've killed many people. We managed to escape—Sheldon, Mara, Greer and myself. That's why they're wearing guards' uniforms; they were assigned to protect me. Then, after meeting up with Durham, we went to the science facility to rescue Curwen. He'd been captured and injected with the disease as punishment. My sister and her boyfriend were left behind as the guards arrived, and we were forced to escape into the mountains. I don't know what has happened to them."

By the time I was finished speaking, finished being honest, Durham was subtly glaring at me. Then he gave a close-mouthed smile to the council members and said, "Well, of course there are a lot more details, but those are the main points."

One man was about to say something when the oldest man—perhaps the AO—asked me, "Why were you going to marry Gigandet?"

We stared at each other, his dark eyes surrounded by wrinkles. He knew the truth. He knew I wasn't supposed to marry Gigandet. Maybe he was the one who had told Gibson about the correct interpretation of the curse. Or maybe all the AOs had known the truth. But, he was the last one living. Everyone was staring at me, waiting for my response. But when I didn't speak fast enough, Greer answered, "To break the curse and stop the people from dying." It was the first time I'd heard his voice all morning.

The old man coughed. "But she's the mark, not the match. She's not supposed to sit on the throne. Your sister, is she your twin?" I nodded.

"Well, she is supposed to sit on the throne—not you." Curwen's eyes met mine. "And you don't appear surprised by this."

"This morning I'm not," I said. "I was surprised when I found out yesterday."

Durham stood up. He was shocked by this. "Wait, what are you saying? It's always been that the one with the mark had to marry the king to break the curse."

"No," the old man said, "it's always been that the original language was translated improperly, perhaps purposely. And, she doesn't have to marry the king. She simply has to become queen. It doesn't have to be through marriage."

All of us appeared shocked at that last revelation. That meant Gigandet wasn't needed. He could be dead or deposed—it didn't matter. Greer did not appear okay with that. "Why should we believe you?" he demanded.

"Because he's the Ancient One," Mara said with respect for the old man.

"We're supposed to seat Laney on the throne," Durham said like a question, more to himself than us.

Greer stood up now. "You will not dethrone Gigandet!"

"News flash: he's already been dethroned," one of the councilwomen said under her breath.

Laura stood and demanded everyone to sit down. Durham and Greer hesitated, but obeyed.

Another woman, who'd been quiet until then, asked, "I'm sorry, but is Gigandet still alive? You didn't say."

I shrugged and shook my head. "We don't know. He'd been shot in the leg the last time we saw him. He ordered us to leave him behind."

"So, what is it you want from us?" James asked. I just wanted a place to rest, to plan, to recharge. But I remained quiet, curious to see what Durham wanted from them.

He shifted on the stone seat, scooting forward a little. "Well, for years our resistance group has been preparing to force Gigandet to release some of his power, and to accept a more representative government. We weren't anticipating Whirl to come along and disrupt the process."

The AO scoffed. "You made the mistake of underestimating him. He's been planning this ever since Gigandet's father had his parents killed."

"That's his motive for all of this?" I asked.

"Well, he was already a disturbed young man who may have done this regardless of his parents' deaths, but I'm sure it helped to spur him on."

Curwen looked confused. "How did Gigandet not know this?"

"Whirl changed his name and identity before joining the military. And Gigandet was just a boy at that time."

One of the women seemed frightened. "Well, he has to be stopped. Once he has the city under his control, it will only be a matter of time before he comes here to round us up and enslave us again."

Durham knew this was his moment. "That's what we want from you. Fight with us to defeat him."

Another man said, "Who is us? Just the six of you?" He seemed like he wanted to laugh.

"No," Durham said. "I lead a group of about seven hundred. Your people could join us."

"Most of them are not fighters," Laura argued. "Almost a third of them are children. You may have a group ready for war, but we do not."

"War is not a glorious thing, son," an older man said to him. "It's a horrific thing. To watch people die. To be the one who killed them. To be the one who survives." His face was stern, every wrinkle telling a story. He was no stranger to battle.

"Well, we don't want to kill anyone," Durham explained. "We just want to take back the government."

"Well, that comes at a price. And they have guns. People will die," the same man said.

"Well, I have guns too," Durham announced, like he was putting another one of his cards on the table. This was the first we'd heard of it, and there was silence as everyone stared at him.

Curwen broke the silence in anger. "What? You've been smuggling guns into Antonia?"

"No, of course not," Durham said nonchalantly, giving Curwen a look that said *what kind of fool do you take me for*? "I bought the crates from the black market before Whirl could get them."

Sheldon, Greer, Mara, and I all exchanged glances. We'd seen the crates at the black market when we'd gone to seek the Ancient One, to try and find an alternative to marrying Gigandet. But we'd only found Yadriel and a stash of guns that he'd smuggled into Antonia for Whirl. "Why would Yadriel sell them to you?" I asked. "He wouldn't even let Greer make an offer." The AO gave me a sharp look; if what the young woman at the market had told me was true, then Yadriel was his grandson—and a criminal.

"Maybe I had more to offer him," Durham said with a crooked smile. "Anyway, I've got them hidden away. My people should be practicing with them now."

It seemed like he wanted us to applaud him. But then Greer said, "Well, we don't know how to use guns, and we don't want to use them. We don't want to kill people. Antonia has always prided itself on nonviolence."

There was a quiet moment before laughter rippled through the group, growing louder and more unified. These people had been bodies, slaves. They knew all about Antonian violence. Greer looked angry with embarrassment. He'd meant Antonia prided itself on nonviolence against Antonian citizens. But even that could be said no longer. Whirl had brought violence to them as well.

When the laughter settled, Durham tried again. "Over the last twenty-five years most of the bodies who have come to join your community only escaped because people from my group helped them. And who is it that brings you the goods that you request? Us. You wouldn't be thriving like you are without us."

"So, we owe you?" Laura asked. "Is that what you're saying?"

That's what it sounded like to me. But he shook his head slightly. "I'm saying we can help each other. It's already been said…Whirl will come here next. He's not going to ignore the bodies in the mountains like other leaders have done in the past."

They weighed his words. "Do you have a plan?" Laura asked.

"We can create one together," he said—a shocking response from the man who always seemed to want control of every situation.

"You've given us a lot to consider," James said. "We'll have an answer for you in the morning—if and how we might help you. Please return to your campsite—don't say anything to anyone about any of this. You're welcome to come down to the main fire this evening to grab some food. Otherwise, keep to yourselves." They dismissed us from the meeting.

Waiting until morning, waiting another twenty-four hours seemed almost unbearable. I could tell the rest of our group felt the same, but nobody said a word. Nobody pressed for a more urgent decision because they deserved the time to make a wise choice for their people. But it felt so urgent for *my* people, for Laney and Hollister, for the children, and the rest of the slaves.

As we returned to our campsite, I pulled Curwen aside, wanting a minute alone with him to check in. We perched on some large rocks by the river.

"How are you doing?" I asked him.

He shrugged his shoulders. "Well, at least I'm not dying."

"I'm so glad." My words and close-mouthed smile were completely sincere.

"But I'm still Antonian," he asserted after a moment.

"Of course you are. You were born and raised here." Although, he could have ended up as a test subject or a slave, but I didn't say that. Instead, repeating Sheldon's words, I added, "You're about as Antonian as they come."

He cut his eyes at me briefly and then back to the water.

"Curwen, about what happened at the science facility…I'm sorry you had to kill Anderson."

"Please, don't apologize."

"But you didn't even really need to…and you knew it."

He looked at me in appalled disbelief. "What? I was supposed to let him kill you just because I knew you aren't the one to break the curse?" He shook his head. "Why would you even think that? You're always willing to sacrifice everything, but you need to learn to fight for yourself—not just for others."

"I do fight for myself," I said defensively.

"Oh, really? When? I haven't seen it yet."

I tried to think of an example, something to spit back at him, but nothing came to me. Maybe he was right. Did I only fight when it was for the sake of others? But wasn't that a good thing, to think of myself less and of others more? It's what my mother had always taught; it's what she had displayed with her life.

His face ashamed, he said, "The thing that bothers me the most is that I…I wanted to do it, you know? I wanted to take his life the way he had taken Muriel's and was trying to take yours. The way he had taken mine when he ordered that injection. I wanted him to be no more. Now I'm a killer. And I keep wondering, have I always had that in me?"

I placed a hand on his shoulder. "I think we all have it in us, given the right circumstances. I should have at least wounded him with my shot, instead of intentionally missing. I should have known it wouldn't do anything to scare him. Perhaps if he'd been wounded, it would have given us more time to find Laney and Hollister."

He shook his head, "We wouldn't have had time to find them. Whirl's soldiers were arriving." We sat in silence, listening to the water rush by. Then he stood. "We have a fight ahead of us, whether they join us or not, so we should rest while we can. You look exhausted."

So did he. We needed sleep. But I couldn't help thinking the only sleep I'd get would be fitful, filled with fear, loss, and…death.

CHAPTER 12

(HOLLISTER)

A ladder led down into the dark. As soon as my feet hit the ground, I dug for the flashlight in my bag and clicked it on. It did seem like the tunnel may have been newly constructed. The concrete brick walls seemed freshly built. The floor was hard-packed dirt, the dust still settling. "The room we're looking for should be down on the left," I said.

"What if the room is occupied?" Etienne asked. I hadn't considered that, too focused on a safe place to rest.

"Here." I flashed the light into the bag. "Each of you take a flashlight and a weapon." Etienne grabbed an electric baton, and Rick picked a stun gun. I took a baton as well. Slinging the bag over my shoulder, we continued down the tunnel, in the only direction it went. About half a mile later, we came to a metal door on the left. Part of me was tempted to keep going, to see where the tunnel led, to try to get out of that place for good. But my whole body was weak and worn, so I stopped, praying that the key card would grant access to the room. Sliding it through the slot, the tiny light changed from red to green and it beeped. We were in.

I reached my hand inside, feeling along the wall for a switch and turned the lights on. The room was small, and thankfully, empty. It contained two bunk beds, a small bathroom, and a cabinet filled with food. Etienne grabbed a box of crackers from the shelf and plopped down on one of the bottom bunks. "Man, what I wouldn't give for a delicious, hot meal after all this time," he said. He'd been in Antonia, in captivity, for four years. The thought of it was unbearable.

Scanning the limited food options, I asked him, "What would you have if you could have anything?"

He paused to think, and then smiled. "Cassoulet with a side of poutine."

Rick chuckled. "You're such a Canadian."

"French Canadian," Etienne clarified.

"You don't have a French accent though," Rick said.

"Because we moved to Toronto when I was young. Mom still spoke French with us though."

As I grabbed a can of nuts, I found some folded papers underneath. They were pamphlets that said horrible things about Gigandet, blaming him for the deadly sickness being spread throughout Antonia, accusing him of being a weak ruler. It assured more freedom and power to any who would stand against the king. And most frighteningly, it promised an expansion of Antonia through the travel light…into our dimension, with plans to infiltrate our governments. Handing them to Etienne and Rick, I asked sarcastically, "Need some good reading material?"

They scanned them. "Whirl's been busy," Etienne said. "No wonder so many have followed him, if they believe these things." He tossed it aside as he stood. "Guys, mind if I take a quick shower? Been a long time since I've had a real one."

"Go for it," I said. I'd had my shower for the day. I shivered remembering the cold, rushing water in the pit, my hair still not completely dry.

Rick was sitting on the top bunk, studying the pamphlet. "You think he'd really come to our dimension?"

"I think he'd really like to. Imagine him infiltrating our government. Even worse, imagine us trying to tell them about it and them not believing us."

"Then it wouldn't matter if I went home to Angie and Caleb." He was suddenly angry. "This evil place will still come after us." He crumpled up the paper and threw it across the room; it hit the concrete wall and then fell on the other top bunk.

"That's why we have to stop them," I said. After a moment, I decided to tell him, "You know that curse we heard about, about the Antonians getting sick?"

He nodded. "Yeah."

"Well, according to the legend, Laney is the one who can break the curse by marrying Gigandet. That's why the whole town ended up here… because Whirl was trying to find her and Leela."

"Are you kidding me?" I'd fueled his anger even more. "We were kidnapped because of some stupid legend?" When all I did was nod, he gave me a questioning look. "Wait…do you believe this curse is real?"

I shrugged. "Maybe. Leela has the mark described in the legend. Laney is her match. It makes sense, and all the Antonians seem to believe it…"

Rick shook his head. "No, dude. We're getting out of here, and we're gonna celebrate your engagement to Laney for real this time. She's not marrying anyone but you. Nothing's breaking you two up." I wanted to find assurance in his words. When I yawned, he said, "We can't do anything unless we're well-rested. Get some sleep. I'll keep first watch."

"Okay, wake me up for second watch," I said as I crawled into the bottom bunk. It was a tight squeeze with my feet hanging off the end. I munched on some nuts and thought about what he'd said. *Nothing's breaking you two up.* But I couldn't stop imagining hundreds of different things that could break us up—death being number one, my willingness to die for this cause. I knew that had hurt Laney, made her feel less important to me, when I wanted to come back here, when I wanted to fight. But I wouldn't be a man worthy of her if I was willing to leave our people in slavery. I hoped she'd come to understand that.

It felt like I'd just fallen asleep when I felt someone shoving my shoulder. The lights were out, so I couldn't recognize who it was. "Is it already time?" I asked, rubbing sleep from my eyes, assuming Rick was waking me like I'd asked.

"It is," the man replied. I didn't recognize his voice.

Sitting up quickly, I hit my head on a metal bar, forgetting I was too tall to sit up in a bunk bed. The noise alerted the guys who were immediately on guard. Rick jumped down from the bed above onto the back of the man who was crouched beside me. "Get off of me!" the man ordered, standing up, trying to shake Rick off. "I'm here to help."

Etienne flipped on the light. Rick was still holding onto the man. He hadn't met him, so he didn't know it was the guard who had tried to help us escape earlier. "How'd you find us?" I asked the guard.

Jerking his arm out of Rick's grip, he said, "Uh, I did mark this room on the map. Figured you might come here if you got away. You all are just here sleeping, like you won't get caught."

Rick looked down, ashamed. "Sorry, I must have fallen asleep on my watch." I shook my head to let him know it wasn't a big deal. It could have been a big deal. But it wasn't, thankfully.

The man said, "We don't have much time. The guards are searching for you, especially the one you left in the pit." Etienne smiled at me over the man's shoulder, and I could tell he was suppressing a laugh. "I can lead you out from here, take you to the resistance headquarters. We need to go now. This will be my last effort at helping you."

I was torn. I knew we needed to go. We needed to get out in order to come back with more people, maybe a small army of our own. But it felt like I was abandoning all the others…again. They'd already executed five of us. They'd already performed the blood-swapping on Rick. They were going to begin experiments on the children soon. They weren't wasting any time. What else would they do before we returned? Would there be anyone left to come back for? If I stayed, Rick would never leave, but he needed to go home to his wife and baby. I gave the man from the resistance a nod and said, "Okay, let's go."

We grabbed our stuff. He flipped off the overhead light, clicked on a flashlight, and cracked open the door. Listening closely, all seemed quiet. It reminded me of how quiet and dark it had been the morning I'd left the cave and headed for town. Corey had been deep asleep, and there hadn't been a sound coming from the girls' tent either. But, as I knew now, at some point Annabelle had snuck out and followed me. I'd missed any sign that she'd been awake or aware of my departure. I'd made it three-fourths of the way across the field before the lightning had struck me. She'd been watching, and I had never noticed. Were they—the guards—watching us now without us noticing?

According to the map, the exit shouldn't be that far, but then we'd be in the woods. "How far to the headquarters once we're above ground?" I asked.

"A few miles," the still-unnamed man said. "We'll remain hidden among the treeline until we reach another hatch leading to our bunker. Let me check my radio again, see if any updates in the search are being transmitted." He shut the door. We stood in the dark as he fumbled with the dial on the radio attached to his shoulder.

Static, static, static, then a voice. "Priority is 327. Surveillance footage shows them entering the cleaning closet. What's that about?" The man didn't seem to have knowledge of the hatch in the closet floor.

But the one who responded did. "I know what it's about. We're nearby. We'll take care of it," he said with confidence. 327. The number they'd assigned to me as a body. I was their priority.

"We need to go *now*," Etienne said, clicking on his flashlight and charging out the door. The man from the resistance pushed past him, asserting his leadership position, and led us out of the room to the left. We were moving at a quick pace, me taking up the rear, when suddenly bright lights turned on overhead. I hadn't noticed before that the tunnel ceiling was lined with lights. These tunnels were definitely an upgrade from the ones beneath the city. They were coming. I gripped the baton more tightly, ready for a fight. We all paused for a moment, listening, sensing they were close, but the man from the resistance urged us to hurry. Even with the lights on, I couldn't see the end of the tunnel; it seemed to just keep going and going.

From far behind me, there came a loud thud of metal—the hatch door closing. It echoed through the tunnel. We couldn't be caught again. Not all of us, at least. They needed to get free. Etienne was 3227—not their priority. Rick was 1027—not their priority. The memory of his beaming face when he first told me he was going to be a father flashed through my mind. I would do everything possible to make sure he got to be a dad, a better dad than either of us had experienced.

It was no longer just our feet pounding the earth. There were others behind us, moving faster than we were. Looking past the guys' heads, I could see an open doorway in the distance, but the tunnel continued far beyond that. The map must not have been drawn to scale. The metal door locked from this side, perhaps a security measure for the science facility. We were just passing another tunnel on our left. It was unfinished, went nowhere. But I knew what I had to do. I was their priority. Only a bit further.

As soon as the guys passed through the open doorway, I shouted to them, "Just keep going," and then shut and locked the door. They couldn't come back. They had to go on without me. The door handle rattled. They banged on the metal. I could hear their protests, but couldn't make out the words. Knowing they probably couldn't understand mine either, I still shouted again, "Just keep going!"

Eventually the yelling subsided, and it became quiet. I hoped the man from the resistance had urged them on. Turning my back from the door, I could see the guards now, tiny, moving black specks coming closer. I backtracked to the other tunnel, moving closer to them as well, and when I was sure they recognized me as 327, I turned down the tunnel, praying they would follow me. I was the one they wanted.

They followed me. Just two of them. This tunnel wasn't very long. I was almost near the end, which was just a wall of dirt and rock. When I reached it, I turned to face the two men hurtling towards me, my feet firmly planted and my knuckles white around the baton.

CHAPTER 13
(LEELA)

"Hey." My eyes opened to the sound of a voice and tapping on the center tent post. It had taken a while to fall asleep, but I'd actually slept. No nightmares. No waking up gasping for air. Mara stood a couple feet away. "We're going into the village to get dinner, if you want to come." She'd been distant for the most part, and when she did speak to me, there was a coldness in her tone. I'd come into her life and caused a massive disturbance, at least that's how it seemed she saw it. They'd come into mine and done the same, their lightning reaching down from the sky and snatching us from our home, taking my parents, killing my mother. I wanted to be cold back, but anger took too much energy, a need for constant refueling. I needed my energy for better things.

"Hey, are we okay?" I asked her, sitting up.

"Yes," was all she said before exiting the tent. We were okay, but we'd never be friends.

I stood, stretched, and followed her. The sun was low in the sky and would probably set in another hour or two. The air was cooler at the higher elevation. The guys were waiting for us. Even Greer was there. He'd been distant too. How did he feel when he'd heard that I wasn't the one he needed to be protecting? He should have been assigned to Laney. He should go back and save her, guard her. The AO said she doesn't have to marry Gigandet; she just has to sit on the throne. As far-fetched and strange and unbelievable as it was, there was a peace inside of me, like it all made sense. It made sense that Laney should be a queen. Not Gigandet's wife. But a queen, all her own. And she could choose her king.

I fell into step beside Greer as our group walked the path along the river, downhill to the valley where the camp was nestled. I nudged his elbow so he'd pay attention to me. "What do you think about going back to rescue Laney?" I asked quietly. "She can stop the disease from spreading anymore."

He didn't look at me, but his jaw tightened. "My orders were to protect you."

"That's because Gigandet didn't know. Why did he never consult with an AO about the curse?"

"Because there were none to be found. They were all killed or exiled during the rebellion. This AO…how do we know he's really an AO? How do we know he isn't lying? Maybe he's just trying to dethrone Gigandet."

I shrugged. "Maybe. But maybe not. It's a huge risk you're taking, if he's right."

"What do you mean?"

"Staying with me, instead of going back for her."

"Hmph," he grunted. "Maybe you're just trying to get rid of me." I smirked, but said no more. I'd planted the seed. Maybe I'd wake in the morning to find him gone. Then, Laney would maybe be safe. *Safety's an illusion*, I heard Jace's voice say again. But maybe not, I argued back. Maybe it could be real. Maybe she could be queen. Maybe, maybe, maybe.

We'd reached the entrance to the camp, row after row of tents. It reminded me of how armies used to set up camp before battle. Would these people become the army we needed? Or would they wait for the new dictator to come to them? It almost made more sense that they should. They could fight him in their own territory. The Antonians were afraid to come here.

There was a wide central pathway, which led to the main fire, as James had called it. People were sitting outside of their tents. Others were standing in line waiting for food. Some shy children snuck a peek and a smile at me. Some of the adults seemed fearful, grabbing their children and moving away as we approached the line. But most of the adults appeared curious. What had their leaders told them? Had they been instructed not to speak with us? Through the crowd, I glimpsed Laura and James monitoring the food distribution. Or perhaps they were there to make sure none of *us* interacted with any of *them*.

As we neared the front of the line, a lady sitting nearby, stood and asked, "Durham? Is that you?" She scrutinized his face. It was one of the only times I'd ever seen Durham shocked. He was speechless for a moment as he took a step toward her.

"I thought you were dead," he nearly choked out—one of the only times I'd seen him overcome with emotion too.

The woman's eyes scanned the rest of us until her gaze fixed on Mara. I gasped quietly looking back and forth between them. When Mara and I had been imprisoned in a cell beneath the palace, she'd told me about the day her parents had disappeared. She'd come home from school to find them gone. Eventually Durham, a friend of her parents, had arrived to take her home with him, and that's how she'd become a part of Durham's family, his little trio of orphans. Mara had never known whether her parents had been taken by the government and killed or if they had escaped into the mountains.

The way this woman was looking at her, the way they looked alike, I knew she had to be Mara's mother. She could have been Mara, only twenty years older—the dark skin, the almond-shaped eyes, the long black hair in braids. Mara's hair was gone though. Whirl had shaved her head bare just a few days earlier. But there was no mistaking their resemblance. They stared at each other for a long moment, letting it sink in. I imagined Mara wasn't the same little girl her mother remembered. But she was hers. The woman ran the short distance and wrapped her arms around her daughter, her body shaking with sobs. Mara, caught off guard, hesitated for just a moment before her arms locked tightly around the woman's torso, holding her up.

I only noticed my own tears when one of them fell from my chin, the salty drop landing on my arm. It was the kind of reunion I had hoped to have with my own mother. But she'd barely recognized me, disoriented and confused, and when it finally did register in her mind who I was, she'd been upset that I'd come to rescue her. Our reunion had ended quickly in separation…and death. But here was Mara's mother, still alive, never dead, as they had thought. I smiled through my tears watching them. Curwen and Sheldon's eyes were glistening too.

I felt fingers wrap around my arm and turned to find a young man I'd never seen before. Pulling away from him, I asked, "May I help you?" Glancing back at Mara and her mother, I didn't want to be interrupted from witnessing their coming together. Everyone else was focused on them as well; they didn't seem to notice the strange man beside me.

"My apologies," he said, taking a small step back. "My name is Heri. I'm the apprentice to the AO, and he's requested your presence at dinner." He spoke quietly, like he didn't want to be heard by anyone else.

"My presence? Me—alone?"

"Yes, he'd like you to join him. Alone." When I hesitated, he added, "He wants to discuss some things with you that may be able to help your sister."

My eyes narrowed with suspicion and intrigue. The AO was supposed to know everything. Perhaps he did have some knowledge, some other way to cure the disease that didn't involve Laney. Mara had wanted to find the Ancient One more than any of us; she would have loved an invitation to dine with him. But that night she would get to have dinner with the mother she hadn't seen in more than two decades. I nodded at him. "Follow me," he said.

After we left the crowd behind, I asked him, "How long have you been here?"

"Too long," was all he said. He led me between the tents down narrow dirt pathways. They'd been trampled so much the grass had died. Every so often we'd see a few people, but it seemed like most were at the main fire.

"Is there always a meal at the main fire?" I asked.

"Every other night, yes. All other meals are your own responsibility, unless you can't physically provide for yourself, then others take turns providing meals."

"How do y'all provide food for so many? Everyone appears healthy and well-nourished."

"We have some crops nearby. Some are skilled hunters. And, the river always has an abundance of fish."

He stopped at what seemed to be the far corner of the camp, completely opposite from the guest campsite, and even somewhat secluded from the other tents, as if the AO had been bestowed his own private space. His was also one of the permanent wooden structures; it was one of the nicer ones I'd seen, though it only had a flap of cloth for a door. There was a fire burning outside, and I could smell something good cooking in the pot hanging above it. Heri pulled back the cloth door and gestured for me to enter the little shack.

It was just one large room with a dirt floor. In the rear left corner was a bed. Across from it, in the right corner, was a cot like the one Curwen had used at the medical station. I assumed it was where Heri slept. Immediately to my right was a set of shelves and to the left of the door, a trunk. In the center of the room there was a small table with two chairs. The AO stood beside one of the shelves, used as a counter it seemed, and poured something into a cup, something from a glass tube that looked very similar to the one I'd seen Laura with when she'd prepared the treatment for Curwen. The old man stirred the liquid in his cup. Was he sick? He was a short, but stocky man. Though he appeared old because of all the wrinkles in his forehead and at the corner of his eyes, I doubted he was as old as he looked. My eyes bounced from the vial to his cup. He saw where my gaze landed.

"Yes," he admitted. "I too was injected with the disease when they held me in captivity."

"How long ago was that?" I asked. How long had this treatment kept him alive?

"I've been here for a few years."

"How do you like it?"

He rolled his eyes slightly. "It's fine, but I long for my city. I know I won't set foot in it again though."

"Why not?" I asked. "You should. I know Yadriel would love to see you."

His eyes narrowed. "You were quite clever throwing his name around in the meeting this morning."

"I wanted to see if you would react, to confirm whether you were the same AO related to him."

"Of course I'd react—to find out my grandson is running the black market and smuggling guns for Whirl. He should be as ashamed of himself as I am of him." Though Yadriel had pointed his gun at us and refused to help us, for some reason I felt bad for him, to hear his grandfather talk about him that way. The AO was still shaking his head in disgust when Heri came to the doorway with two bowls in his hands and set them on the small table.

The AO instructed Heri to leave us, and when he was gone, I asked, "So, he's your apprentice?"

"Well, I have to teach *somebody* everything I know before I die. Heri has a good memory. He'll need to teach others, if we are to create a new generation of Ancient Ones."

"The keepers of history," I said. "Why not just write it all down in a book?"

"It has been," he said. On a shelf beside him, he set his hand on a four-inch thick hardbound leather book. He very gently opened it to a random page for me to see. That book contained everything about Antonia, and my excitement grew as I stepped closer. Squinting in the lantern light, I could see some letters were smudged, but even so, I couldn't read the words. They were in another language. The AO smiled as though he'd tricked me. "That's why I must teach someone. The Antonian language stopped being taught more than a century ago."

"But why?"

"When light travel became extremely popular, and every citizen was allowed to travel as he pleased, the government decided to begin teaching English in our schools. It started as a second language at first, but then over time became preferred. It was a way to keep our people safe when they traveled as well as keep them from tipping anyone off in your dimension that there were people showing up all over the place speaking an unknown language. We didn't want any foreign governments suspecting or investigating."

"So, Heri can read this?" I asked, still studying the page.

"He's…getting there. There are a few distinguished Antonian families who hold to tradition and ensure every generation can read the old language. I requested an apprentice from one of these families. I got Heri.

He was taught, but he didn't retain much. So, I have to teach him the language and then the history before I die."

"Why not just translate it into English?"

He appeared shocked at the suggestion. "Never! No, never. We couldn't risk one of your kind reading it and learning everything. And, if it were ever brought to your dimension…" He stopped talking and continued to shake his head, his eyes wide with fear and apprehension at the thought.

"I meant no offense. Just that…if you die before you finish teaching Heri, he'd have a book he could read."

"Well…no." He shook his head again. "I'll just have to live long enough. Now, will you please have a seat? Let's eat while it's warm." It was a steaming stew of meat and vegetables, and I was starving. We sat in silence for a few moments, taking our first bites, before he asked, "So, tell me, what do you know about the curse?"

"I clearly know very little, and what I do know seems to keep changing. Tell me, why did you request my presence this evening?"

He chuckled softly and took a sip of his tea. "We've waited hundreds of years for the one with the mark. It would be a shame not to have her for dinner, even if it's in humble circumstances."

"But I'm not the important one. You should be dining with Laney. She's the one who can make a difference."

"On the contrary, she cannot fulfill her role without you." I gave him a questioning look. "Without a mark, there can be no match," he explained. "If you were to die, she would be useless in breaking the curse. I heard you've already had a couple of attempts on your life already. You need to be careful and protected."

"Yes, and one of them made it clear that I wasn't needed."

"Because he doesn't understand the legend of the curse properly. On purpose, it was created as a riddle. The body who created it wasn't going to make it easy for the Antonians to figure out—then it wouldn't be a punishment for them. Over time it has become even more distorted as people have passed it along orally."

The AO should have said he *didn't* understand the legend. Anderson was dead. Curwen had killed him. How come I still felt his breath on my neck and voice in my ear? Why did I suddenly feel like I was under water again?

"Leela, are you okay?" I heard the AO ask. He was standing over me, concerned, but he sounded and looked far away. That's when I realized my hands were covering my ears.

I pulled them away, taking deep breaths to calm myself. "I'm fine. What happened?"

"I don't know. Perhaps what you'd call a panic attack." I looked at him in confusion. He explained, "You've been sitting like that for at least a minute gasping for air, like you couldn't breathe."

"What?" I didn't remember that. "Maybe I should go now." As I stood, I had to grab the back of the chair to balance myself. What was wrong with me? My head was throbbing, my mind foggy, and my ears felt like they were clogged with water.

"Will you be able to find your way back in the dark?" he asked, his hand on my elbow to steady me." Heri hasn't returned yet to guide you." As though he'd been summoned, he appeared in the doorway. Had he been waiting just outside? "Heri, please make sure Leela gets to the guest site safely."

I almost groaned out loud remembering how far away it was. My eyelids were heavy, but my feet even more so. Each step felt like I had bags of rocks around my ankles. We moved slowly as we exited his dwelling and began the long journey to my tent. Where I could sleep. Sleep. Sleep sounded good.

After we had passed through the tents, quietly as Heri had instructed, he said, "You ate all your soup and quickly too."

I nodded. "It was good. What did you put in it?" I asked, interested in the recipe and if he'd used any ingredients native to Antonia. Then I paused. What had he put in it? Cutting my eyes at him, I asked, in a slur, "Wait, *what did you put in it?* Did you drug me?" His white teeth gleamed in the moonlight, admitting his guilt. I should have been afraid, but there was a disconnect between my mind and fear. Fight or flight was not kicking in. Instead, I asked, "Why would you do that?" Whatever he'd put in the stew made me curious, not wise.

He tucked one arm under mine to support me as we continued strolling at a slow pace. "You want to know what I've been doing?" he asked, sounding excited to tell me. I nodded like a child ready to hear a story. "Well, you know how the AO was infected with the disease?" I nodded again. "Well, I have to empty his pot every morning, and do you know where I take it?" I shook my head, looking up at his face. My eyes must have been glazed over. "I've been taking it down river and dumping it in the water supply that runs to the city, to all their crops and drinking sources, hoping that it would spread the disease more quickly."

I gasped in shock, but still not fear. "Why would you do that?" I asked in awe.

"The sooner they all die, the sooner we can return to the city and start over," he said. I nodded as though it was a smart plan that made complete sense. I wanted to sleep. It felt like I would fall asleep any second, leaning on his shoulder. Were my feet even still moving? I looked down to see them, to check. Yes, they were moving, but blurry. "But, you know what would ensure that none of them survive the disease?"

"Huh?" I mumbled, still watching my feet as one moved in front of the other. They were both doubled, like I had four feet. They looked funny. I almost laughed.

"Are you paying attention?" he demanded, sounding annoyed. He'd taken away my faculties, but wanted me to pay attention. I picked my head up and looked at him again. "What would ensure that none of them would survive the disease is. . . if there is no mark."

"No mark?" I asked. "But I'm the mark." I laughed and repeated, "I'm the mark. Can you believe that? Can you believe any of this?" I laughed again. "None of this is real. None of this is real." I couldn't stop laughing.

But he wasn't interested in my drug-induced breakdown. He grabbed my shoulders and shook me. "Stop it! Don't you understand what I'm telling you?"

I shook my head, smiling and laughing softly, attempting to suppress it because he looked so angry. He'd had enough. His hands moved from my shoulders up to my throat. Slowly he began to apply pressure. He was stronger than his scrawny figure made him seem. Or maybe it was an illusion; maybe he seemed strong only because he'd weakened me. Now the fear began to rise inside my chest as I struggled uselessly against him, my arms weakly hitting his chest, my feet simply kicking up dirt. Whatever he'd put in the stew had destroyed my cognitive abilities and all the self-defense

Hollister had taught me. Heri pushed me backwards, pinning me against a tree as I strained for life and breath. His grip became tighter, his fingertips digging into the back of my neck and his thumbs pressing harder on my throat. This was my end. This was how the mark would die. *She cannot fulfill her role without you*, I heard the AO's voice say.

Then suddenly someone else was there, grabbing him around his neck and pulling him away. I slumped to the ground gasping for air, the tree my only support. I was only vaguely aware of the struggle happening just a few feet away. A few punches, some thuds. And then I was lifted from the ground. Someone was carrying me.

I opened my eyes briefly and glimpsed Greer's face. He'd honored his word to Gigandet. He'd kept me safe once again.

There was a bright, distant flash in the night sky. Before passing out, I asked, "Was that lightning?"

CHAPTER 14

(LANEY)

"Stay with Chuza tonight," Phaedra said through the phone. "I'll see you in the morning."

She was brief. It was as I'd expected—I'd exhausted her patience. I didn't even get to ask her about Hollister, or if Jace was okay, before she hung up. When I set the phone down and turned around, the four sets of eyes were still staring at me. "Which one of you is Chuza?" I asked.

"That'd be me," the woman said, her voice deep and smooth. She appeared to be in her late thirties; she was tall and slender with tan skin, dark hair and eyes. She was beautifully intimidating. "I live around the corner. We can go as soon as the rain stops. Looks like you could use some rest."

All three men continued to remain silent. The two others, besides Clive, didn't introduce themselves.

"Thank you," I murmured, glancing at them and then at the table between us. There was a large paper spread across it. I stepped forward to get a better look. It was a map of Antonia. Not just the city itself, but the tunnel system as well as the mountains were marked in detail. "What are we planning?" I asked.

"We?" Chuza asked, raising an eyebrow. "Are you a part of us?"

I shrugged. "I think we have similar goals."

"What are your goals?" she asked.

"Defeat Whirl, end the sickness, free the slaves."

"Free the bodies?" asked one of the men finally, sounding appalled at the idea.

I glared at him. "They're not *bodies*. They're people who've been kidnapped and enslaved, including everyone from my hometown." I hit my palms on the table as I said this, emphasizing my anger and the injustice of it all.

"You're Laney," Chuza said with a slight smile. "I've heard about your temper. Did you really hold a knife to Curwen's throat?" She seemed impressed, but the three men gasped. It felt like she said it so that they would fear me, or at least take me seriously.

"How do you know about that?" I asked, slightly embarrassed. Curse my anger preceding me.

She shrugged one shoulder. "Word gets around."

"I can't imagine Curwen would want to share that."

"Probably not," she agreed. "But he included it in his reports. And I read all the reports." She began folding up the map. "Guys, you're dismissed. We'll reconvene with Phaedra in the morning." The two men from the table left quickly, but instead of going out the front door like I expected, they headed upstairs. Did they live here with Clive? Chuza must have seen the curiosity on my face because she explained, "Their houses aren't as close as mine. They can't be caught out past today's newly imposed curfew. It's better for us to have the team together anyway."

"What team is that?" I asked.

"Strategic operations."

"Are you planning an attack?"

"We are waiting for further instructions, but preparing as best we can."

"Chuza, that's enough," Clive chided her. He didn't want her to tell me anything else, but she dismissed him with a roll of her eyes and a wave of her hand as she turned to pack the map into her bag. She went to the counter where there was food spread out—fruits, vegetables, cheese, meats, and bread—and began piling it into an empty container. "Hey…" Clive protested.

She looked at him and then looked at me. "When's the last time you ate?" she asked me.

I couldn't remember. "I haven't today."

"I don't have any food at my place, and we need to eat," she said to Clive. He grunted, sighed and left the room. The first time I'd met him, his appearance had reminded me of my father, but now I knew that was the only thing they had in common. My father would give a stranger the last speck of food from the pantry, no questions asked. Chuza snapped a lid onto the container and pulled her jacket's hood over her head. "Come on. Let's get out of here."

As we passed by Clive, he was sitting on his couch, crouched over the coffee table. I paused to get a closer look at what he was doing. There was a handgun on the table and a second one he'd taken apart to clean. "Where'd you get the guns?" I asked.

Without looking up, he said, "Phaedra assigned them to me this morning."

"Do you know how to shoot?"

"That's why she assigned them to me." He didn't like my nosy questions.

"Where'd she get them?" I asked. Curwen had always been firm about no guns in Antonia. Obviously Whirl had them, but did the resistance too?

Chuza answered when he wouldn't. "Durham purchased them on the black market. He didn't want Whirl getting to them first. And it's a good thing too. Our reports are showing that without that shipment, Whirl hasn't been able to arm all his soldiers."

"Are there enough to arm the resistance?" I asked, still unsure how many members they had.

She nodded. "And then some. Now, come on, let's go."

She cracked the door open and peered out. The rain was a light drizzle, and the street was empty. Whirl's soldiers must have had better things to do. She stepped out and motioned for me to follow, closing the door silently behind us. There was a coolness in the air I hadn't felt before. It had come with the rain, but it suited the atmosphere, the mood that had settled over the quiet, dark, imprisoned city. Chuza walked at a quick pace, staying in the shadows of the houses and making no sounds with her steps; I mimicked her as best I could. It reminded me of hunting with my dad, the way he tried to teach me to walk silently through the woods. I had never been very good at it. Leaves would crunch and twigs would snap, and I'd scare all the prey away. But I was the prey now, trying not to be caught.

Before I could let the panic build, worried that at any moment a guard might appear, Chuza rounded the corner and stopped in front of the first house. It looked just like the rest with its white stucco exterior. When she opened the door, it had the same layout as Curwen's place—kitchen to the right, living area to the left, a flight of stairs in the center. There was no red flower in her windowsill though—it wasn't marked as a safe house for the resistance. But I hoped it would be that night. A safe place to rest.

I did rest. Despite everything I slept without disruption, no tossing and turning, no nightmares. Chuza had made sure my belly was full, offered me a hot shower, and a warm bed. And I slept like I hadn't slept in a long time. When I woke, the clock showed that it was almost noon. I'd missed the entire morning, and I'd missed whatever plans Chuza had discussed with her strategic operations team. After changing into new clothes from the closet, I cracked open the bedroom door. I could hear voices, and I crept down the stairs as quietly as possible, hoping to hear what they talked about when I wasn't around. They were in the living room.

"What do you think is the best move?" a woman asked. From her voice, I knew it was Phaedra.

"The new tunnels are almost complete," Chuza said. "We just need a day or two more. Then we can make the move."

"What about Curwen's report?" Phaedra asked.

"I think it will work out perfectly."

"Laney," Phaedra called. "You can come and join us now."

Rounding the corner, I stepped into the room. Phaedra rose from the couch and came toward me. She hugged me, but it didn't feel the same as it had days earlier when we'd first met. There was a sternness in her now, the way my mother used to get when she was upset with one of us. "You two have made things much harder than they had to be," she said, pulling back to look at me.

"Us two?" I asked. Did she mean me and Leela?

"You and Hollister. Neither one of you know how to follow directions, how to submit to someone else's instructions. Always thinking you know best."

"Where is Hollister?" My stomach dropped in panic. "Is he okay?"

"I can't honestly tell you. He wouldn't leave the science facility. Not without his men."

"He's willing to die for them," I said quietly, more to myself than to her, remembering his words to me. This is bigger than us. *They are important enough that I'm willing to die for them*, he'd said that day in the rain. I'd just gotten him back, but he wanted to go and sacrifice himself for others. He didn't want to forget them. He didn't want to choose comfort over sacrifice. I needed to be more like him. I needed to remember the dead child in my arms. I needed to remember what we were fighting for. I needed to be able to let Hollister go. That thought nearly knocked the breath out of me.

As Phaedra led me to the couch, I asked, "What was that you were saying about Curwen?"

"Curwen was able to call me this morning," she explained.

I gasped. "They actually made it out? They're okay?" I hadn't believed it until that moment.

She nodded slightly. "For the most part. The group, minus you and Hollister, were able to make it to the mountains and have been staying with the community there."

"There's a community there?" I asked. It was the first time I'd heard of anyone living outside the city.

"Yes, most of them are escaped bodies. Some are Antonian fugitives."

"And they're okay?" Anxious for my twin, I asked, "How's Leela?"

"Well…she was almost killed last night, for the second time. Anderson nearly drowned her in the fountain at the science facility, and last night another man attempted to strangle her. But Curwen assured me that she's okay, at least physically. When we spoke, he hadn't had a chance to talk with her since the incident. The man got away, so Curwen was out searching for him. They think he may be on his way back to the city."

Two men had tried to take my sister's life. My stomach felt sick. Anderson had murdered Muriel and then gone after Leela. "Did Anderson get away too?" I asked.

"No…" She hesitated. "Curwen shot and killed him." I could tell from her face those were words she had never thought she'd say. Her son had taken a life. But he'd also preserved one too, one of the most important ones to me.

"I'm so sorry that happened," I said.

"I'm just glad we got you out of there," she said, squeezing my hand. "You don't know how important you are."

"I do know," I said. "I know I'm the one who's supposed to marry Gigandet. But Gigandet is already married."

"Well, then it's a good thing you don't have to marry him," Chuza said. "You just have to be queen."

"What do you mean?" I asked, confused.

Phaedra nodded. "It's true. Curwen told me this morning. You *could* have married Gigandet to break the curse, but you don't have to. We just need to seat you on the throne."

I shook my head. "You want me to rule Antonia, by myself, when I don't even belong here?"

"But you do belong. Antonians have been waiting for you for hundreds of years."

"I'm not a monarch."

"But you could be," Phaedra said, encouraging me.

"What if I don't want to be?"

"That probably means you'll be a good one," Chuza said.

Before I could protest further, Phaedra's phone began to ring. Could it be Curwen again? Perhaps I could talk to Leela.

"Hello," she answered. I could tell from her face it wasn't who I had hoped. She listened for a moment, and then asked the caller, "The man has requested to speak with Laney?"

"Who?" I asked. "Hollister?"

She shook her head. "Another man who escaped the facility. His name is Rick."

Rick. He was alive. The last I'd seen him he'd been hooked up to a machine being drained of his blood. I nodded frantically, reaching for the phone. "Put him on," she told the caller before handing it to me.

"Rick?" I asked.

"Laney," came his deep voice. "I'm so sorry." He sounded like he might be close to tears.

Now I felt as though the blood was draining from my body. "Why?" I said. "What happened?"

"Hollister," he said. "He was with us in the tunnel. Right with us. But then there was a door…when we went through, he shut and locked it. He purposely stayed behind. I think he wanted to lead the guards in another direction, to give us a chance to get out."

"So…we don't know what's happened to him," I said. It wasn't a question, just something I needed to hear out loud. "He could still be okay…"

"The guard who helped us escape said he's going to try to find out," Rick said. "Maybe he was able to find another hiding spot."

I pointed at the map Chuza had spread on the coffee table, and asked her, "Where are the tunnels beneath the science facility?"

"There's only this one that leads out," she pointed to it. "It's relatively new. There's a vault door here," she pointed to it, "and then it exits through a hatch door in the forest not too far away."

Hollister must have shut the vault door. Staring at the map, I already knew the answer, but I asked anyway. "So, there's no other way to escape without going through the door?"

She followed the tunnel with her finger. "Here's the door. The only other way he could have gone leads to a dead end. That tunnel hasn't been completed yet."

"So, he'd be trapped," I said. Again, it wasn't a question. I just needed to hear it out loud.

"I'm sorry, Laney," Rick repeated.

"How long ago was this?" I asked, ignoring his apology. It wasn't his fault. There was nothing he could have done.

"We've been here at the headquarters for a couple of hours now, so maybe three hours ago. It took that long to finally convince them to let me talk to you."

Suddenly, there was a loud horn, something like a tornado siren sounding through the streets outside. My first instinct was to crouch down in fear. "What is that?" I asked the women who seemed unfazed.

"There's a government broadcast for us to watch," Chuza explained, walking over to a cabinet and sliding the doors open. There was a screen inside; she pressed a button to turn it on. We were looking at the front steps of the palace, the same place I'd been the day before to witness the royal wedding. There was a podium set up. Beside it was a poster-size photograph of Leela. She looked beautiful, but I could tell that her smile had been forced. The wedding gown she wore—the same one Elodie wore yesterday—was not yet stained with blood, which meant it had been taken before Whirl's massacre.

"Are you watching this?" Rick asked. I had forgotten I still had the phone to my ear.

Phaedra grabbed it from me, said, "We'll be in touch," and ended the call.

The siren finally stopped, and our eyes were glued to the screen. There was no crowd in front of the palace this time. This time they weren't trying to make it appear like a joyous occasion. Or, perhaps they didn't want to risk bringing any citizens out of the lockdown zone. Either way, there were only guards lined up along the front of the steps and against the palace wall. But then the engraved wooden doors began to open, and Whirl walked out. He approached the podium, and the camera zoomed in for an up-close view of Whirl with his cold blue eyes.

"Good afternoon, citizens of Antonia," Whirl began. "We come to you today to ask for your help. The woman you see in this photograph," he gestured to his right, "is a dangerous criminal. She's not from here. She traveled through the light and attempted to infiltrate our government by pretending to have the mark. She pretended that she could end the terrible sickness among us! As you can see from the photograph, Gigandet fell for her tricks and almost married her, but I arrived in time to stop the wedding. But this woman escaped. There are actually two of them, twin sisters. And we have it on the authority of a witness that both of them are in Antonia. We need to find them as soon as possible. Once they are found, the lockdown can be lifted, and the city can return to safety. These *bodies* need to be captured. If anyone has information about either of them, where they can be found, please get in touch with the nearest guard. They will be stationed throughout the living quarters. You will be generously rewarded for any accurate and helpful details."

He paused, then looked back at one of the guards and gave a slight nod. The massive doors began to open again. I assumed he was preparing to exit the stage, but no. Instead, three figures were coming out of the palace—two guards and one prisoner—Hollister. His hands were shackled, and so were his feet, so that he could only take small steps. It reminded me of the picture Annabelle had drawn of him. Had she seen the future, or was this the second time he'd been bound this way? As he was brought closer, to the right of the podium, the camera zoomed in on him. He had a black eye, a swollen lip and blood stains on his shirt. And he wore a shock collar once again. Tears were pouring down my cheeks. Now we knew what had happened to him. He had been trapped, as we had predicted, and caught.

Whirl cleared his throat. "If either of the women—criminals—would like to turn themselves in, we will spare this body's life." He gestured to his left at Hollister. "This body is an accomplice, and we apprehended him this morning after he attempted escape." Hollister glared at Whirl with a face of stone, his whole body tense, ready for a fight.

When Whirl paused and there was silence, Hollister yelled, "He's lying to you all!"

Almost immediately he was on his knees from the shock of the collar. As he went down, I went up, springing to my feet, lunging toward the screen as if I could actually help him, lift him from the tiles. Phaedra pulled me back and put her arms tightly around me as we continued to watch the scene unfold. Whirl attempted to suppress a scornful snicker. He returned to the mic. "You see, bodies will do anything to manipulate you. Do not trust them. Do not approach either of the young women, but report immediately to a guard. We need your help to make Antonia safe again. Thank you."

The screen went blue, and I went for the front door. Chuza was quicker and closer. She blocked my path, her back against the door. "Move," I demanded. "I need to save Hollister."

"You're not going anywhere," Chuza said.

"Is that what Hollister would want you to do?" Phaedra asked from behind me.

No. I turned around to look at her. "They're going to kill him," I said, defeated.

"We'll find a way to get him out of there," she assured me. "But it's not this way. Everyone will be searching for you. Everyone will want the reward. Your picture will be posted everywhere."

"Leela's picture," I corrected.

"Leela isn't in Antonia. Leela doesn't have blonde hair anymore," she said. "It's *your* picture now."

CHAPTER 15

(LEELA)

"Leela," someone spoke my name softly. A woman. "Leela, can you wake up and tell me how you're feeling?" It was Laura. She was sitting on a short stool beside my cot inside the dimly lit tent. It was just the two of us. I vaguely remembered hearing voices throughout the night, sometimes raised in heated conversation, before drifting back into unconsciousness. Laura's had been among them.

My own voice was hoarse as I tried to answer her. "My head is pounding, and I'm so thirsty."

She handed me a glass of water as I sat up. "The headache will go away once you get some water and food in your system. Can you tell me what happened last night? What do you remember?"

Instantly my hand went to my throat as Heri's face flashed through my mind. "Heri brought me to have dinner with the AO. But soon after eating, I wasn't feeling well, so Heri was instructed to bring me back here. I can't remember much from there, except for Heri choking me…"

She clicked on a small flashlight and gently moved my hand so she could examine my neck. "You definitely have bruising consistent with your story."

"It's not a story," I said defensively. "It really happened." Even if I couldn't remember all of it.

"I believe you. Greer gave a similar account. Did Heri give you any indication why he would do this? Any motive?"

There was something. Something he had revealed. Something important. But it escaped my memory. I couldn't grasp it. "He put something in my soup…to drug me," I said slowly. "But I can't remember why." Tears of frustration filled my eyes. What had he said? Why did he want me dead?

"It's okay." She gave my shoulder a squeeze. "It might come back to you. Greer took us to the place where the incident happened. There was some blood on the ground."

"Whose blood?" I asked.

"Probably Heri's. It seems Greer beat him pretty well."

"Where's Heri now?"

"We haven't been able to locate him."

The last man who had tried to kill me was dead. I didn't have to fear him coming after me again. But Heri was still out there somewhere in these mountains. Not that I wanted someone else to be killed on my behalf—I certainly didn't want that. I wished death on no one. But I wanted his location to be known, for him to be locked up and guarded. She must have seen the concern across my face because she said, "Don't worry. We have some of our skilled hunters tracking him, and you will not be left without protection at any time. I suppose Gigandet was wise in assigning guards to you." She stood. "I know they're all anxious to see you."

"Wait," I said, grabbing her wrist as she was turning to leave. "Was the AO behind this?"

She shook her head. "No, we don't believe so. He's expressed great concern for you and been nothing but helpful in our search for Heri. He's still being watched, but at this point we believe Heri acted alone. Eat some breakfast. Get some rest. I'll come back to visit you soon." She disappeared through the tent flap, sunlight shining in for a split second before it fell closed, back to darkness.

I welcomed it. I could think better in the dark. My head was sore to touch where he'd slammed it against the tree. I remembered that. But the why…I couldn't remember the why. My thoughts raced into nothingness. They stopped at the realization that he'd drugged me and began again with his hands around my throat. The in between was lost. Before I could shed more frustrated tears, Sheldon spoke from outside the doorway, "May I come in?"

"I'm coming out," I said, standing and wiping the sleep and the tears from my eyes. My whole body ached.

As soon as I stuck my head out, Sheldon was waiting there, his body blocking the sun from blinding me, his dark figure outlined by its glow. "How are you?" he asked, anxious and impatient to know. I stared into his green eyes, blinking back more tears, not wanting to shed anymore or cause worry. But he instantly wrapped his arms around me. When I had impulsively hugged him before, when he'd been released from the prison, he had shyly pulled away. But this time he initiated and didn't seem to want to let go. "I'm sorry we weren't there."

"How could we have been?" came Durham's voice. I pulled away from Sheldon's chest and looked at him seated on one of the benches around the firepit. "You didn't tell us where you were going. Why did you go off like that without one of us?" He was stern and sounded like my father. But was he really concerned for my life or more worried that my death might have ruined his plans for Antonia?

"Hey, she didn't know the AO's apprentice was dangerous," Sheldon said in my defense. "This isn't her fault."

"I assumed it would be safe to talk to the AO," I added quietly.

"You can't assume anything is safe," Durham said. "Safety is an illusion."

There it was again. Jace had said the same thing a few nights earlier.

"You're right. How could I forget?" I asked sarcastically, taking a seat on an empty bench. "Did you teach that to Jace—safety is an illusion?"

"I teach it to all of those who join our group. Some understand it more than others." His eyes cut to Sheldon for a brief moment. "Jace gets it. Curwen gets it. Mara gets it. But Sheldon, he's always been different. More trusting. More willing to hope for the good in people." Sheldon just looked at the ground. "I think he actually believes there's such a thing as a 'safe place.'" Durham spoke these things with a kind of disappointment, like he expected better from Sheldon. I wasn't sure why he'd even started criticizing his own son, if something had happened or if this had always been the nature of their relationship.

"If you don't believe that a safe place can be achieved, then why are you bothering to try and change Antonia?" Sheldon argued. "You've spent your whole life fighting for it. You must be hopeful for better things too.

Don't criticize me for having hope that safety doesn't always have to be an illusion. It can be real."

After the past few days, I wasn't sure if it could be. Would I ever be able to let my guard down? Would I ever feel safe again? Durham didn't have a chance to respond before Greer emerged from the other tent. He didn't look like he'd been in a fight. He was nearly twice the size of Heri. I could have defeated Heri, if I hadn't been drugged. At least, that's what I wanted to believe. Greer stretched his arms upward and then took a long drink from his water bottle. "How are you?" he finally asked me.

Before I could answer, Durham piped in, "Bet you're glad he didn't leave to go protect Laney now, aren't you?"

He had somehow eavesdropped on yesterday's conversation or Greer had told him what I'd suggested. But I couldn't understand why this leader of the resistance was being so antagonizing. "Yes, I'm very grateful," I stated firmly. "Thank you, Greer."

"Not necessary," he said. "It's my job."

That stung. "And if it *hadn't* been your job?" I asked. I would have died. They would have found my body.

"He still would have done it," Sheldon said quickly. Trying to see the best in people. I used to do that too.

"Maybe," Greer said. "But then again, I wouldn't even be here if it wasn't my job."

Durham cleared his throat, and then said, "Well, then Gigandet's orders worked for our benefit. This time."

I was disgusted with both of them. I was just a means to an end for them, exactly what Curwen feared I would be, the reason he had never wanted to bring me here. Changing the subject, I asked, "Where is everyone?" By everyone, I meant Curwen.

"Mara stayed with her mother last night," Sheldon explained. "Her father passed away a few years ago. She has brothers she never knew. They wanted some family time together." I was happy for her, even if I couldn't *feel* happy at that moment. "And Curwen went with the search party to find your attacker."

"How long have they been searching?" I asked.

"When I brought you back here last night," Greer began, "nobody was here. They were still with Mara's family." His tone sounded a little accusatory. "So, I had to wait for them to return before one of us could go report what had happened to Laura and James. By that time, a couple hours had passed and Heri had plenty of time to get away. I should have left you and gone back for him myself, but I was too worried you'd stop breathing or something. I didn't know what was wrong with you or that you'd been drugged. But, the team's been searching since then…since a couple hours after the incident."

The incident. How many people in their camp knew about the incident? Was leadership keeping it quiet, or had they spread the word about the murderous man among them? And what about the AO? Was he really innocent? He had invited me for dinner. But he hadn't prepared the food. "Have any of you seen or spoken with the AO?" I asked.

"I did," Sheldon said. "I went with James to question him. He was shocked and extremely upset…kept saying over and over that you must not die."

You need to be careful and protected, he had said to me at dinner. But then his own student tried to kill me.

"Speak and he appears," said Durham, looking beyond me. I rose to my feet and turned to see the AO coming over the hill with Laura. His steps were very slow, and he used her arm for support. Sheldon came and stood beside me, as did Greer, even though the old man was clearly not a physical threat. It seemed like forever before they reached us, and I couldn't bring myself to make any movements toward them.

When we were face-to-face, a foot apart, the bench the only thing between us, he said with sincere remorse, "I'm so sorry this happened, Leela. I should have made you stay last night. I shouldn't have trusted him to escort you. I'm so sorry." He was near tears, as was I. I couldn't speak for fear my voice would break. He continued, "Heri always was a little odd. That's why his family wanted to send him away to be trained by me. But I never imagined he was capable of this…"

It wasn't the AO's fault, and I didn't want to talk about what Heri had done. It was already on repeat in my mind. So instead, I asked, "Who will you teach now?"

"I'm not sure I have enough time to train anyone new. I can feel my life coming to an end, and fear I will not have a successor."

I almost felt worse for him than for myself. Without someone to train, the history of Antonia would die with him. He knew what no one else knew. An idea came to me, a long shot. "Durham, do you have anyone in your network who can read or speak the Antonian language?"

He paused to think before shaking his head. "Most of them are too young to know what it looks or sounds like. The only one who had knowledge of it was Muriel." The kind old woman I had only heard about, the one who'd been executed in front of Laney and Curwen. We were all silent for a moment, but then Greer began speaking to the AO in a foreign, guttural language.

A huge smile spread across the AO's face as he said something back in the same language. Then he said, so we could understand, "Your speech is perfect! Can you read just as well?" Greer nodded. "Are you from one of the noble families?"

Greer shook his head. "Just had grandparents who saw the value in teaching us our language."

The AO looked like he could leap for joy. "We must start your training immediately."

Greer took a step back. "Sir, I have other duties. We have to defeat Whirl and end the sickness."

The AO's smile was replaced with pursed lips. "We have to preserve our history."

"I have to preserve Leela's life," Greer said. "She's obviously not safe anywhere."

"Anyone can do that job," the AO argued. "You are the only one qualified for *this* job."

I could sense the struggle inside of Greer. He was supposed to obey his sovereign, the king to whom he'd pledged his life. And that king had ordered him to guard me with that life. I didn't think his loyalty would let him do anything else. Did he even want to become the next AO? As the only one qualified, did he have a choice?

I turned to Greer, placing my hand on his shoulder. "It's okay," I assured him. "You've done your duty. Gigandet would be proud. Even if it was just your job, I'm forever grateful. But it's okay. You can go with the AO."

His eyes still appeared conflicted. He looked at the AO. "I will come with you for today and begin learning. But when it's time to fight, I'm fighting." Then turning to Sheldon, he commanded, "Don't let her out of your sight."

Sheldon gave a single nod. "Not a chance."

Greer took Laura's place supporting the AO as the three of them disappeared down the hill.

It was already midday. I ate some lunch and then decided to rest in one of the hammocks, still not feeling well. Most of me wanted to retreat into the darkness of the tent, but I knew I needed to choose sunlight and the shade of a tree. It would be better for me than trying to hide.

A few hours later, as the sun was beginning to make its descent, I heard Durham shout, "They're back!"

I assumed he meant Curwen and the search party. Did they have Heri with them? I remained frozen with fear, hidden inside the hammock, my own little cocoon. Sheldon asked, "Leela, are you awake?" But I ignored him. The only person who should have been returning to our camp was Curwen. I didn't want to see anyone else.

But then I heard another voice—one I knew well—yell my name. I struggled to untangle myself from the cocoon as quickly as possible. When my feet finally hit the ground, I gasped. It *was* who I'd thought it was. It was my brother Corey, running in my direction. But how? My mind raced until I remembered the flash in the sky the night before, the last thing I could recall before losing consciousness; it *had* been lightning. It had been Corey.

Walking toward him, I demanded, "Corey, what are you doing here?"

Curwen, Laura, James, and another man I didn't know were with him. I shot Curwen a questioning look. He shook his head, clearly frustrated with the situation. Before I could say another word, Corey threw his arms around me. I cried and embraced him, squeezing tightly. I had thought I would never see him grow up. In my heart, I'd already said goodbye to him and locked away any hope that we'd ever meet again. But here he was, already taller than me, his voice sounding different, deeper. I pulled away and asked again, "Corey, what are you doing here? Laney said you were supposed to be taken back to dad at the cabin."

"I was," he said. "Gibson did take me there. But then Annabelle had a vision of you being attacked. We decided to come help and join the fight."

"You're not joining any fight," I said firmly. "You shouldn't even be here. Dad has already lost his wife. He doesn't need to lose three out of four children as well."

"Oh, come on," came a gruff voice. It was the man I didn't know. He was rough-looking with graying, shaggy hair. I assumed he was Gibson. "The boy's fourteen now. That's how old I was when I first traveled." Corey was fourteen. We'd missed his birthday. I had counted on missing all his birthdays.

"Even so," Curwen countered, "it's illegal to bring a minor to Antonia."

Curwen had always been unyielding about Corey not coming here, but Gibson just shrugged, gave a crooked grin, and said, "I've always been a lawbreaker."

Durham approached him, and the two hugged, clapping each other on the back. They were cousins. There was a resemblance between them, except Durham was clean shaven, groomed and ten years younger. Gibson had been in control of the resistance before he had to flee through the travel light to avoid being caught by the government. That's when a young Durham had taken over.

"So, how do you think you're gonna help us, old man?" Durham asked him.

"What do you have planned already?" Gibson asked instead, seeming like he wanted to wait before sharing any of his own ideas. But we didn't have any ideas of our own, at least none that had been shared with me.

Durham glanced at James and Laura who were standing nearby. "I'm not sure yet," he said. "We're still waiting for a decision from the leaders here on whether they'll fight with us."

Gibson grinned again, and then said quietly so only we could hear, "Oh, they will. Annabelle saw it."

"Annabelle doesn't see the future," I argued. She'd only had visions of things as they were happening, at least that's what we had assumed.

"No, Leela. She can now," Corey said, excited. "She's had a few visions that she said haven't happened yet."

"Why don't we all have a seat?" Laura suggested to the group. "We have a lot to talk about, I'm sure."

Curwen came close and said quietly in my ear, "Laney's okay. How are you?"

I shrugged and gave a half-smile. "Better now, to hear that. How do you know?"

"A ways down the mountain, my phone had service. I called Phaedra."

Eavesdropping, Laura interrupted, "Like I said, there's a lot for *all* of us to talk about. Everyone take a seat, please." Corey sat on my left, Curwen on my right. Durham and Gibson shared a bench to the left of us.

James and Laura were across from us. And Sheldon claimed the final bench as his own after stoking the fire. It was strange not having Mara or Greer there. The team had changed overnight. I had changed overnight.

"First things first," James started, "Heri has not been found."

"We tracked him down the mountain though," Curwen added. "We believe he's gone to the city." He was going to the city. Something didn't feel right about that. Something I couldn't remember. "I told Phaedra to have some of our members searching for him."

"What's the update on the city? On Gigandet? Did he die?" Durham asked.

Curwen shook his head. "He was or is alive, but injured. Whirl forced him to have a public wedding ceremony with Elodie. They're married now. Nobody's seen them since."

"But she'll die," I said softly. Elodie, of all people, didn't deserve that.

Gibson said, "That's why he did it. Went to school with Whirl as a boy. He was always doing something sadistic."

Curwen turned to look at me. "Laney's safe with Phaedra. They're keeping her hidden."

"What about Hollister?" Corey and I asked at the same time.

"They tried to get him out of the science facility," Curwen said. "But he wouldn't leave without the others."

I sighed with frustration. Corey stomped his foot and exclaimed, "Dang, Hollister!"

"Sounds like he was doing the honorable thing," James said.

Yeah," Corey said. "Honorable, but stupid."

I grabbed his wrist, gave it a squeeze, and motioned for him to stop talking.

"What others?" Laura asked.

"The men from his barrack, I think," I said. Laney had mentioned it as his personal mission. To Curwen I said, "I wonder if he knows the children are there too."

"Children?" Laura asked, eyebrows raised.

"The ones from my hometown," I said. "They're locked in a wing of the facility."

Corey gasped. He didn't know about that, and I didn't want to worry him. Changing the subject and gesturing to Corey and Gibson, I asked, "When did you find these two?"

"They found us," Curwen admitted. "They'd been hiding all night."

"Well, actually, we were looking for this place all night," Corey said. "I wanted to make sure Leela was okay. But eventually Gibson made us take a rest." He cut his eyes at Gibson as though he'd been so annoyed with him.

Nodding, I said, "I saw the lightning last night."

"You never mentioned that," Laura said, sounding almost accusatory.

"I didn't think it was real."

She scrutinized me with her eyes for a brief moment, but didn't say anything. Nobody spoke for a long time. Until Gibson broke the silence. "I've kept quiet about this because I was trying to make sure I was right, and wondering why y'all haven't figured it out yet." He cleared his throat as everyone stared at him. The sun had almost set behind him. "Laura, Curwen is your son. Curwen, Laura is your mother." It was as if he was introducing them for the first time—which he was—but it sounded odd.

I could tell from her expression that was the last thing she had expected him to say. There was confusion, then disbelief, perhaps mixed with some anger in her eyes. I felt Curwen stiffen beside me, his jaw clenched as was his habit. But Laura did not look at Curwen. She glared at Gibson. "No," she said with confidence. "My son died."

Durham had told us Curwen's mother had been a teenager when she'd been struck. Against the law for minors to be struck. He'd said they hadn't known she was pregnant. Also against the law for pregnant women to be struck. Two major offenses had been committed against her. Against Curwen too. Laura had confirmed she'd been sixteen when the Antonians had taken her.

"No, he didn't die," Gibson countered. "I found out the scientists were going to use your baby for their experiments, so I got word to Durham and organized for Curwen to be smuggled out of the facility, to safety."

There was that word again. Safety. An illusion. Clearly.

"You organized for my baby to be taken from me?" Laura asked. She still didn't glance at Curwen.

"Your baby was going to be taken from you no matter what. At least I made sure he lived, rather than being a human lab rat where he most certainly would have ended up dead." Gibson sounded so certain he'd made the right decision.

I placed my hand over Curwen's as it rested between us. He flinched but didn't pull away. It was my way of silently saying I was glad he was alive. Still looking at the ground, he finally spoke, his question directed at Gibson, "You couldn't have organized for her to be smuggled out also?" He turned his head and glared at Gibson too. With the same dark eyes. Like mother, like son.

"I did!" Gibson cried defensively. "How do you think she escaped to the mountains? Not on her own."

"You know what," Curwen said, pausing to take a deep breath, "this isn't important right now. What's important is that Annabelle's vision showed Whirl's army coming here." He pointed at the ground between his knees. "The battle takes place here in the mountains."

"Have her visions ever been wrong?" James asked.

"Not yet," Corey said with pride, not fully grasping the seriousness of the situation.

"When does it happen?" Laura asked with concern. "We need to prepare."

"I'm ahead of you," Curwen said. This was the first conversation between them as mother and son. "I told Phaedra to have some guns delivered to your usual drop point."

She nodded. "But when is it happening?" she repeated.

Corey pointed at me. "As soon as Leela provokes him."

With those words, a shudder ran through my body.

CHAPTER 16

(HOLLISTER)

The massive, beautifully carved wooden doors closed behind us, a guard on every side of me. Several guards lined each wall. All of them appeared to be armed. The cameras were gone. Whirl had just issued Laney an ultimatum. Had she been watching? I knew she'd want to do it. She'd want to turn herself in to spare my life. But I'd heard the guards talking. They weren't planning to spare my life—or hers—and I prayed she'd stay away. I prayed they, the resistance, would keep her away.

Whirl was just a few feet in front of me. He was barely six feet tall, medium build, in his late forties or early fifties. I imagined what it would be like to strangle him with the shackles around my wrists. If I could just get the chain around his neck. Or, I could grab the gun from the belt of the guard to my right before they activated the shock collar again. My aim would be accurate. It could be over in seconds. Whirl turned around and peered at me curiously with his light blue eyes, still holding the remote in his hand, the one that controlled my shock collar. As though he'd been reading my thoughts, he asked, "You're plotting all the ways you could kill me, aren't you?" When I didn't respond, he smirked. "I'd be doing the same thing in your position. So you see, we're not that different."

"We're completely different," I said, wanting it to be true. "I value human life."

Whirl laughed and asked rhetorically, "Who has time for *that*?" Then he smiled. "Although, I hope Laney does. Do you think she'll come? Does she love you enough?"

I started to lunge at him, but the shackles around my ankles tripped me up, and my knees hit the hard stone tile. This time Whirl laughed hard, the sound echoing throughout the high ceilings of the great hall. Some of the guards joined in, but as I observed the others, the ones lining the walls, they remained expressionless and didn't seem to take pleasure in Whirl's games. Would any of them help me? Were any of them undercover agents from the resistance, like the one from the science facility?

He handed one of the guards on my right the shock collar remote. "Get him up," Whirl ordered. "Take him to his cell."

Both guards grabbed under each of my arms and lifted me to my feet. If I went for the gun, they would immediately shock me back to my knees. My entire body, all my muscles, ached from the beating I'd received in the tunnels and from the repeated shock treatments. As they led me down the hall towards a door on the left, I focused on the floor. It was encrusted with jewels of every size, color, and shape. At the halfway point, near the thrones, I could see large red spots. At first I thought they were jewels, but then realized it was blood. The massacre had occurred here. Whirl had had the bodies removed, but the blood puddles remained. It seemed he liked to keep tokens of death. Like the four dead bodies behind door number ten in the science facility.

When they had captured me in the tunnels, that's where they'd put me, in that room with the decaying bodies of men I had once known—Calum, Miguel, Adam, and Xavier. I had vomited more than once from the smell. And even though it was probably no more than an hour before Whirl had me transferred to a cell beneath the palace, I would never forget the minutes I'd spent with the dead.

As we approached, my feet shuffling along, two other guards opened the wide wooden double doors for us. On the other side was a small landing and then a curved staircase of white stones. With my ankles shackled, it had taken some time and skill to climb them earlier; I hoped going down would be easier. The entire room we were entering was stark white—the walls, floors, ceiling, stairs. It reminded me of the building at the cemetery where my grandparents were buried. Going down was easier with the guards supporting my elbows. I was tempted to ask them questions, to see how strong their loyalty was to Whirl, but I had tried that earlier with the guards who had brought me there—they'd shocked me multiple times and ordered me to be silent. They hadn't wanted to hear what I had to say.

At the bottom, there was another door. One of them inserted a keycard, and then it beeped and slid open. We were entering a short corridor, lined with cells on both sides. Everything was white here too, with bright fluorescent lights. From Laney's description of her time here, I figured these had to be the same cells she, her father, Curwen and Sheldon had been kept in. They were all empty now. Whirl wasn't keeping prisoners; he was simply killing everyone. I was sure I wouldn't be there long, certain I would be the next dead body.

They stuck me in the first cell on the left, leaving my hands and feet shackled. Even though I felt weaker than I ever had, it seemed like they finally saw me as a threat. My entire time as one of their slaves, their *bodies*, the shock collar had been enough. I'd walked around, my feet and hands free. Because of my size, it had always seemed like more guards watched me. But nothing like it was now. Now this *body* required extra restraints because this *body* had fought against them.

The cell didn't have metal bars, but a thick wall of plexi-glass. It was unbreakable; I had tried earlier. There was a tray of food on a small table inside the cell. I had no appetite, sick with worry that Laney might try to come here. I might have vomited again if I'd had anything left in my stomach. Instead, I lay down on the cot, my legs hanging off the end. This body was exhausted; it had no desire to move or think or feel. I closed my eyes, attempting to shut out the harsh lighting above. After a few minutes, the lights went out. Whether they were watching me and decided to turn them off or whether they were motion-sensored, I didn't know. But I welcomed the darkness. *Laney should be with Phaedra. She'll keep her safe*, was what I kept telling myself until I fell asleep.

Some time later—again, it felt like I had just fallen asleep—a sound woke me. It was a beep, and the outer door was opening. Were they back for me already? Had Laney arrived? Panicked, I stood as quickly as possible, once again almost forgetting my chains and nearly falling. The lights in my cell came back on. I decided they were motion-sensored. I stood against the plexi-glass, waiting to see who would enter. There were two guards, ones I had not seen before, and a new prisoner, someone I'd only seen once. I'd seen him the night he had sent us home, the night they'd dragged me from the barracks to the field behind the palace. I'd had no idea what was happening until I saw Laney. Even then I hadn't known what was happening. I had thought they were going to kill us all. But instead, he had sent us home through the lightning.

It was Gigandet, the dethroned king, a man who appeared even more defeated than me. He was a completely average-looking man, nothing remarkable about him that you'd think him royal. I was slightly shocked to see him. He was still alive, but limping. Leela had said he'd been shot in the leg. What was Whirl's purpose in preserving his life? Why would he keep him alive and risk Gigandet being restored to power?

After a few steps, he glanced in my direction; his eyes went wide with surprise and then squinted in confusion. He had freed me only for me to end up back in bondage. But he hadn't freed all the other slaves, *bodies*. They placed him in the cell directly across from mine. There was a small slot in the glass wall I hadn't noticed before; they opened the one on Gigandet's cell and then turned to open the one on mine. The guard met my eyes directly with a strange look I couldn't decipher. Was he resistance? Was he loyal to Gigandet? I couldn't tell. They obviously wanted us to be able to communicate, but why?

When the guards left, Gigandet sat on the floor near the open slot, but he didn't look like a man who wanted to talk. I sat beside the slot in my cell also. "They'll be listening to anything you say," he warned me. I nodded but didn't speak. After a moment, he asked, "What are you doing here?"

"You let me go…but not the others," I accused. "I had to come back for them."

Even though I could only see one side of his face, it looked as though he rolled his eyes. Shaking his head, annoyed, he said, "I didn't create the system. I inherited it. I, and my mother before me, have worked to reduce the number of bodies struck in order to phase it out."

"Phasing it out isn't good enough," I said. "You should have just let them all go."

"And what would I have done with them?" he asked. "Sending them all home would be a disaster, exposing Antonia. They'd never be able to assimilate in Antonian society; they'd never be seen as equal. Would you have me send them out into the wilderness where they could create a new home?"

"It'd be better than slavery. There are already some who live in the mountains." I regretted saying it immediately. What if *they*, the ones listening, didn't know about the ones in the mountains? Immediately, I changed the subject, saying, "And you haven't reduced the numbers. You just took over two hundred people from my hometown, including *children* who are being prepped for experimentation."

"Whirl did that. Not me. I never authorized that. I *did* authorize for you to go home though. How did you get back?"

"Curwen."

"He's back too then?" he asked. I nodded. "Do you know where he is?" he asked. Then before I could answer, he said, "Wait, don't tell me." He pointed up at the ceiling. I knew he was referencing the speaker I had seen earlier in my own cell. He didn't want them to hear.

"I couldn't tell you even if I wanted to. I've been stuck at the science facility most of this time, separated from my group." After some silence, I asked, "So did Leela choose to stay here when we left, or did you threaten her?"

"Not at all. It was her idea…I didn't know she had the mark until you all were gone." He sighed deeply. "It doesn't matter though. She's free. I cannot marry her."

He still thought he was supposed to marry Leela. He didn't know it was Laney. I wasn't going to tell him, just in case they were listening. I wasn't sure if Whirl knew or not. I couldn't figure out if he wanted Laney to come here because he knew she was the one, or if he was trying to lure Leela here as well. Instead I asked, "Why can't you marry her?"

He turned his head and looked at me, surprised. Then after a moment, he said, "You must not have heard. Whirl forced me to marry Elodie yesterday."

Relief flooded through me. Every tense muscle relaxed as I leaned back against the wall. She couldn't marry him now. We'd never discussed it, how she felt about it, how I felt about it. I'd never given myself a moment to consider it. Gigandet didn't sound relieved though. It felt like I was missing something, like I'd forgotten something. Then it came to me. If he married anyone other than the match of the one with the mark, she would die. It's why we had rushed back to Antonia to stop his marriage to Leela. "How is Elodie doing?" I asked.

"She's already begun showing symptoms of a sickness," he explained. "The fever began immediately after the ceremony. They brought me back to this cell, so I wasn't with her. But they allowed me to see her this afternoon. The curse is real, even though part of me always doubted."

Part of me still doubted. "Maybe it isn't real. Maybe Elodie was exposed to the sickness in order to make it *seem* real."

Gigandet shrugged his slumped shoulders. "Either way, she's going to die."

He'd been stoic until that point, but once he spoke those words, he broke. He heaved with sobs, burying his head in his knees. He was mourning her before she was gone. My own body had shaken with sobs once. Late one night in the barracks, shortly after I'd been struck and enslaved, I had attempted to stifle my pain, despite the dozens of men sleeping nearby, as I grieved the life that Laney and I might have had together. Gigandet needed a moment, however limited his privacy, to grieve the life he wouldn't have with Elodie. I retreated back to the cot and lay motionless until my light went out.

CHAPTER 17
(LANEY)

Although I'd spent the afternoon and part of the evening trying to persuade them, they just wouldn't let me leave. They wouldn't let me out of their sights. Phaedra even had a couple of men from the resistance come to Chuza's house to keep watch over me. They may have been our allies, but at that point, they were no longer on my side.

"You said everyone will want the reward," I said. "What about the members of the resistance? Can they be trusted? Because if I'm going to be turned in by one of them, I may as well surrender myself and obtain Hollister's freedom."

Chuza shook her head, saying, "Whirl said nothing about freedom. He said he'd spare him from death—but he won't. I've studied him for a long time."

"What about the man from your strategic operations team?" I argued. "He didn't seem to care for bodies. Would he turn me in?"

She shook her head again. "He's not as progressive as the rest of us, but he's loyal to the cause."

I could tell she believed that, but I wasn't as confident. Most of our time in Antonia, we'd been required to blindly trust people we didn't know. We didn't have a choice. We needed them, and I hated that we did. As if Phaedra could see the anger building inside of me, she put her hand on top of mine and inched a little closer to me on the couch. "We do not want to be unkind, nor do we want to threaten," she said. "But we will do what is necessary to ensure you become queen in order to end this sickness among us. You were down there with them. I made sure you went to the quarantine infirmary so you could see the sick and dying. Do you not want to help them?"

"I do," I said. I felt the weight of the dead boy in my arms and heard his mother's cries. At the same time, I saw Hollister fall to his knees, his face twisted in anguish. There had to be a way to help everyone. "Hollister needs help too though."

She frowned slightly, her lips pursed. "We tried to help him not once, but twice. Both times he chose to stay behind. Do you know how hard it has been for our members to infiltrate the guard? We cannot continue risking their undercover positions for someone who has his own agenda. Hollister is wonderful. I'm sure he believes what he is doing is good and noble. But we have to stay the course and await further instructions from Durham."

Tears were forming in my eyes. "But you said earlier that we'd find a way to get him out of there…"

"We tried," Chuza said. "We've gone through every possible option, and there's just too much risk. We'd have to spend too many resources on a mission that would probably fail. We have to save everything we have for the big attack. I'm sorry, but that is the reality we're working with."

I turned to Phaedra. "If it were Durham, you'd do it." She loved him. She'd loved him for many years.

She disagreed. "Durham wouldn't be in this situation. He would have come with us the first time we sent help." She was right. He would have left men behind and only saved himself. "And, even if he was in this situation, he wouldn't want us to take the risk of sending a team to rescue him."

"Look," Chuza said, "you're meant to be our queen. If Hollister manages to survive, maybe he can be your king. But he's going to have to make it on his own for now."

If Hollister manages to survive. I glared at her choice of words, and I was done talking to them. It was dark outside. The broadcast had happened hours earlier. Something terrible—I dared not think the word *death*—could have already happened to Hollister. I went upstairs to the room I'd slept in the previous night. I shut the door, but then quietly cracked it open in the hopes of overhearing something helpful as I brainstormed how to get out of there and what I would do if I did. I just needed to find a guard, right? Or any person really, anyone who would alert the authorities about me. The day before I'd been filled with fear the guards would discover my identity; now I hoped they would. *Is that what Hollister would want you to do?* I heard Leela's voice in my head.

Out loud, to the empty room, I said, "I don't care what he wants. What he wants has gotten us into this situation."

What he wants is good, I heard my mother's voice join the internal conversation. Sitting on the bed, it felt like I was back in my childhood bedroom with Leela and my mother, both of them giving me the advice they thought I needed. Even though I had rarely listened, and would never admit it to them, they had almost always been right. I couldn't admit it to my mother now. The Antonians had worked her to death. I would never see her again. I might never see Hollister again either. I curled up, buried my face in a pillow, and cried myself to sleep.

When I rolled over and opened my eyes, the clock displayed that it was almost six. I'd slept through the night without waking. Someone had shut the bedroom door. I went to the bathroom and pinned my hair properly so I could put the black, curly wig on my head. It was time to break out of that place and find someone to report me to the authorities. When I felt like I was suitably disguised, I cracked the door and peeked out, listening for any sounds. The other bedroom door, Chuza's, was closed. The house was dark except for a faint glow coming from the kitchen. I crept down the stairs, my back against the wall.

The guard sitting beside the front door was asleep, his head leaning to one side in an uncomfortable-looking position. But I could hear the fridge being opened and closed, glass clanging, and bags being ripped open. The other guard, the one who should have been at the back door, must have been getting something to eat. The thought of food caused my stomach to rumble so loud I feared he would hear it. I'd reached the bottom of the stairs. If the sleeping guard opened his eyes or the hungry guard turned around, I would be caught. As soon as the guard in the kitchen moved to the sink and turned the water on, I slipped past them both, retreating to the rear of the house. The door beeped when I opened it; I prayed the sound of him washing dishes would cover it. It was my only chance. I couldn't pause or freeze to see if I had been heard. I just had to go.

Outside the air was warmer. There was a faint hint of light in the sky as the sun began ascending, overtaking the darkness. I walked around the corner of the house to the small alleyway and rested against the wall for a moment. A small tinge of doubt was creeping in. Is this a mistake? The members of the resistance had helped us, one part of me argued. *But on their own terms*, the other part rationalized. But maybe they are right, the first part argued. I could go back inside, go along with their plans, and hope that Hollister would still be alive whenever they launched their big attack. Or I could continue on my way and be exactly as Phaedra had described me—stubborn, unable to follow directions or submit to someone else's orders, always thinking I know best.

But what was best? This time I didn't know. All I knew was that Hollister was in danger, and while I knew he wouldn't want me to come to his aid, to take Whirl's bait, I just couldn't leave him. I couldn't just sit around and hope that he would manage to survive somehow, as Chuza had said. I began to move toward the street, but then I heard voices and froze in the shadows. Two men were approaching, and they seemed to stop at the front door.

"This lockdown needs to end soon, so the market can open," one of them said as he knocked on the door. "My family's running out of food."

"Well, Whirl said the lockdown would end once that girl is found," the other one said.

"You think that's who we've been sent here to guard?" the first one asked quietly. They were the replacements, the next shift of guards from the resistance, and they hadn't been told about me specifically. They knocked again, a little louder. I pictured the sleeping guard startling awake.

"What if she is here? You gonna turn her in so you can get some food?" the second one asked, laughing and sounding only half-serious.

"Hey, when your kids are hungry…" the other one said as the door was finally opened to them, and they disappeared inside. If the lockdown didn't end soon or Whirl's army didn't start distributing food, the people would have a food shortage. Did Whirl want to starve them? Perhaps it was a tactic to make them grateful when he finally did give them relief. I also couldn't help thinking about Chuza's reassurances that no member of the resistance would turn me in. People will do anything if they're desperate enough.

I waited until the previous night's guards left before I moved. They still didn't know that I wasn't in my room upstairs, and I was sure Chuza would be checking on me soon. Once they had gone around the corner, I hurried in the opposite direction. There weren't any people. I had expected to see Whirl's guards at every corner, but the streets were empty. The people were still sleeping or hiding in their homes. They had no reason to get up, no work to do, no business to tend to. The lack of guards made me wonder if perhaps Whirl's army wasn't as large as he wanted it to seem, perhaps he didn't have the men to spare. Or, maybe he did have a massive army, but it was occupied elsewhere. I imagined the massacre in the Great Hall as Leela had described it to me, and a shiver ran through my body.

I began to suspect that I must have been in the far corner of the living quarters, away from the gates that led to the working or meeting quarters, nowhere near the palace where Hollister was confined. But the outer wall ran parallel to Chuza's house, and I guessed if I followed it to its end, then turned left, it would lead me back to the main gate where Curwen,

Hollister and I had been just a few nights earlier. There had to be some guards there who would report me.

But just then I heard whistling. My heart leapt with hope, and at the same time my stomach knotted with fear. It was getting louder, coming closer, and then a man appeared around the corner. The first person I had seen. He appeared to be in his early twenties with a slight build and dark hair and eyes. Before I could think about changing my mind, I rushed up to him. He stopped in his tracks and looked surprised when I stood directly in front of him, only inches away. "Sir," I began, "I'm the one Whirl is looking for. If you turn me in, you can receive the reward."

His eyes narrowed and he glanced around suspiciously, as if to make sure I wasn't playing a prank on him. He asked, "Why would you want me to turn you in?"

"I just want to save Hollister," I said with desperation, letting him know I was serious.

"The prisoner in the broadcast?" he asked to clarify. I nodded. "Okay, come back to my place. Let's get you out of sight. I don't want anyone else to see you and collect the reward before I can." When I hesitated, he gestured to a house I had already passed and said, "It's just down here." It went against everything I had ever been taught about going anywhere with strangers, but sizing him up, I knew I could take him. We were the same height, and probably the same weight. I nodded and allowed him to lead the way.

As he slid a keycard through the slot and unlocked the door to his house, I asked, "What's your name?"

He stepped inside, holding the door for me. Smiling, he said, "I'm Heri. And you are?"

"Laney."

He shut and locked the door behind us. "In the photo in the broadcast, the suspect had blonde hair," he said.

"This is just a wig," I explained, pulling it off, wanting to prove my identity.

He nodded. "If you would just take a seat in there," he said, gesturing to the couch in the living room, "I will make a call to the authorities about your location."

This was it. I would be in custody soon and probably come face-to-face with Whirl.

I took a seat on the couch as he'd suggested, while he walked into the kitchen. The house had the same layout at Curwen's and Chuza's, but it seemed cozier, like perhaps a family lived there. There were pictures of smiling children hung on the wall, a vase with flowers on the coffee table, and a brightly-colored rug—little touches I had noticed in other Antonian homes.

"Yes," I heard him say from the other room. "I know the location of the young woman in the broadcast. Would you please send someone?" He paused for a moment, then said, "Thank you," and hung up the phone. He appeared in the entryway. "They're sending someone," he explained.

"How do they know where to send them?" I asked. "I noticed you didn't give an address of any kind." I never could figure out how they gave directions in Antonia. There weren't street signs or house numbers.

"If you call from the house phone, they automatically know which house it is," he explained with a smile, taking a seat in a chair across from me.

We sat in silence for a moment. Then I pointed to the pictures and asked, "Whose kids are these?" The man seemed too young to have children their ages.

"Oh, those are my nieces and nephews," he said. "Technically the children of my cousins. But they've always called me 'uncle.'" When all I did was nod, he added, "They're very smart children. All of them were accepted into the Advanced Ones." He paused for a moment, and then a frown crossed his face. "I didn't test high enough to go to school with the Advanced Ones. My family was embarrassed by me. In the end, they exiled me to the mountains to live with *bodies*." His lip twisted in disgust. "I've only just returned."

His words alerted me. "You've been living in the mountains?" I asked. He nodded. "When did you get back?"

"Oh, just last night." He gave a slight, closed-mouth smile that I couldn't decipher—it was either polite or wicked.

This man must have been with the same group that Leela was with. Had he met her? Had he known who I was the moment I'd walked up to him? What had Phaedra said? They think he—the man who had attempted to kill Leela—may be on his way back to the city. Was Heri that man? Phaedra had never told me his name. I had never asked.

"The city is on lockdown. How did you get inside the living quarters?" I asked, attempting to determine if he was a potential murderer.

"The owners of this house have been digging a tunnel from their basement to the outside." He wasn't the owner of this house. The owners had been digging a tunnel. Was this one of the tunnels Chuza had mentioned, one they were waiting to be completed? Heri explained, "I saw a man outside the wall, and I watched where he went. Then I followed him inside the tunnel, and it led me here."

Dread was beginning to fill my stomach. "So, are you not really related to the children in the photos?" I asked, almost afraid to hear the answer.

He shrugged. "Well, my nieces and nephews do look similar to them."

I took a deep breath before asking, "So, where are the owners of this house?"

"Oh, they're upstairs," he said casually. But then he gave a big smile, and there was no mistaking that it was wicked.

I jumped up to make a run for the front door, but he was closer and quicker, blocking my way, pulling a gun from his waistband. It had a silencer on it. "Come on, let's go meet the owners," he said, gesturing toward the stairs with the gun.

"Are you the one who tried to kill my sister?" I asked, unmoving.

He whistled. "News sure does travel fast. If I had succeeded with her, then I wouldn't have to do this to you."

"You don't have to do this, Heri," I said, my hands raised in a sign of peace and surrender.

He raised the gun higher. "Get upstairs now."

If he killed me there would be no chance of helping Hollister. Had Heri really called the authorities? Was anyone on their way, or was I on my own? When I had sized him up earlier, deciding I could take him, that was before I knew he was armed. I took some steps toward the stairs and began ascending them slowly with him close behind. I could feel the hard metal pressing into my spine.

"Why are you doing this?" I asked, hoping to stall and distract him as I considered my options. I was halfway up the stairs, and I could see into one of the bedrooms. The carpet was stained with dark blood, and I could see the back of someone's wounded head. They had gray hair. The owners must have been older, and it appeared that he'd killed them with blunt force. Perhaps the children in the pictures were their grandchildren. They must have been members of the resistance.

Ignoring my question, Heri said, "At least the man completed his mission of building the tunnel before his death."

"Before his *murder*," I corrected him.

If I didn't do something, I would end up like the owners. I had reached the landing, and he was one step below. It was my best chance. It was time to take down the scrawny man, gun or no gun. I turned quickly, swinging my arm out as I did, clotheslining him in the neck and then pushing his chest to make sure he went down. The gun went off as he fell backward, but the bullet went into the ceiling. He dropped it as he fell hard, hitting his head on several steps until he lay motionless at the bottom. I paused for only a moment with concern that I might have killed him, but it instantly passed when I saw his chest rise and fall. I grabbed the gun from the middle step and rushed down the stairs past him, no time to waste.

But instead of running out the front door, I headed down the hallway to the basement, flying down the flight of stairs. The light was already on, and I could see the opening to the tunnel the old man had built. If I could get outside the city walls, then perhaps I could re-enter through the tunnels that led to the palace, the ones Leela had come out of just a few nights earlier. Then I could get to Whirl…and Hollister.

CHAPTER 18
(LEELA)

The plan was for me to provoke Whirl. Laura and James didn't want Whirl or his army to come to their camp. They didn't want to risk the lives of the people they had cared for all these years, especially the ones who couldn't fight for themselves. But Laura and James had explained things to the camp, and the people had voted. The majority realized that Whirl would come to them sooner or later, and they preferred for it to happen in a way that they could control, so they would be aware and prepared. The council was already organizing their people. Our group's plan was for me to fulfill Annabelle's vision, to stir Whirl up to action. I trembled at the thought of it, not ready to face him.

Curwen had left early in the morning, by himself, to travel a ways down the mountain until he had service to communicate with Phaedra. I think part of him just wanted time alone to talk to his adoptive mom about his biological mom. There hadn't been any further discussion about Gibson's revelation from the previous night. I don't think Curwen or Laura knew how they were supposed to respond; they'd both, for decades, thought the other one was dead.

When Curwen returned, he sent some men from the camp to their usual drop spot to collect the guns that Phaedra had somehow delivered to us. But other than that, he didn't have good news. "Whirl has Hollister," he began. "They aired a broadcast yesterday offering a reward for anyone who knew the whereabouts of Laney or Leela. He said if Laney or Leela turned themselves in, then he would release Hollister."

"Do you believe he would?" I asked. All the men sitting around— Curwen, Durham, Gibson, Sheldon—shook their heads. "Then, what should we do?"

"Wait," Curwen said. "That's not all." He paused before adding, "Phaedra tried to keep Laney under guard, but she somehow escaped, and they don't know where she is."

"She's going to Hollister," I said. "Of course, she is." I wanted to roll my eyes and be annoyed, but I understood. It was Hollister. If I was in the city, I would probably do the same thing—but maybe in a different way. She'd snuck away from the care and protection of the resistance and was on her own. I had an entire team surrounding me. "So, what do we do?" I asked again.

"This doesn't change our plans," Durham said. "Our plans may even help Laney if we're able to get Whirl out of the city before she gets caught."

"Do you really believe Whirl will come here?" I asked, still doubtful. "How do we know he won't just send his army?"

"Either way, it's an advantage to us," Gibson said. "If he remains in the city, the resistance will capture him. If he comes here, we will. We need to get going though."

They sounded confident, and I wanted to believe it would happen that way, so easily, but I hadn't seen anything in Antonia go according to plan, so my concerns were valid. I stood and pulled my backpack over my shoulders. We—Gibson, Sheldon, Curwen, and I—had to make a small journey to an old, abandoned communication station on the other side of the mountain. Sheldon was going to hack into the Antonian's broadcast system and air live footage of me to the entire city. I was going to get my chance to tell them the truth, to correct the lies Whirl had spread. I wanted to be articulate, strong, endearing, likeable. If Laney was going to be their queen, we needed to win them over. I could imagine her being queen, but I didn't think she'd want the position, especially if Hollister wasn't by her side.

Greer had been checking in with us regularly, and he'd wanted to go with us to the communication station, but I had insisted he remain with the AO, and to my surprise, he reluctantly agreed. He actually seemed to have a great interest and passion in the work, in learning and preserving Antonia's history. I was afraid to tell him that the rest of us had decided that when the battle began, we wouldn't allow him to fight. He was the only potential future ancient one; neither his life nor the AO's could be risked. They would be hidden away in a cave with the children and other adults who were unable or unwilling to fight. Even though I was a pretty good shot with a gun, they wanted me protected in the cave as well. It seemed almost poetic to me that this Antonian experience had begun in a cave and would potentially end in one too.

Mara had visited our camp once also, to get updates and assure us that she was still ready to do whatever we needed her to do. She was in it for Antonia—not for me or Laney—and I was okay with that. I'd always suspected we'd never be friends, but I knew she'd risk her life for mine, if necessary. She spent most of her time with her mother and siblings though, making the most of their reunion and helping them to pack and prepare for the move to the cave.

As we began our trek to the communication station, Gibson led the way through an old pass, a trail he was familiar with. He'd been there before, many times, twenty-five years earlier during the rebellion. They had used it to broadcast subversive messages, to draw support for their cause. Now we would use it to draw Whirl out of the palace into unknown territory. Curwen fell in step beside me. "How are you?" he asked. "I'm so sorry I wasn't there the other night, and that I wasn't able to find Heri."

I shook my head slightly. "It's not your fault. I shouldn't have gone off by myself." I doubted whether I'd ever feel comfortable going anywhere by myself ever again, in Antonia or at home. *Home.* Would we actually make it home? I had to get Corey back to my father, somehow.

"I wish I'd never brought you here," Curwen said. In some ways, I wished he hadn't either. But then I wouldn't have been able to see my mother one last time before she died. I may not have gotten my father back. I wouldn't have met Sheldon. I would never have realized how much I wanted to live by being brought so near to death…over and over again.

"It was good that you did," I said after a moment. "How are you, though? With all the new revelations."

He shrugged. "Not really sure who I am anymore."

From behind us, Sheldon said, "You're still the same Curwen you've always been."

"I'm glad you see me that way, brother," Curwen said, placing a hand on Sheldon's shoulder. "But at the same time, my identity is completely new and foreign to me. It might take some time for me to figure it out." In many ways, I felt like I knew exactly what he meant. I wasn't sure who I was supposed to be anymore, who I would become after this was over.

"You three stop yapping back there," Gibson shouted to us. "We need to hustle. Pick up the pace."

We did as he commanded, catching up to him. He was right; we needed to get the broadcast out as soon as possible. Curwen prepped me on the way, telling me all the details about Whirl's two public appearances since taking control—Gigandet and Elodie's marriage ceremony and the plea for my and Laney's capture. Other than that, he had not spoken directly to the people to explain what was happening. All the information they had came from propaganda newspaper bulletins or from Whirl's guards as they subdued the peoples' protests. We all discussed what I should say, what would inform the people but also provoke Whirl. I felt better prepared and grateful that I would be speaking to a camera—not to his face.

When we reached the top of the next peak, I spotted the communication tower not far off. It was a small stone building that almost resembled a cozy cottage. There was a window spanning the side of it that faced the city. The land was flat and the purple-leaved trees surrounded the building, adding to its charm. There was even a picnic table outside. I could imagine it would have been nice to live and work there, secluded yet connected to everything.

"Why did they shut this station down?" I asked Gibson.

"This station was mostly used to report about travel activities. You could see every bolt of lightning from this location," he explained. "But once travel became restricted, there wasn't as much use for it. And those stationed here began to get attacked by groups from the camp who wanted the mountains to themselves. So, the monarchy removed the workers and began to warn that it was dangerous for citizens to come to the mountains, for their own protection."

That's why Greer and Henley, and even Mara, had been afraid when I mentioned going to the mountains. They'd been raised to believe they were dangerous, that they would die, and they had developed all kinds of superstitious reasons why. The monarchy must not have wanted to report the truth—they didn't want Antonian citizens going there because runaway slaves, *bodies*, lived there.

We reached the building; up-close it was more worn and weathered with vines growing up the sides. Gibson cut through several of them to get to the metal door. To my surprise there was no lock or keycard needed. It was rusted and the hinges creaked as he opened it and ushered us inside. "There's a shower inside, Leela," Gibson said. "You need to take one."

"Will they believe I've been roughing it in the mountains if I'm squeaky clean?" I asked.

"They need to be able to recognize you from the picture," he said. "Your hair's already a different color. Your face doesn't need to be dirt-stained too. When you're done, braid your hair, so they can easily see the mark on camera. And here," he pulled some red clothes from his bag, "put these on as well." We entered a dark, narrow, musty hallway, and Gibson directed me to the bathroom. Curwen stood guard outside the building while Sheldon and Gibson got the system up and running. He was planning to call Phaedra when we began filming to make sure it was working, that it was being successfully broadcast to Antonia.

I found refuge in the tiny bathroom, a few moments by myself. In the quiet moments alone, I often questioned my sanity, doubted if any of this was real. This was my summer before medical school. I should have been at home, helping my mom in the kitchen, swimming in the creek with Corey and Annabelle, celebrating Laney and Hollister's engagement, studying with my dad in the evenings. That should have been my current reality. Instead, I was in Antonia, attempting to overthrow a military dictator who wanted me dead. If we ever made it home, there was no way we could tell the truth. They wouldn't believe us. They *would* think we were insane.

Wiping the mirror with a towel, I stared at my reflection. My new dark brown hair felt both shocking and natural at the same time. It did make my blue eyes pop, as Mara had said, perhaps the only compliment she had ever and would ever give me. My hands went to the bruises on my neck, and then my fingers wandered up behind my ear, grazing the stitches of my head wound. They were ready to come out. I found a first aid kit in the cabinet. Using the tweezers and small scissors, I began to remove the sutures slowly. When I'd reached the last one, Gibson rapped on the door, startling me, nearly causing me to cut myself. "How come I don't hear the water running? Hurry up in there!" he ordered. *Yes, hurry up, Leela. Laney needs you to hurry up*, I told myself, turning on the faucet. I showered quickly, once again realizing that no amount of water could ever wash me clean from the things I'd experienced in Antonia.

Braiding my wet hair, I entered the control room to see if they were ready to film. "How's it going?" I asked.

"This is some old equipment," Sheldon said. "Good thing Gibson is here to help out."

"Don't be calling me old, boy," Gibson joked, and they both laughed.

I wanted to laugh, but I found no humor in anything. I was in serious mode, which to be honest, was my usual mode. Laney was the lighthearted twin, well at least she was before the lightning struck. I hoped she would be that person again. Staring out the large window, I surveyed the land and the white city in the distance. On the far side of the city, there was a single, dark cloud of smoke rising into the sky. Had Whirl set fire to a section of the city? "What's that smoke?" I asked the men, pointing to its location.

Gibson didn't even look up from the computer screen, but he knew what I was talking about. "That's the smoke from the cremation center. I imagine it's probably been running non-stop."

I sighed, my stomach feeling heavy. I knew he was right. They had to cremate the sick. They had to cremate the men Whirl's army had murdered. They had to cremate bodies they worked to death. Sheldon glanced at me. "You okay?" he asked with concern. I nodded. "All right. I think about ready," he said. "Where do you want to film?"

"Definitely outside," Gibson answered immediately. "They need to see the trees so there is no mistake about her location." Gibson led us outside. He knew exactly how he wanted this to go. He positioned me in front of a cluster of the purple trees. A slight breeze caused a few pink flower petals to fall around me. "If that happens during filming, that will be a nice effect," Gibson commented, more to himself than me. "When she mentions the mark, you need to zoom in," he told Sheldon. "And Leela, you need to turn slightly so the back of your neck is more visible. Here, put your braid on the other side." He wanted every detail to be perfect. I wasn't sure what he did back in our dimension, but he could have a career in directing. He placed both his hands on my shoulders. "You know what to say?" he asked.

"Yes." I nodded. "I'm ready."

He smiled. "Good. Good." He turned around and said, "Curwen, get Phaedra on the phone."

Sheldon had the camera set up on the tripod, the long cord trailing back into the building, connected to the monitor in the communication room. Gibson would be inside, controlling the broadcast alarm system and the live broadcast itself.

"I got Phaedra," Curwen confirmed.

"Good," Gibson said. "Give me the phone and come with me." As he was walking into the building, he turned back and said, "As soon as you hear the horn stop, begin recording. Leela, wait three seconds before you begin speaking."

When they disappeared inside, Sheldon asked, "Are you really ready?"

I took a deep breath and nodded. It was tempting to let my nerves take over, but instead I thought of all the things that made me angry. My mother's death. My siblings growing up without her. My father losing his wife. People kidnapped from their homes and enslaved. Laura who never got to raise her son. Curwen who never knew his true identity. Gigandet's forced marriage. Elodie's inevitable death. Whirl importing guns and having dozens murdered. Whirl injecting Curwen with the disease. Whirl threatening Laney and Hollister's lives. Anderson attempting to drown me. Heri trying to strangle me. Whirl desiring to kill us all. I was ready.

As I said firmly, "I'm ready," I could hear a faint horn coming from the city. If we could hear it on top of the mountain, I dreaded to hear how loud it was down there. It seemed like it went on forever, but was probably only thirty seconds. As soon as it ended, Sheldon clicked the record button and a red light turned on. He held his hand up, raising one finger at a time, counting the three seconds for me.

I took a breath and began. "Hello, Antonians. I am Leela, one of the women Whirl has introduced to you as a dangerous criminal. I'm here to tell you *he* is the dangerous criminal, and *he* is a liar. Yes, I have the mark." I turned slightly as Gibson had instructed to show the camera as Sheldon zoomed in. I waited a moment before facing the camera and continuing. "Yes, Gigandet and I were going to get married…because we wanted to spare any more of you from dying from the unknown disease. But before the ceremony could begin, Whirl and his guards stormed the palace and murdered dozens of the king's men. I barely escaped with the help of faithful men. You must not believe the tale Whirl has twisted. Did you notice the bloodstains on Elodie's wedding dress? That's because it was the same dress I was wearing when the massacre occurred. Did you notice Gigandet limping? That is because he was shot.

"It's true that you needed to find the one with the mark to end the curse. But more importantly, you needed to find *the match* of the mark. Both the mark—myself—and the match—my sister—are necessary to save all of your lives. After speaking with the only living AO, it has become clear that my sister—not me—is supposed to become your queen in order to break the curse. So, I'm asking for my sake, for her sake, for *your* sake, that if any of you find her, do not turn her in to the authorities. Hide her and protect her. *She* is your only chance of getting rid of the sickness among you. Do not trust your new leadership. Fight for your freedoms. And if Whirl wants *me*, he can come get me himself."

With a fierceness meant to challenge Whirl, I stared hard into the camera until I saw the red light go out and Sheldon said, "You're good." My body relaxed, and I released the air I'd been holding in.

Curwen appeared in the doorway with a smile on his face. "Phaedra said that was perfect," he said.

"Heck yes it was!" Gibson exclaimed with glee as he pushed past Curwen. Sheldon smiled broadly at me, his green eyes looking proud. I wasn't sure how to respond. It was over, but it was also just beginning. Would Whirl take the bait? Would he come for us? Could I trust in Annabelle's drawings, the visions of my five-year-old sister? Gibson clapped me on the shoulder. "You done good. Now, let's get everything put away and get back on the trail. We've got to prepare for battle."

When we approached the camp, it was midday, and we could hear gunshots. The gun supply Phaedra had dropped off must have arrived. They were having target practice, and I knew that's where Corey would be, even though he wouldn't be participating in the fight. There were a lot of men and women from the camp lined up across the valley, choosing targets and aiming for them. I could tell that several of them had previous experience, but others would need a lot more practice. Corey was actually instructing a couple of them. A genuine smile of pride crossed my face. Durham saw me watching, and called to me. "Are you as good a shot as your brother?" he asked.

I grabbed the pistol he held out to me. Mara and Greer, who were standing nearby, stopped what they were doing to watch me. They'd seen me with a rifle before in the tunnels—and they hadn't liked it—but they'd never seen me use it. None of them knew the skill I possessed with a gun. In the science facility, Curwen had seen me shoot and intentionally miss. But this time I wouldn't miss. They had set up a row of little rocks halfway across the gap. Most of them were still in one piece because most of our fighters couldn't hit them. I raised the pistol, took aim, and fired, hitting one rock after another—five total—until Durham said, "Okay now, we've got to preserve our ammo for those who need the practice." I handed the gun back to him. "Too bad you won't be in the fight with us. But, think you can give the rest of us some pointers?"

"Sure," I said. They needed all the help they could get. Even then, would it be enough? I was almost certain it wouldn't. I felt sick, like I had when Greer announced I'd be marrying Gigandet, like something was coming that couldn't be stopped, like I had just set things in motion with that broadcast—things that didn't need to happen yet because we weren't prepared. This time I walked behind a tree and threw up in private.

CHAPTER 19
(LANEY)

The tunnel was narrow, just wide enough for one person, with rough edges. It wasn't like the other professionally built tunnels beneath the city. How many men had been working on it, and how long had it taken? The ground was covered in rocky debris, which slowed me down, as I tried to make sure I didn't twist an ankle or get my foot caught. There had been several helmets with lights in the basement; I'd put one on, so that my hands would be free from holding a flashlight. I needed my arms for balance, both of them touching the stone walls for stability. The gun was tucked into my waistband. There had actually been several guns in the basement. Were they the ones Durham had bought at the black market, or had the resistance been arming itself as well?

It was a gradual decline, which felt like it took forever as I continued to fear that Heri would regain consciousness and come after me. But eventually I saw some light coming through as I neared the opening, and when I arrived at the entrance, I could see trees—it let out at the edge of the woods. The sunlight filtered through the leaves. I stepped out and removed the miner's helmet, realizing I'd left the wig behind and had nothing but my pinned up blonde hair to reveal my true identity. If my sense of direction was correct, then I was on the opposite side of the city from the entrance to the palace tunnels. I'd have to walk the perimeter.

Where I stood, the sun was intense, so I walked a ways into the woods for shade, for a few moments to figure out my next steps. Still worried Heri might appear any second, I sat down at the base of a large tree, hidden from view. If he did come out of the tunnel, it would be good to see which direction he went. He'd tried to kill Leela. She'd nearly been murdered multiple times, yet I had never felt it, never had any twin intuition. I had always wished we'd had a stronger connection. We were close, but we'd never had that special bond that other twins would describe. I felt like I'd let her down. I'd had the opportunity to kill the man who'd almost killed her. But how could intentionally take a life? I had only briefly considered it when Curwen had arrived at our home, a complete stranger threatening to expose us. Now Curwen—not I—was the one who had killed someone in defense of Leela.

My thoughts were getting jumbled and incoherent even to me, so I closed my eyes to focus, to picture Antonia like an aerial-view map in my mind and decide what my best option was. Soon, I dozed off, and instead of picturing Antonia, I was back home, in the woods, not far from our camping cave. It was dark and raining. There was lightning in the distance. The thunder rumbled a few seconds later. My feet were bare as I walked through the underbrush, leaves crunching and twigs snapping, as it felt like I sunk deeper into the earth with each step toward the cave. I pushed my wet, stringy hair off my forehead and out of my eyes. Crossing the small creek, my foot slipped on a slimy rock, and I came down hard on my knees, my clothes soaked anew. I crawled my way out and stood up. Just over the hill, I just needed to get over the hill. I knew Hollister would be waiting for me there. At the top, I paused to catch my breath and squinted to see through the rain and darkness. Finally, I caught a glimpse of him, standing just inside the cave. When he saw me, he began hollering for me to go back. "Don't come here!" he yelled. The ground began to shake, and my feet slipped on the wet leaves until I was on my stomach, sliding back toward the creek below.

Someone shook my shoulder. "Laney," a man's voice woke me. My reflexes were quick as I grabbed the gun from my waist and pointed it at the man. I looked up, fearing I would see Heri's face. But, it was Rick. He'd stepped back and raised his hands. "It's okay," he said. I dropped the gun and burst into tears. He crouched down and put his arms around me. "It's okay," he said again, his voice soothing and familiar.

After a minute, when I caught my breath and could speak, I said, "We have to help Hollister."

Don't come here, Hollister had said in my dream. He'd yelled those same words in previous recurring dreams from before I even knew Antonia existed. Had it always been a warning from him? Was he now warning me not to go to the palace to rescue him? Or did I simply know subconsciously that that's what he would tell me to do?

"I know," Rick said. "We are working on a plan." When he said we, I finally looked around and took notice of the two men standing twenty feet away watching us. "This is Etienne, a man who was in the same barrack with me and Hollister. And this is Rune, a member of the resistance who's been assigned to assist us." It was clear Etienne had been a body. His clothes were worn and dirty, and his skin was tan from being in the sun. Rune was a half a foot taller than Etienne, clean, fair-skinned with black hair, but the most striking thing about him was his uniform. It was a deep, scarlet red. I'd never seen anyone in Antonia wear that color.

Glancing back at Rick, I asked, "They're going to assist you in getting to Hollister?"

"Hopefully. That's the plan," he said. "I'll explain more, but first let's get you into the bunker before you're spotted. You had all of us so worried this morning. How did you get here?" He grabbed my upper arm and helped me stand, picking the gun up at the same time. "And where'd you get this?" he asked.

I took it from him, turned the safety back on, and returned it to my waistband. "From the man who tried to kill Leela and then tried to kill me," I said bluntly.

Rune and Etienne led us for about half a mile in the direction of the warehouses, but still in the woods. When they stopped, I wasn't sure why until Rune bent over, twisted and pulled a lever, and opened a hatch door in the ground. It was permanently covered in grass and leaves, so that it was always completely camouflaged, and I never would have known it was there. A flight of stairs led down into the bunker, as Rick had called it. Part of me wanted to resist going down there, still angry at Phaedra and Chuza, and the rest of the resistance, for being unwilling to help Hollister, for simply hoping he would "manage to survive." They didn't seem to see him as their equal. He was just a body who happened to be important to the body they wanted to seat on the throne. But if anyone would be my ally, if anyone would want to help Hollister as much as me, it would be Rick. He hadn't given up, and I would listen to what he had to say.

When we reached the bottom of the stairs, we were in a long concrete hallway that ended with a vault door. Rune entered a series of passcodes into the keypad before he was able to turn the wheel and open the door. Once cracked, I immediately heard many conversations, so many voices all speaking at once. How many people were down here? Through the door was a large, brightly-lit room, almost the same size as the quarantine room I'd been brought to beneath the hospital. The walls, floors, ceiling were all concrete, some smooth, some rough. There were several tables spread throughout, couches and chairs lining the walls, a small kitchen area in one corner. The red flowers of the resistance were displayed in the center of every table. People occupied every space, all of them clothed in the same red as Rune. Some of them were eating, some were playing cards, and some were cleaning guns and sharpening knives. There had to be more than one hundred men and women in that room.

All of them turned to stare at us, a hush falling over the group. It felt like a million eyes were on me. Suddenly, one young man stood and began to come toward me, saying, "Laney, you're okay." It was Jace. "I'm so sorry I lost you in the crowd," he apologized. "If I hadn't gone with the guard, it would have drawn attention and possible danger." He was in front of me now, and I could tell his eyes were glistening with unshed tears of apology and relief. But he was also in front of his comrades, and he wouldn't let them see him cry. As one of the youngest among them, they probably already teased him in a million other ways.

It seemed like he may have received a severe thrashing for leaving me behind, so I simply smiled and placed a hand on his shoulder, giving a small squeeze. "It's okay," I assured him. "I made it out okay." He released a sigh of relief. "You've been a great help to me and my sister," I added. He nodded, but clearly did not believe he'd done a good enough job.

Just then, the loud, tornado-siren horn began to blow, the one that announced a broadcast. My stomach dropped, and I instantly felt like I might faint. What if Whirl was back to announce the death of Hollister? What if he was going to perform a public execution? The room started to close in on me. Rick and Etienne supported my arms, while Jace grabbed a chair from one of the tables. "What if it's bad news about Hollister?" I cried to Rick, near tears.

"Shh, it's okay, Laney," he said. "We received a report thirty minutes ago that Hollister is still alive."

"A lot can happen in thirty minutes," I said. His eyes admitted he knew that was true.

Someone turned on the screen across the room and turned up the volume. It was still just a blue screen. But then the horn stopped, and the screen became fuzzy as the broadcast tried to come through. It wasn't Whirl. It was Leela. I still wasn't used to her dark hair; I hadn't seen it in daylight. She was clothed in the same red as the resistance fighters; it had always been her color—I guess mine too. Behind her were the most beautiful trees I'd ever seen, their purple leaves contrasting with the red. How was she being broadcast across the Antonian network? She was supposed to be safe in the mountains. What was she going to say? I held my breath in anticipation.

"Hello, Antonians. I am Leela, one of the women Whirl has introduced to you as a dangerous criminal. I'm here to tell you he is the dangerous criminal, and he is a liar. Yes, I have the mark." The camera zoomed in to show it, but I could only notice the bruises, the ones Heri must have left on her when he'd tried to choke the life out of her. Anger welled up in me. I should have killed him. When the camera zoomed out, she continued, "Yes, Gigandet and I were going to get married…because we wanted to spare any more of you from dying from the unknown disease. But before the ceremony could begin, Whirl and his guards stormed the palace and murdered dozens of the king's men. I barely escaped with the help of faithful men. You must not believe the tale Whirl has twisted. Did you notice the bloodstains on Elodie's wedding dress? That's because it was the same dress I was wearing when the massacre occurred. Did you notice Gigandet limping? That is because he was shot.

"It's true that you needed to find the one with the mark to end the curse. But more importantly, you needed to find the match of the mark." At this remark, many in the room shifted in their seats and looked at me. I couldn't tell what they thought of me, if they accepted me or saw me as a body. "Both the mark—myself—and the match—my sister—are necessary to save all of your lives," Leela said. "After speaking with the only living AO, it has become clear that my sister—not me—is supposed to become your queen in order to break the curse." When she spoke those words, I felt like I'd betrayed her. I hadn't told her the truth; she'd found out from someone else—Curwen, the AO, someone other than me—that it was me, not her, who had to be queen. She continued, "So, I'm asking for my sake, for her sake, for your sake, that if any of you find her, do not turn her in to the authorities. Hide her, and protect her. She is your only chance of getting rid of the sickness among you. Do not trust your new leadership. Fight for your freedoms." Then she paused, her eyes becoming intense, before saying, "And if Whirl wants me, he can come get me himself."

When the screen went blank, the entire room burst into cheers. Some of them began to hit the butts of their rifles on the ground. Those without guns began to stomp their feet in unison. They were ready for battle. Leela had inspired them with her words, with her bravery. She was a better leader than me and would make a better queen.

"All right, all right," Rune eventually silenced them, his voice deep and commanding. "The Mark has done her part. Continue to prepare as we wait to see if it works. We must be ready to move when the time comes." When they all went back to talking amongst themselves, Rune sat down in a chair beside me. He nodded to someone nearby who set a drink and bowl of soup down on the table in front of me. Then he asked, "Is the Match ready to do her part? Will she stop causing us trouble, stop trying to get herself killed?"

I glared at him, wanting to take offense, but instead I asked, "What is the plan? Why did Leela do that?"

"We're hoping it will provoke Whirl and his men to go into the mountains, so we can retake the city," Rune said.

My eyes widened with fear. "But what about Leela? And Curwen? Durham? All the people who live there? Whirl's army will destroy them."

"It was their idea," he said nonchalantly. "They planned it all. We take our orders from them."

Rick was crouched between us, ready to join the conversation, but Etienne stood back, leaning against the wall, observing. He hadn't said a word yet. "What do you think of this plan?" I asked him.

"It seems like our best option," he said. "To divide his forces gives us a better chance of taking the city. And if they're able to capture or kill him, that would be even better."

"How will they do that?" I asked. "Do they have weapons?"

Rune nodded. "We've dropped off a supply to them."

I turned to Rick. "You said something about getting Hollister. How are we doing that?" I asked.

"We'll get him when we take the palace," Rune answered instead. "He's being kept in the palace prison."

I leaned toward him, angry. "But we don't know when that will be! Whirl could kill him before then. He could decide he's no longer necessary now that Leela's given this speech."

Rick placed a hand on my shoulder. "Laney, if we go in there now, we'll all end up dead and be no help to him at all. With this plan, there's a chance. We've been getting regular updates from someone on the inside." Rick was Hollister's best friend. I knew and trusted him, but it was difficult to hear that I could do nothing, that they would do nothing unless Durham's plan worked.

"So, what's my part?" I asked Rune. "If Leela's done hers, what's mine?"

"Your part is to do exactly what Leela said. Let us hide and protect you, so that when the time comes, you can be queen."

What if I don't want to be queen? is what I wanted to say, but I knew what that would sound like. It would sound selfish. Leela had been willing to do it, and she hadn't even seen the sick and dying in the quarantine area. She said in her speech that we were both necessary to save all their lives. It should have made me feel important…special, and maybe it would eventually, but in that moment, I could only think about both Leela and Hollister still being in danger, while I did nothing. "So I'm just supposed to wait here?" I asked to clarify.

Rune nodded. "Yes. There are rooms down that hallway there," he pointed behind me, "if you need to rest or just want some privacy. The door we came in is the only entry point, and everyone in this room has been instructed not to let you leave."

"So, I'm a prisoner of the resistance?"

"You're being protected for the sake of everyone." With those words, he stood and walked away.

So, I waited. For a couple of hours Rick, Etienne, and I talked about everything that had happened to us since Antonia had disrupted our lives. I told Rick in detail how I'd seen Angie and the baby the afternoon after they had all been struck, how she'd brought the police to the town square and they'd instructed her to evacuate the town. "When I saw a news article about her, it said she was staying at her mom's house," I said.

He had tears running down his face. "I'm sorry," he said. "I cried the first time Hollister told me, but hearing it from someone who actually saw her, makes it feel even more real. She didn't get struck. She's home and well, with our son."

"And missing you."

"I'll be home soon, I hope."

When he said those words, it hit me hard that I might never be home again if the resistance had its way. That's when I retreated to one of the rooms Rune had mentioned, to cry and sleep and try to create within me the same strength and bravery that Leela had. I woke to the sounds of cheers and stomping. Entering the common space, I spotted Jace and asked him, "What's happened? There wasn't another broadcast, was there?" I hadn't heard the siren.

He shook his head. "No. We just received word from one of our undercover agents that Whirl is mobilizing his troops to move out. Leela's speech worked."

CHAPTER 20
(CURWEN)

Durham had put me in charge of communication and assigned me as a watchman, so I sat alone most of the afternoon waiting for Phaedra to call me with updates about Whirl's response to Leela's broadcast. Knowing Whirl the little bit I did, I couldn't imagine he wasn't provoked. He was a bitter man, fueled by jealousy and pride and rage. Leela had chosen her words perfectly. I was sure her beauty must have captivated the Antonians, but I hoped even more that they were moved by the things she had said, that they had believed her, or that she had at least planted a seed of doubt in their hearts about Whirl.

Leaning against the tree, my back ached. It had been hurting for days, injured from the beating I had received from Anderson at the science facility. The shock collars and stun guns aren't enough for men like Whirl, Anderson, and Heri. They're the kind of men who want to be hands on. Anderson had wanted to break a sweat during the beating. He had wanted to feel the pain in my body. He had wanted to make sure I felt like a walking bruise.

It almost didn't feel real that I had used a gun to kill him. There had been no time to think. He was drowning Leela. He was killing her. The one promise I had made to myself was that I would keep her alive no matter the cost. And every part of me felt that he deserved to die. He had murdered Muriel, he had injected me with the disease, and then he was trying to take Leela's life. There was no other option but to take his, and I felt no regrets.

Then Heri had tried to take her life, his hands around her throat. And I hadn't been there. My promise broken. I hadn't kept her safe. Every time I saw the bruises on her neck, anger welled up inside my chest. I had created this mess. Whirl's coup would have happened no matter what, but I could have kept Leela and Laney out of it. They could still be in their little farmhouse, wondering what had happened to their loved ones. Or, I could have reported them to the authorities, so they would have been removed from the empty town and put somewhere safe where they might never have been found by Gigandet or Durham or Whirl.

But then all the Antonians would die; the sickness would wipe them out. Not me though. I'd be the last man standing, alone. Or were there others who had been deceived into believing they were Antonian? I still couldn't believe there wasn't any Antonian blood in my veins. If Laura hadn't been struck, I would have been born and raised in southern California. I probably would have been taught to speak Spanish from Laura's mom—my abuela. That night after Gibson's revelation, Laura had pulled me aside privately to share these things with me. She understood that we might never have a real mother-son relationship, but she wanted me to know where I came from. Her high school boyfriend was my father, and I couldn't help wondering what he must have thought when Laura disappeared. Did he think she had run away, or did he fear that she had been kidnapped and murdered? She had only just found out she was pregnant; he didn't even know I existed. Laura had cried during the conversation—the first sign of vulnerability I had seen from her—and hugged me.

Early evening, as the sun was beginning to set, the phone rang—my other mother calling me with news. "Whirl has ordered his army to mobilize," Phaedra said. "He wants them in position to attack at dawn."

"Have they started toward the mountains yet?" I asked.

"No. They are still preparing. I think it will be a few more hours yet before they head in your direction," she said. "I'm waiting to hear an update from K."

K was one of our undercover guards, a member of the resistance it had taken a long time to put in position. K had worked his or her way up the ranks, earning the trust of some of Whirl's most respected soldiers. That's all I knew about K. I couldn't imagine the things K must have had to do to gain recognition from Whirl. Had K been at the palace massacre? How many people had K been forced to torture or kill in order to maintain his or her place in the guard? When I thought of K, I was grateful I had only been sent undercover to gain Gigandet's trust and friendship. K had been sent to impress Whirl—and the one thing that impressed Whirl was cruelty.

"Did K confirm if Whirl would be with his army?" I asked. He either needed to come here and be defeated or the resistance would have to take him down as they regained control of the city. I couldn't decide which would be better. Part of me wanted him to stay in Antonia, far away from Leela.

"Yes," Phaedra said. "He'll be with them."

"Okay," I said, sounding disappointed. "Let me go so I can inform the group."

"Wait," she said. "Let them know that Laney is back in our custody. She's being kept safe, even if she doesn't like it. She was also threatened by Heri. He made it to the city, like you predicted."

"Is she okay?" I asked. Leela would want to know.

"Yes, she knocked him unconscious and got away."

"Good." If Laney had been able to overpower him, I was certain Leela would have been able to also, if she hadn't been compromised. "I'll be out of range for about an hour," I told her. I wanted to go see Leela.

"All right," she said. "I'm sure there won't be anything to share before then."

When she hung up, I immediately got on the radio and announced to the team that Whirl was mobilizing and wanted to attack at daybreak. It was going to be a long night. "That's great," was all Durham said in response. I knew he was worried. In some ways he seemed more confident with Gibson by his side, but I could tell underneath it all, he doubted whether the mountain people could fight the well-trained armed guard. I think we were both expecting major casualties, if not complete defeat.

"Where's Leela?" I asked whoever would answer me.

Sheldon responded. "We're just arriving at the cave."

Of course they were. Of course they were together. I rolled my eyes to myself. Even though we hadn't talked about it, it was obvious to me that Sheldon had been interested in Leela from the moment he had met her.

I stood and stretched my aching muscles. Laura and James had shown all of us the cave location earlier in the day, so that if a retreat was necessary, we could all fall back there and defend those who couldn't defend themselves. Although it had become clear to everyone who had witnessed Leela and Corey with guns that *they* could defend themselves, if they were armed. But because we had a limited amount of guns, they would only have one in the cave with them.

By the time I arrived at the cave, they had all the children settled inside, as well as any of the adults who couldn't or wouldn't fight. The cave was deep and extensive with plenty of crevices to hide, and most of the people had already claimed their spots. Mara was sitting with her younger siblings, telling them goodbye. Her mother was there too, even though she had wanted to fight, but Laura and James had refused to let her because she was already a single parent and couldn't leave her children orphaned. Leela stood with Greer and Sheldon as I approached. Her hair was still braided, and she was still wearing the red uniform Gibson had given her, showing, as she had explained, her solidarity with the resistance in the hope that its members would save Laney and Hollister.

Leela saw me first and walked toward me with a hesitant smile. "So, it worked?" she asked. "He's coming?"

I nodded. "He's coming."

She inhaled deeply. "That's good, right? You don't sound so sure."

"I guess we'll know if it's good when we see what happens," I said, trying to sound positive when I didn't feel it. "I wanted to tell you first, before announcing it to the team, that Laney is okay. She's back with the resistance, and they're keeping her safe. Although, from the sounds of it, she might be giving them a hard time."

Leela's eyes glistened with tears that she blinked away. "Now, *that is* good to hear."

I momentarily debated whether to tell her the rest before saying, "Heri did make it to the city, and he did threaten Laney." Leela's eyes went wide with concern, so I added quickly, "But she knocked him unconscious and got away." This time she exhaled deeply. Sheldon and Greer were listening to the conversation, but I needed a moment alone with her. "Will you take a walk with me for a minute?" I asked her. "We won't go far."

She glanced back at them and then nodded at me. We walked side-by-side beneath the purple trees down to the river, to the edge of a cliff where it flowed over into a waterfall. "Are you okay?" she asked when we stopped.

I nodded and turned toward her. "I just wanted to give you this without others watching," I said, pulling the transporter from my pocket. "I took it from Gibson when he wasn't looking. It's already programmed to take you back to the cabin where your father and Annabelle are." I took her hand, placed it in her palm, and closed her fingers around it. "If anything goes wrong, you take Corey and go," I said firmly.

She shook her head, this time not blinking back the tears. "I can't leave all of you like that. I can't leave not knowing what will happen to all of you. I can't leave Laney and Hollister like that." I only cared that she was alive and safe. But she wouldn't be Leela if she didn't care about everyone else. She tried to give the transporter back to me, but I gently pushed her hand away.

"You can leave if you have to," I assured her. "It's up to you. But please keep it. Just in case."

Instinctively, I stepped forward and wrapped my arms around her.

"It feels like you're saying goodbye," she said, her head on my chest. Maybe I was. Maybe this was it.

We stood in a silent embrace for a long moment until Corey's voice interrupted. "Hey, Curwen!" he shouted, emerging from the treeline.

Leela pulled away and quickly stuck the transporter in her pocket. I sighed with relief. Giving her the transporter felt like the last thing I could do to protect her. "Corey's not happy about missing out on the action," Leela explained.

"I'm not surprised," I said. "Laney doesn't seem happy about it either."

We walked to meet Corey halfway and continued on to the cave. "Curwen, can't you convince them to let me fight?" Corey asked. "I'm the best shot here."

"Sorry, man," I said. "I don't have that kind of authority, and even if I did, I think it's better for you to be here with your sister." So they could leave together, if they needed to. I tousled his reddish-brown hair with my hand. He moved out of my reach, annoyed at my response.

Greer was standing in the same place we'd left him, but Sheldon was helping bring food and other supplies into the cave. We didn't know how long the battle would last or if they would need to remain hidden until the mountain was secure, but I felt deep inside that it would be over quickly— whether it would end in victory or defeat, I couldn't say. When Sheldon emerged from the cave a second time, I approached him and asked, "Where does Durham have you assigned?"

"I'm leading a fighter group," he said.

"Do you feel confident?" I asked. That was the question we always asked each other before any of the missions Durham assigned us to.

"As confident as I can be. They gave me some of the more experienced shooters from the camp."

I had watched Leela give him pointers with the guns earlier that afternoon, and he'd picked up the skill immediately. He had always had good aim. Greer didn't want a gun, preferring the weapons he was used to. Some in the camp who were willing to fight also preferred their bow and arrows to guns, choosing to be at their optimum skill level with inferior weapons than to shoot poorly with superior ones. I wasn't sure what Mara had decided; she hadn't been around or spoken much to me since we had been reunited at the science facility.

"All right," I said as I gave him a quick hug. It was like Leela had said. It did feel like I was saying goodbye. "Turn your radio on when you're able, so we can communicate."

"Will do," he said. "Stay safe."

Simultaneously we said, "Safety's an illusion," and then laughed. Durham had been telling us that since we were boys. I squeezed his shoulder as I turned to find Mara. She was sitting with her mother. It was strange to think that both of us had found our biological mothers in these mountains. I remembered her mother from when I was a little boy; she had always been kind to me. Even now as I came near, she smiled wide, her white teeth gleaming.

Mara stood. I said, "I wanted to check in before heading back to my post."

"Thanks," she said. "I'm just getting them settled before joining Laura. I'll be with her group." Mara hadn't been there when Gibson revealed the truth about Laura and me, but from the way she said Laura's name, I knew someone had filled her in.

"I'm sure she'll be a great leader," I said.

"Yeah. My mother has told me many things about how Laura has led them well." She smirked, and then said, "You're a lot like her."

It was a compliment. But I didn't feel as though I had led anyone well. As I walked away from all of them, I turned back to get one last glimpse of Leela. She was kneeling on the ground helping a child bandage his knee, while also threatening to tie Corey up if he didn't stop complaining about not being able to join the fight. I made eye contact with Greer and then nodded in Leela's direction. He glanced where I indicated and then gave me a single nod, silently affirming that he would take care of her.

I decided I would carry out my duties as watchman at the communication station, somewhat because it wasn't too far from the cave— from Leela—but mostly because I could see the city perfectly from there and give notice of Whirl's movements. I could see how many men he had and in what path they were traveling, and then I could report to all the scouts who were in place to monitor his army's position. I could also keep in touch with Phaedra and the resistance as they prepared to take the city. I grabbed some food, a sleeping bag, and binoculars from inside the building, and then camped out on the balcony that protruded from the side of the mountain. I sat on the edge with my feet dangling in the air, my elbows resting on one of the railings.

The sun had set long before I saw, through the binoculars, the guards began to gather outside the city walls. I had planned on counting them, estimating how many there were as best I could, but in the dark, with their black uniforms, it was hard to tell them apart. Only the spotlight that occasionally passed over them had alerted me to their presence. We were outnumbered. There had to be at least three hundred soldiers. How many of them followed Whirl because they truly believed what he was doing, and how many of them only obeyed out of fear? It wasn't until midnight that Whirl appeared. That's when the phone rang; Phaedra was calling with an update.

"They should be heading out any time now," she said. "They're going by way of the science facility, like you all did, believing that to be the easier, more gradual terrain. But I have some good and bad news. K has been ordered to stay behind and command the units controlling the city. That's good for us down here, but he—"

"He won't be able to give us anymore intel," I interrupted, finishing her sentence.

"Right. So you're going to have to rely on your scouts."

"If they're in range…" I muttered to myself, knowing we had just lost an advantage.

"Exactly," she said. "Share this information with the team. Then get some rest, Curwen, so you can be ready for what's to come. I love you, son."

"Love you, too," I said before ending the call.

I turned the dial on the radio so that I would only be talking to the home base team and relayed everything to them. James responded, saying that they would increase the number of scouts to make up for missing K. Durham was optimistic that the resistance would be able to take control of the city with K in charge. I switched back to the main station, and Durham came through, saying as a reminder to everyone, "We don't kill unless we have to. Save your ammo for when it's needed. If a guard surrenders, accept their surrender. They can face the consequences of their treason before the Antonian people."

Not everyone was happy with his instructions, and there was some conversation among different group leaders for a while, but once the radio went silent, I watched until Whirl's army disappeared beyond the treeline, marching in the direction of the science facility. Around three in the morning, when I could no longer see them, I lay down in the sleeping bag and rested, falling asleep without any trouble.

My eyes didn't open until the sun was cresting the horizon. It was daybreak. Had the battle already begun? Had Whirl's army attacked yet? I stood and stretched. I hadn't heard anything from the radio, and when I checked the phone, there weren't any missed calls. Suddenly, I heard a man's voice shout, "Curwen!"

Peering around the corner of the building, I saw a man running uphill toward the communication station. He had a bloody eye. This was not part of the plan. I took a deep breath, not allowing panic to consume me. Rushing toward him, I asked, "What's wrong?"

He paused to catch his breath before he could speak. "I was monitoring the army's progress up the mountain, when all of a sudden, I noticed Heri was with them. He and Whirl were together, and they were leaving the group, going off by themselves somewhere. I was about to announce it through my radio when one of their soldiers found and attacked me. I managed to get away, but he broke my radio. Once I got my eye to stop bleeding, I ran here as fast as I could."

"Does Heri know where the cave is?" I asked, feeling like I wanted to throw up.

"Of course. Everyone from camp does. It's always been our safety plan."

Why hadn't we thought of Heri helping Whirl? Why hadn't we thought that he would lead Whirl straight to Leela? I took off running before the scout could say another word, almost yelling into the radio, "Heri is leading Whirl to the cave!"

Greer at least would hear it. He would have his radio on. He would do something. Every muscle burned as I willed my body to move faster.

CHAPTER 21
(LEELA)

When Curwen had walked away, I'd wanted to call after him, "Stay. Don't leave." But he had a job to do. He had to leave, and he'd left me with a dilemma burning in my pocket. I kept checking my pocket to make sure the transporter was still there, while Curwen's words continued to cycle through my brain. *If anything goes wrong, you take Corey and go*, he had said. It was so tempting to want to take Corey outside and send him home, but I knew he wouldn't go without me, and my work in Antonia was not done. There were a few lanterns lit throughout the cave, giving off a warm glow. Most of the camp residents had gone deep into the recesses of the cave, but I only went far enough in that I couldn't be seen from the entrance, around a curve, hidden from view. Everyone was asleep—they all felt safe here— but Greer and I couldn't lower our guard. We sat next to each other with our backs against the hard rock wall, and while he was dozing a little, I knew he was never fully asleep, always maintaining a level of alertness.

Corey slept soundly a few feet away. He'd never had trouble sleeping. The whole world could be falling apart and it would still seem like he had no anxieties or fears, nothing that would trouble his sleep. I only wished I had that kind of confidence. My mother had been like that—before Antonia—so sure that things would work out well. I wanted to know how this was going to work out. If only Annabelle could tell me. I wanted to hold her little body in my lap as she drew what would happen next. Deep down, I knew there was going to be death. Battles come with death. My mind ran through different scenarios of who and how many.

At least the resistance would have an easier time taking the city with their undercover agent in charge of the remainder of Whirl's guard. K was what they called him…or her. He could surrender without a fight. They didn't have to lose any lives. And Laney was being protected, even if it was against her own will. Heri had found and attacked her because she had refused to stay put and listen to Phaedra. I prayed this time she would allow herself to be guarded. We all needed her. I hoped Hollister would still be alive when the resistance stormed the palace.

I had almost fallen asleep, my head on Greer's shoulder, when his radio crackled. He'd turned the volume down so that it wouldn't disturb the others, but I heard it clearly in my ear, Curwen's voice, yelling that Whirl and Heri were on their way to us. Did I hear it correctly? The look on Greer's face told me I had. I put my finger to my lips, warning him to be quiet, as I reached for the gun on the ground next to me. We both stood and creeped in the dim light toward the cave entrance. "You should stay," Greer whispered. But I shook my head. He didn't know how to use the gun. He hadn't wanted to learn. I couldn't blame him. The first time my dad had taken me hunting, I hadn't wanted to touch the gun, much less the trigger. Eventually, I became a good shot, though I never enjoyed the taking of life. Greer didn't want to take life. He only wanted to subdue it, knock it out, shock it, capture it—not kill it.

We paused just inside the opening of the cave. "You need to go back," Greer ordered through clenched teeth.

"What good will you be against two armed men?" I asked. "And how do we know he doesn't have more men with him?"

"They should have given us more fighters," he said, annoyed that it was just the two of us against whatever was coming our way.

I shook my head. "They're already outnumbered. They needed as many as they could get. Let's find a good place to hide so we can ambush them."

He agreed, but as he took a step forward, there was a loud click and then a bullet flew into Greer's right shoulder. He stumbled backward, gripping his shoulder with his left hand, his face in shock. Whoever shot him must have had a suppressor on his gun. There was a second clicking sound. I ducked, assuming it would be aimed at me, but the bullet hit Greer's left thigh. His knee buckled and hit the ground as he groaned in pain, his body being used for target practice.

I started to raise the rifle in my hand, even though I had no idea where my enemy was, but a man threatened, "Put the gun down or I will finish him." I knew the voice, and I knew from his aim that it could only be one person. Whirl wasn't being led to the cave. He was already there, hidden behind a tree about thirty feet away. From experience, from witnessing the way he'd perfectly executed Elodie's uncle at the wedding ceremony, I knew he'd have no trouble following through. It'd only take one more shot for him to end Greer's life.

I glanced at Greer who leaned against the rock wall, trying his hardest to remain upright on his knees. His right arm hung limp, while he clutched at his thigh with his left hand. He grimaced in pain and shook his head at me, telling me not to put the gun down. He wanted me to use it. But I knew my reflexes wouldn't be fast enough to position the rifle, aim and shoot, especially when I wasn't sure which tree Whirl was behind. I wouldn't stand a chance. Whirl would execute Greer. Greer *could not* die. He was the next AO. He would be the keeper of Antonia's history and a part of its future. "I'm sorry," I told him, as I bent slowly and set the gun on the ground. "I'm going to lead them away from here. Don't say anything or alert anyone until I'm gone. We don't need to put them in danger. Get inside the cave, out of his sight. Put pressure on your wounds, and keep Corey safe."

"Leela…" he said in weak protest, as he began scooting himself backwards.

"It's okay," I assured him. I raised my hands in the air and began walking toward the trees. "It's okay," I kept repeating. I had to convince myself it would be okay. With each breath, I pushed the fear deeper and deeper down, burying it, steeling myself to face the men of my nightmares. They weren't ghosts or boogie men. They were real monsters.

When I was three-fourths of the way to the woods, Whirl ordered me to stop. He stepped out from behind the tree, but his focus and his aim never left Greer. It was strange that he looked like he had aged in the past few days since I'd seen him. His hair seemed grayer, and the wrinkles in his forehead were more pronounced. But his icy blue eyes hadn't changed. "Cuff her hands quickly," he ordered someone.

Heri came from behind another tree. My breath caught in my throat, and I almost allowed the fear to resurrect itself. On a scale, I was certain Whirl was more evil, but I still had the bruises on my neck from where Heri had wrapped his fingers around my throat. I wasn't drugged this time though. While he approached and smiled at me with glee, I stuck my wrists out and glared off into the woods, ignoring him, refusing him any attention. He grabbed the cuffs from Whirl's belt. I saw the keys dangling there as well. "Hurry up," Whirl said with annoyance. *Yes, please hurry so that Greer doesn't get shot, so that Corey doesn't wake up to find me gone.*

After plenty of fumbling for such an easy task, Heri secured the cuffs. He seemed to be nervous in front of Whirl, like he wanted to impress him. Whirl grabbed my elbow, and we began walking through the woods toward the river, the same path Curwen and I had taken the previous evening. Heri trailed just behind. "What are we going to do with her, sir?" he asked Whirl. "Can't we just kill her now? Where are we taking her?"

I glanced sideways at Whirl's face. His jaw was tight, and I could tell he was losing patience with his young companion. He preferred to be obeyed —not questioned. He stopped suddenly, causing Heri to bump into me. "Heri, come in front. Face me," Whirl said. Heri did as he was told. "You want us to kill her now?" he asked the young man. Heri reluctantly nodded. From Whirl's tone, that clearly was not the right answer. "Without any witnesses? How would I prove to the Antonian people that I captured her?"

"We captured her, sir," Heri said. My eyes went wide and my jaw nearly dropped at the risk he'd just taken to correct Whirl. And he didn't stop there. He wanted credit too. He added, "You couldn't have done it without me."

It was so silent for a long moment as Whirl stared at Heri, almost emotionless. I couldn't read him, but I knew in the pit of my nauseous stomach that something bad was about to happen. Finally, Whirl spoke. "You're right. You've been very helpful. But now, I think I've no more use for you."

He raised the suppressed pistol and shot Heri directly in the forehead. An involuntary cry escaped my mouth as I tried to turn away, as Heri's body hit the earth. Whirl jerked my elbow. "Get it together," he commanded. "That man tried to kill you." He squeezed my arm harder and dragged me along, leaving Heri's body behind. "Now we won't have to listen to his incessant talking the whole trek back. You should be thanking me."

I focused on my feet, attempting to match the speed of his steps. We'd reached the river's edge, and it seemed like he planned to follow it all the way down the mountain. Without Heri, he wouldn't know how to navigate the mountains. He didn't want to kill me yet. He wanted to show the Antonian people that he had caught the criminal, and then perhaps execute me publicly. If the resistance regained control of the city, they would be able to rescue me before anything could happen. There was still hope that I might live, and a greater chance that the people in the cave would be all right. I had done the right thing by leaving with him. Everyone would be okay.

"Leela!" someone was calling my name. "Leela!" It was Curwen. He was behind us. He was running toward us, his voice becoming louder. Whirl sighed and rolled his eyes. Terror gripped me. He was going to do it again.

"Please, don't," I begged him, tears already streaming down my face.

"They just won't leave us alone," Whirl said as he turned us around. Curwen was running down the riverbank, maybe fifty feet away.

"Curwen, stop! Don't!" I yelled. But it was too late. Whirl had already raised the pistol, aimed, and pulled the trigger. It felt like slow motion as Curwen's body did stop, blood beginning to pour from his shoulder or his neck. I couldn't be sure from the distance and the tears blurring my vision. Whirl pulled the trigger a second time, hitting Curwen in his abdomen. "No!" I cried, this time in anger. I attempted to knock the gun from Whirl's hand, but he shoved me to the ground. Curwen teetered on the edge of the river, his hands clutching his stomach, before he fell into the water. The current was swift, bringing him in our direction. I tried crawling toward the water, hoping he would be able to grab my shackled hands as he went by, but Whirl blocked my path, standing over me, the pistol pointed at my head this time. Curwen's body floated quickly downstream toward the waterfall. I watched until he went over the edge, and then sobbed harder, my face in the grass.

"Whew," Whirl said, releasing an audible breath. "You don't know how long I've wanted to get rid of him. Such a pest. A hindrance to my plans. Always whispering in Gigandet's ear."

What do I do? What do I do? What do I do? kept repeating in my head.

But before I could decide on any action, another gunshot rang out, this one loud and unsuppressed. I peered up from my position on the ground to see blood staining Whirl's chest, some coming out his mouth. He stumbled for a moment, and then dropped to the ground. He'd been shot directly in the heart. I looked behind me, at the treeline, from the direction of the shooter. Corey. Frantically, I reached for the keys on Whirl's belt and unlocked the shackles, tossing them in the dirt beside his body.

"Corey, are you okay?" I called. He nodded and lowered the gun.

I ran to the edge of the cliff, falling on my knees on a large, flat rock, and looked down into the water below, searching for any sign of Curwen. All I could see were whirling rapids, the water rushing downstream around and over massive rocks and boulders. I don't know how long I stared, mesmerized by the ripples, but suddenly someone was beside me. It was Sheldon. He knelt and put his arms around my shoulders. "Are you okay?" he asked. "What happened?"

"Curwen…" I said.

"What about him?" he asked, grabbing my shoulders and forcing me to face him. "Where's Curwen?"

I pointed at the river. "Whirl shot him twice, and he fell into the water."

Before I could say another word, Sheldon stood, dropped his backpack and weapons, and began removing his vest and boots. I hadn't noticed, but his team members were with him—men and women from the camp standing around, observing us. I couldn't tell if they had fired their guns or experienced any fighting, but it was obvious they had raced here as each of them tried to catch their breaths. Sheldon ordered them to begin searching the riverbank, but they had to go the long way down and around. Sheldon wasn't going to waste that kind of time. He grabbed my hands and pulled me up from the ground. "You need to go help Greer and Corey," he said firmly, like an order. "I'll be back once I find Curwen." He squeezed my hands for reassurance, and then he took a few steps back so he could get a running start. I felt the breeze as his body passed mine, flying into the air over the edge of the cliff, falling forty feet into the plunge pool below.

I didn't want to move, frozen in place, trying to follow his figure as he got caught in the current, fearing that he'd get slammed into a rock, hit his head, lose consciousness. But after a few seconds, he was able to gain control and swim to the opposite riverbank and climb out. His team members would search one side; he'd search the other. Once he got to his feet, he looked back and waved at me. *You need to help Greer and Corey, his words* repeated in my head. Turning around, I found my brother sitting along the treeline with the rifle still in his grip. Corey seemed to be in shock, staring upstream at Whirl's motionless body. He'd proved he was the best shot. He'd killed a man…in my defense, in defense of all of Antonia. I ran to him, fell on my knees, and wrapped my arms around him. "Corey, it's okay," I said softly in his ear.

"He shot Curwen. He was going to hurt you," he said without emotion, without taking his eyes from the body. "I had to do it." *Somebody* had to do it; I just wish it hadn't been my fourteen-year-old brother.

"Come on," I said, grabbing the gun from him. "We need to help Greer. He's probably lost a lot of blood." I took the gun from his hands and coaxed him to stand, forcing him to look away from what he'd done. I kept my arm around his shoulders as we walked through the small patch of trees back to the cave. We passed by Heri's body, and I shielded Corey's eyes as if he hadn't already seen it.

Just inside the mouth of the cave, Greer lay on the ground unconscious, either from the pain or the blood loss or both. Mara's mother was leaning over his body, putting pressure on the right shoulder, while her teenage son pressed on the left leg wound. The woman looked relieved to see me. "We have a doctor in the camp. He was assigned to the same team as Mara," she explained.

"Might have been a smart idea to keep him in the cave," I said. I imagined there would be many in need of a doctor. I removed the radio from Greer's good shoulder, pressed the button and said, "This is Leela. Whirl is dead. Greer has two GSWs. We need the doctor to come. Curwen was shot and fell in the river. Sheldon and his group are searching for him."

Laura's voice came through the speaker. "We're coming now." She'd just found Curwen, just been reunited with the son she had thought was dead. Now he might actually be. I couldn't think about that though. Sheldon would find him. He would be okay. Everyone would be okay. *Everyone would be okay*, I kept telling myself as I used all my medical knowledge to stop Greer from bleeding out.

CHAPTER 22
(LANEY)

It was three in the morning before Rune received the call to action. I woke in the bedroom to his voice booming from down the hall. As I entered the main gathering room, he was saying, "If they fire, we return fire. If they surrender, we accept surrender. Our goal is to disarm and subdue, to avoid killing if at all possible. The resistance has always been about peaceful change. We do not allow the illegal importation of guns to change our goals. We do not become like Whirl or his followers. We do not harm any civilians. We need them to rebuild a better Antonia. They are part of us."

I could feel the sense of unity among them. Even Rick and Etienne had joined their ranks, now wearing the scarlet uniforms. I approached Rick and asked, "You're going with them?"

He nodded. "There will be two teams. We'll be with the one entering the palace."

Etienne added, "*Our* specific mission is to find Hollister."

"I can help," I said, desperate to see Hollister. "I've been in the tunnel that leads to the palace. I know the way."

"We know the way in," Etienne said. "We've already gone over the maps with our team." When I began to protest, he interrupted, "Laney, you're not going with us. Hollister never spoke a word about you to me. I'd never heard your name until yesterday. He kept you secret because of how important you are to him. We're gonna keep you secret too. You'll stay here. Even if we wanted you to come—which we don't—*they* wouldn't allow it."

"Why are you all so controlling?" I demanded through clenched teeth.

"Why are you so controlled by your emotions?" he asked. "There are more important things than how you feel." I could tell Rick was as shocked as I was at the way he spoke to me. After seeing our expressions, Etienne added, "Look, I'm not trying to sound harsh, but people's lives are on the line, and you just need to sit this one out, and let us do what we've been trained to do."

"How have you been trained for this?" I asked, somewhat as a challenge, but also genuinely curious.

But Etienne didn't answer. Instead, he walked away, joining a small group in the corner. "He's a war vet," Rick explained. "He's usually really lighthearted, but I guess he's in soldier mode now. I know he just wants to keep you safe."

If you're offended, there's probably some truth to it, I heard my mother's voice say. But I didn't want to think about the truth of it, how I'd always been the more emotional one, how my siblings had often bowed to my emotions rather than fight them. Everyone was fighting them now though. Everyone was willing me to submit. I knew the right thing, but didn't *feel* it. *Sit this one out, Laney*. I released a deep breath, knowing that's what I had to do.

So, that's what I did. I sat there stoically as they all filed out, one red uniform after another, and then Rune locked me inside—"for my protection." They had to secure the city before I could enter it. The only thing I had asked was, "What if all of you die and there is no one to let me out of here?"

Rune had smirked and said, "We're not gonna die. Trust me, someone will come get you."

It was the longest five hours of my life, waiting for someone to come get me. I stared at the clock, I pilfered the fridge, I played with cards, I attempted to sleep—but I was restless. If that was how submission felt, I didn't like it. *But it's for your good and the good of others*, my mother's voice echoed through my head. In desperate moments, I found myself speaking out loud to her. Then I was in tears, realizing that I would only ever hear her in my head for the rest of my life. She was gone. I sat on the floor beside the vault door, remembering everything from childhood until now, always tempted to doubt any of it was real, that Antonia was just a bad dream.

Just as I was about to doze off, finally, the door handle began to turn. It was Phaedra. She stepped inside and smiled softly at me. "Oh Laney, have you been sitting there this whole time?" she asked.

"No. I've sat in nearly every spot in this place," I said, standing.

"Well, if you're ready, I can take you to Hollister now."

My heart leapt. "He's okay?"

She nodded. "He's okay. Most everyone is okay. There was a small group of Whirl's soldiers who wouldn't surrender, so there were a few killed and a few injured, but overall, it was an easy mission thanks to our undercover agent."

When we climbed out of the bunker, there were a couple members of the resistance waiting to escort us. As we walked the long way around the city wall, heading to the tunnels that led to the palace, I asked, "What about the others, in the mountains?"

I could tell from her expression she was worried, her brow furrowed. "I don't know," she said. "I've been trying to call Curwen for the last two hours. He's not answered. I've sent two men up the mountain to find out what's happened." Her eyes were filled with tears. "I just hope they're alive."

I put an arm around her. "Me too," I said, blinking back tears, wanting to be strong for Phaedra. "I'm sure they're fine." I wasn't sure. What if Leela was…I couldn't even think it. Trying to convince myself, I added, "They just haven't had an opportunity to reach out yet." Phaedra nodded, hoping that was true.

There were resistance fighters stationed around the perimeter of the city, some in the guard tower, and a few at the entrance to the tunnel. "Since we're not able to communicate with them, we have to be prepared that Whirl's army might be coming back to attack. We have to be ready to keep them out," Phaedra explained. I shook. *If* they were coming back, that would mean they had defeated everyone in the mountains, that our people had not been successful in victory, that Leela had been captured or…killed. Hollister was okay, but Leela might not be.

The tunnels were illuminated with lanterns hanging along the walls. As we turned a corner, the two men leading us stopped. Up ahead, I could see the sign indicating the hospital basement entrance, the same place Jace had helped me and Henley escape. Now there were resistance fighters directing a group of Whirl's guards, shackled, into the hospital. The members of the resistance wore masks over their faces to protect them from possible infection, but the captured men did not. "Where are they taking them?" I asked Phaedra. "The quarantine area is down there."

"That's exactly where Gigandet has ordered them to be taken," she responded.

"But they could get sick and die," I protested.

"They committed treason," she said. "They've condemned Elodie to death. Gigandet's revenge, of sorts."

"But these men obviously surrendered," I protested. "Maybe they didn't even want to carry out Whirl's orders. They should get some kind of trial or something. This isn't right. Your people have committed treason too. You have to stop this."

When all of them had disappeared into the hospital, the door shut behind them. Phaedra looked at me and said, "When you are queen, you can stop this. *My people* have restored Gigandet to his throne, and they are talking to him now about abdicating and naming you the successor." Did I want to be his successor? Did I want to live the rest of my life ruling a foreign land, a place I didn't want to love or embrace? In the end, did it matter what I wanted? They were determined—I *would* be queen.

I couldn't pay attention the rest of the way. I couldn't help thinking about how those guards were going to pay for Whirl's crimes with their lives. Had they ever foreseen it ending this way? Had they realized what it would mean to follow a man like Whirl? Had they weighed the cost? Before I knew it, we were standing at the bottom of the long, narrow flight of stairs that led to the palace. I'd been there before in our effort to help

Elodie escape. She had refused, desiring to marry Gigandet despite the risk, and now she would die—according to the curse. I couldn't fault her. I probably would have done the same thing if it meant marrying Hollister.

Hollister. He was so close I could feel it. I pushed past the two men who'd been leading us, running up the concrete stairs as fast as I could. I knew the way. At the top there was another resistance member guarding the door. "Open it," I ordered him in a rush. He turned the wheel too slowly, but as soon as the door cracked open, I slipped through and was once again in the hallway of the second floor of the palace, the thick red carpet under my feet. I ran past the bedroom where I'd met Elodie. Only for a split second did I consider pausing to see if she was still there, but I continued to the end of the hall, stopping on the balcony. Gripping the balustrade, my nails digging into the wood, I looked down into the great hall.

Hollister stood near the throne, speaking with Gigandet and Rune. His wrists and ankles were free from chains and restraints. His back was to me, but when his companions glanced up at the balcony, he spun around, almost as if he sensed my presence, his eyes finding mine and a smile spreading across his lips. I turned and headed for the staircase as he also ran toward it. By the time I reached the bottom step, he was there and his arms were around me. Embracing his chest, my chin on his shoulder, I asked in his ear, "Are you okay?"

He was nearly in tears—I could tell in his voice—when he said, "They just told me—you don't have to marry him to break the curse."

I held his face in my hands and gently kissed the bruise across his cheek. "Curse or no curse, you're the only one I would ever marry." It was at that moment, speaking those words, that I realized that would have been my decision. Even if the curse required me to marry Gigandet, even if he wasn't already married to Elodie, even for the sake of the Antonian people, I wouldn't have chosen to do it. I would have had to find another way to help them. Hollister was the only husband I wanted.

"I never got to ask you," he said. "Will you be my wife?"

"Will you be my king?" I asked. "I don't want to do this without you."

"We'll do this together," he said softly, and as his lips touched mine, it felt like home. If he was here with me, Antonia could feel like home.

From behind Hollister, Gigandet cleared his throat and said, "We don't show that kind of affection publicly in Antonia."

Hollister pulled away and said jokingly, "Well, that may have to change."

"Are you ready to be queen?" Gigandet asked me. It was clear from his demeanor he was a defeated man, and I wanted to know how he really felt about it.

"Do you want to abdicate?" I asked. "Or are they forcing you to?"

He shook his head. "I don't want it anymore. I wasn't made for this role. And this is what's best for Antonia. But I would suggest you two get married before the coronation," Gigandet said. "If you are unmarried when you ascend the throne, the Antonian people will insist on you marrying an Antonian. If you're already married, they'll simply have to accept it."

"You're okay with that?" I asked. Did he really not mind having two non-Antonians reigning over his city?

"Antonia deserves to have a queen and king who love each other," he said. "The people haven't had that in a long time. I couldn't give it to them."

"Elodie—how is she?" I asked.

"Henley is with her," he said. "I will go to her as soon as we get things settled here. As soon as we know what's happened with Whirl."

As though he summoned an answer, Phaedra appeared at the top of the stairs. She looked as if she had been crying. My heart beat faster in panic. "Are you okay?" I asked. "Did you receive news?"

"Whirl is dead," she announced stoically. "About half of his men fled beyond the mountains. The other half surrendered. A few were killed. There wasn't much fighting as Whirl never gave the order to attack."

"How did Whirl die?" Gigandet wanted to know.

Looking at me, she said, "Corey shot him."

"Corey?" Hollister and I asked simultaneously.

"*My brother* Corey?" I clarified. Phaedra nodded. "What is he doing here?" I asked in disbelief. "How did he get here?"

"Gibson brought him."

Hollister and I glanced at each, both of us angry. My brother had… killed someone when he should have been safe in the cabin with our father.

"Whirl was supposed to be brought back alive, so I could punish him," Gigandet said, clearly upset at the news.

"It couldn't be helped," she said. "He shot Curwen, and he was going to get away with Leela. Corey did what he had to do."

"Curwen—is he okay?" I asked. That was why she'd been crying. He wasn't okay.

"They…aren't sure," she stumbled over the words, holding back tears. "He fell into the river, and they're still searching for him…or his body…" She slumped down on the stairs. I sat beside her and held her as she sobbed, allowing tears to roll down my own cheeks as well.

The resistance fighters and guards who had remained loyal to the king, the ones Whirl had imprisoned, marched into the mountains and rounded up the remainder of Whirl's army, the ones who had surrendered, and placed them in cells. Gigandet had wanted to send them to the quarantine area beneath the hospital, like he had the others, but we talked him out of it. Their cases would be judged individually, though it would take a long time. It was a few days before the rest of the team came down from the mountains because they didn't want to stop their search for Curwen.

To explain things to the people until then, Gigandet had announced in a broadcast that Whirl had been defeated, and that he had been restored to power. He explained that elections would be held within the week so the people could vote for a representative council that would share authority with the crown—a great victory for the resistance. It wouldn't be until after the elections that Gigandet would step down and name me as their new monarch. Not so many changes all at once, Durham had said over the phone.

Gigandet reopened the working quarters so the people could have some sense of normalcy, to get back to work and to move about freely. Some of them were confused even when presented with the truth, and most of them were incensed about the guns in Antonia, demanding they be destroyed at once. They'd watch as guards had been shot outside their homes—the ones who wouldn't surrender peacefully to the resistance. They never wanted to see anything like that again. I, as their future queen, never wanted anything like that to happen again.

Gigandet did well, restoring order and stability. Within the palace walls, he was teaching Hollister and I as much as he could about ruling

Antonia. "Of course, it will be different now that you're sharing power with the council. Previously, they were simply advisors, and I made final decisions. I'm sure Durham has already determined how it will work," he said. It was clear he was irritated with the leader of the resistance. Even from the mountains where he was searching for his son, Durham had been very involved in orchestrating the aftermath, ensuring there would be little disturbance among the populace—and grating on Gigandet's nerves. He had planned perfectly, schemed for years, to make sure it would all work out according to his vision, or the vision of those before him.

The only thing that wasn't part of his vision was my marriage to Hollister. Durham thought it would be better for me to marry an Antonian; he felt that it would please the people, keep the peace, and bring unity. He said we could discuss it in person. But, we refused to let him make that decision for us. It was our decision to get married before Durham could return to protest, even though it meant Leela and Corey wouldn't be there. Phaedra knew, and supported us, so she kept all members of the resistance away so that no reports could get back to Durham.

Elodie, weak from illness, but full of enthusiasm, had immediately organized a small, intimate ceremony in the palace courtyard with flowers and lanterns, something out of a dream. She had given me one of her chiffon gowns in sky blue—*the color of your eyes*, she'd said—to wear as I walked down the aisle. As I was getting ready, putting the final touches on my hair, there was a knock on the door. Phaedra entered carrying a beautiful bouquet of jasmine. My breath caught. "How did you know?" I asked.

"Know what?" She seemed confused.

"Oh." My voice dropped as I took the bouquet from her. "I guess you couldn't have known. I just wondered if Leela might have mentioned it some time. This was my mother's favorite flower. She grew it around our house. It is the scent of every childhood summer. It's the smell of my and Hollister's first kiss." I smiled to myself and probably blushed. "It's perfect for this evening."

"I'm sorry your family can't be here," she said with sincerity.

"Me too."

I wouldn't look into the crowd and see my mom smiling through tears. My father wouldn't offer me his elbow as the wedding march began. Leela wouldn't stand next to me as maid of honor. Gigandet would officiate, and there would only be a few witnesses—Phaedra, Rick, Etienne, Elodie, Henley, and Gigandet's right-hand man, Anderson. It wouldn't be the wedding I'd always imagined. But it would be the groom I had always wanted, the one *I* had chosen.

CHAPTER 23
(LEELA)

You two are gonna be the death of me. That's what Curwen had said. He'd only been joking, but I'd never forgotten the moment he'd said it or the fear I'd carried in the back of my mind that it would somehow become a true statement rather than a sarcastic punchline. We'd searched for him for two days straight, walking the riverbank for any sign that he'd gotten out of the water, and then following the river for miles all the way to the sea. When we had passed through the fields where the slaves were still working—why hadn't they been freed yet?—a few of them had described seeing a man's body float past the day before, but when they had tried to alert the guards, they'd been brutally silenced, their words not taken seriously. Durham had immediately ordered the arrests of the guards who'd been so negligent, and I believe he might have killed them had there been no witnesses.

It had been two days of searching through tear-filled eyes. All of our eyes were red not just from crying, but also from exhaustion, none of us wanting to waste time with sleep. But when we reached the river delta, the

254

edge of the sea, our feet sinking into the wet sand, I think we all knew the search was over. His body had to be out there somewhere. We had been the death of him. I dropped to my knees, allowing the warm waves to rush over my legs, soaking me to my waist. Corey took off down the shoreline, his determined personality refusing to give up, continuing to scan the water and the beach.

Sheldon sat down beside me, resting his elbows on his knees, the water ebbing and flowing between us. After a few moments, he said in defeat, "I can't believe he's just…gone…"

"I know," I said softly. "I know I only knew him a short time, so my grief cannot compare with yours—"

"Don't do that," he cut me off. "Don't diminish your grief. I could see you two had a connection, no matter how brief…I just…it doesn't feel real that he could…be no more."

No, it didn't feel real. I kept replaying it in my mind. Him running towards me. My name was the last word on his lips—at least the last word any of us heard. I had been the death of him. He shouldn't have come, shouldn't have left the communication station. His job was just to warn us that Whirl was headed in our direction. He shouldn't have come. He could still be alive. Maybe I shouldn't have been in the cave. I should have been somewhere Heri didn't know about. But then they might have hurt the others if I hadn't been there to lead them away. All the things we'd done wrong, all the things we could have done differently, wouldn't stop tormenting me.

Not far from us, James was holding Laura in a firm embrace as she wailed, violent sobs shaking her whole body. I knew she had been suppressing her anguish, refusing to be vulnerable, struggling to hold on to hope. She deserved better. She should have had decades to get to know her son, time for them to form a real relationship, but just as he'd been given back to her, he'd been taken away.

Durham stood further down the beach, motionless and emotionless, staring at the blue horizon. There was no one to comfort him, if he could be comforted. Phaedra was not there, and I imagined she was distraught, and would be in a similar state as Laura. Mara had not come with us. It would have been too much for her. She'd chosen instead to travel with the group transporting Greer to the science facility for medical treatment. Gigandet had ordered all the scientists to be arrested until they could be questioned further to determine who among them had been working for Whirl. The doctor from the camp—he was actually a surgeon—now had full control of the facility to take care of any who had been injured in the mountains or in the city. Before we had left them, I'd asked him to find the children—the ones from my hometown who were locked in the science facility, the ones Curwen had said we'd go back and rescue—to find them and make sure they were all right.

When Corey came back, shaking his head because he didn't find anything—I hadn't expected him to—Durham announced that we needed to head to Antonia. Laura and James decided they would return to the mountains to care for their people, and Laura explained, "We won't come down until you get things stabilized, until Laney is queen, and you determine what you will do with all the bodies and ex-bodies." We followed the river with them until our paths diverged. I hugged Laura tightly, choking back tears and apologizing for everything. She half-heartedly said, "It's not your fault." I wasn't sure if she meant it or if she just felt it was the right thing to say. Other than Whirl, I didn't know who else she might hold responsible for her son's death, and if she wanted to blame me, I would accept it.

James and Laura continued along the riverbank, but Durham led us away from it, up a gradual incline towards the woods, leaving the valley behind us. Unusual for Corey, he didn't utter a word, and he seemed like he would drop any minute. I knew he needed rest—we all did. But we kept on. The best place to rest would be a warm bed. Our food supply had dwindled down to nothing. "How much further?" I asked Durham once we had trudged a while through the forest.

"A couple more hours," he said. "We should arrive just after sunset."

He'd estimated correctly. As the sun began its descent, the warehouses came into view. We paused at the edge of the treeline and watched as guards led a line of bodies back to the barracks, their day's work complete. My father had been among the ones who'd worked in the warehouses; I had the satisfaction of knowing he was home with my little sister. But these bodies, most of them men, needed to be returned to their families too. "Durham, why haven't they been freed yet?" I asked, my voice pained by the injustice.

"They will be," he assured me. "It will take some time. An entire economy can't be changed overnight. Who will take over their jobs?"

I cut my eyes at him. "The Antonians. They can produce their own goods and farm their own fields."

He nodded. "Right. But they have to be taught how to do those things. They'll have to be trained." His answer made sense, but it didn't stop my heart from hurting for all of my people with shock collars around their necks. "The sooner we get back, the sooner we can set all this in motion."

When we reached the main path, the walls of the city rising up before us, I could see watchmen in the tower, wearing the red of the resistance. They had succeeded in taking back the city. Everything had worked out perfectly—except for the loss of Curwen. And for so many that loss was deep and painful, cutting like a knife. There were other members of the resistance stationed around the perimeter of the city and at every entrance. When we were close enough for them to recognize Durham, they let out a loud shout of victory, welcoming their leader home. Two of them approached and offered to escort us to our destination—the palace. We climbed the steep stone stairs and then passed through the gate, entering the working quarter, which was empty since the work day had ended.

"Gigandet opened the working quarter just yesterday," one of the guards explained as if Durham didn't already know that, as if Durham wasn't the one giving the instructions.

Even though I knew he was exhausted, Corey's eyes had been taking in everything, wide with wonder. I wasn't sure he had even blinked, too afraid he would miss something. As we were about to exit the working quarter, a woman came out of one of the shops, locking the door behind her. When she turned and saw us, her wide eyes deadlocked on me. "It's you," she said, rushing toward me. Sheldon stepped slightly in front of me to keep her from coming too close, while I pushed Corey behind me. We didn't know—was she for or against me? "You're the one from the broadcast," she said. "The one with the mark."

I nodded. "Yes, I am."

"Is it true that your sister can save us?" she asked, her voice urgent. "Where is she? My neighbor was just taken to quarantine. I'm afraid my children will be next."

"I'm so sorry," I said, moving in front of Sheldon, placing a hand on his shoulder to let him know it was okay. Taking a few steps forward, I forced her to move backwards—I wanted her away from Sheldon and Durham and the two guards. She may have been exposed to the sickness, and I didn't want her spreading it to them. "It is true, according to the curse, that my sister can help you all."

"Well, is she going to?" she demanded.

I looked to Durham for the right answer. Were we supposed to tell the people about Gigandet abdicating the throne yet? Last I'd heard, they planned to wait until after the council elections. Durham spoke up. "Soon," he said. "But we really must be going." He nodded at her and walked to the gate that the guards had opened for us.

Her eyes looked like they were tearing up—whether from worry or hope, I could not tell—so I gave her a small smile before turning away, taking Sheldon and Corey's arms as we entered the meeting quarter. The first time I'd been there had been with Curwen. It was just as I remembered it with the tree-lined avenue and two long rectangular fountains. There was no one around except for a couple of guards from the resistance resting on benches beneath the trees. They stood immediately when they saw Durham, looking ashamed that their leader had caught them sleeping on the job. But Durham simply shook their hands when they approached.

Both of them seemed to pay more attention to me though. "Thank you so much for helping us," one of them said. The other quickly followed with gratitude of his own. It caught me off guard. I didn't *feel* as though I had really helped at all. Before I could respond, Durham ushered us on. He had called Phaedra to alert her of our arrival, and glancing up the hill at the palace, I could see her, Laney, and Hollister waiting on the veranda, little specks waving at us. Through the small forest and then we would be in front of them. As much as I looked forward to reuniting with my sister, I dreaded seeing the pain across Phaedra's face when Durham would tell her the search for Curwen had ended. Almost as if Sheldon had the same thoughts, he grabbed my hand and held it tightly. He was her only living son now.

The white palace rose before us, the sky a rainbow sherbet of colors behind it. Before we could ascend the steps, Laney and Hollister hurried to us, wrapping me and Corey in their arms, huddled together in a group hug, something I had thought would never happen again. But somehow, we had all survived.

Laney and I spoke at the same time. She said, "Corey, I can't believe you're here," while I said, "I'm sorry we left y'all behind at the science facility."

She held my face in her hands, shaking her head with tears in her eyes. "We're okay." She smiled at Hollister. "More than okay."

"Wait," Corey said. He took her hand from my face and held it up for us to see the ring on her finger. "Y'all are married!" he exclaimed loudly. Durham, Phaedra, and Sheldon had been having their own private conversation, but when they heard Corey's announcement, they became silent.

"You're already married?" Durham asked Laney. "That wasn't part of the plan."

"That wasn't part of *your* plan," she countered. "But if I'm going to give up my home and my family and stay in this place, I'll only do it with Hollister by my side, as my husband."

"Gigandet married them last night," Phaedra said. "We thought it was right."

Durham looked at her, shocked and betrayed. But Sheldon came forward to shake Hollister's hand, offering his congratulations. Realizing I hadn't offered mine yet, I hugged them both, and having heard for years about Laney's wedding plans, I asked, "Was the wedding all you'd hoped it would be?"

"It was magical," she said with a smile. "The only thing missing was my family."

"We're brothers now," Corey said to Hollister with a smile and their special handshake.

Hollister nodded. "We always were."

Their bond was sweet. It always had been. But did Corey realize he would soon be separated from them again? We were going home, and it was an unbearable punch to the stomach when Laney said she was giving up her home and family to stay in this place. I had never expected her to make that decision. I knew it had been the plan, that it was the only way to break the curse and help the Antonians, but a large part of me never believed it would actually happen. Her words had made it real—our inevitable separation.

"I need to speak with Gigandet, now," Durham said, approaching the massive front doors, all of us following.

When we entered the great hall, Gigandet was seated on his throne. The second throne was still beside it—the place I might have sat if Whirl hadn't interrupted our wedding. At the thought of it, flashbacks from that night ran through my head—the gunshots, the blood, the death, but mostly the fear that had paralyzed my entire body as I'd attempted to hold a dead man in my arms. I didn't want to be there, and as soon as we reached Gigandet, before anyone else could speak, I asked, "Where's Elodie? I'd like to see her."

He seemed surprised, but quickly nodded. "I'll have someone take you to her," he said, motioning to a nearby guard, one dressed in white, representing the crown, not the resistance. "Please tell her I'll be with her soon, after I speak with Durham, Laney and Hollister."

Phaedra placed an arm around Corey's shoulders. "I'll take him to the kitchen for a good meal."

The guard led me out the rear, through the courtyard, to the right around the side of the palace, and then down a white stone path. Elodie had told me she lived in a small home beside the palace, and soon enough the guard stopped in front of a little white cottage, a place with character that seemed like it would suit her perfectly. The guard would not enter, unwilling to risk infection, which I fully supported.

I waited until he left before knocking and listening for a response. It took several seconds, but I finally heard footsteps, and then Henley opened the door. Her long black hair was in braids, and she was wearing a mask over her mouth and nose; I could only see her amber eyes glaring back at me. Without her permission, I instantly hugged her—glad to see she was alive, regardless of how she felt about me. She shook me off, annoyed.

Turning away from her, I approached Elodie who was lounging on the sofa in front of the fireplace. She was still as beautiful as I remembered, her hair the color of honey and her eyes gray like a stormy sky. She wore a mask as well, a more secure one, and her cheeks were flushed as she shivered from fever. "Elodie, how are you feeling?" I asked.

"I'm all right," she said softly. "How are you? I heard about Curwen…"

I nodded, taking a seat in the chair beside her. I didn't want to talk about Curwen. "I've brought something for you," I said instead. "When I was in the mountains, I found that they have a treatment for the sickness. It's not a cure. It won't heal you, but it prolongs your life. The AO has been living for years with the disease by taking it."

"You found the AO? What is the treatment?" Henley demanded, coming closer.

I reached into my bag and pulled out a few of the vials the AO had given me. "We'll have to get more, but these are enough to start with. It's a plant, or maybe multiple plants, that grow in the mountains. They didn't tell me how it's made, just that it works." I handed a vial to Henley and said, "Here, put this in some tea for her."

"I'm not sure I should," Elodie whispered when Henley was out of earshot.

"Don't you want as many years as possible with Gigandet?" I asked.

"Won't it prolong his suffering?" she asked, a guilty look on her face.

"No." I shook my head. "It will prolong his joy."

She smiled through tears and took my hand. "Thank you for all you've been willing to sacrifice for Antonia."

"I think I was mostly just willing to sacrifice for the ones I love. You're the one who was willing to sacrifice everything for Antonia."

I walked back to the palace on my own. Other than a few guards, there was no one else around. I assumed they had retreated to Gigandet's library for private conversation and planning—something I wasn't interested in. I trusted Laney and Hollister would assert their opinions and fight for what was right. This would be their home, not mine.

I crept up the red carpeted stairs to the bedroom I had occupied just a week earlier. I wanted to know if it was still there, hidden away in the bedside table drawer. It was. The copy of *Jane Eyre* that had belonged to Curwen, the one I had asked Gigandet if I could keep, and tucked inside its pages was the blonde lock of my mother's hair, the one I had cut when I'd viewed her body in the morgue. I curled up on the bed with both items and cried until I fell asleep.

CHAPTER 24

(LANEY)

The people had never experienced an election process before. Generation after generation had simply been submitted to the monarchy, but there seemed to be great excitement among them that they would have representation in the council. Two dozen men and women were nominated, and then the voting began to determine the final twelve representatives. All the members of the resistance put their votes toward ensuring that Durham and Phaedra would both have spots on the council, but the rest of the elected were ordinary citizens, including a few business owners, two teachers, and a doctor.

The night before my coronation, Hollister and I were enjoying dinner with Leela and Corey in the courtyard. Gigandet and the new council were having their first meeting, and I wasn't allowed to attend until after the crown had been passed to me. I could tell Hollister was nervous, his leg continuing to bounce underneath the table until I placed my hand on his knee and gave him a slight smile. The council would be making a decision about the slaves, and we didn't get to be a part of it, though we had made our position known to Gigandet, Durham and Phaedra. Would the council set them free? Would they let them return home? Or would they continue Gigandet's plan of reducing the numbers and eventually phasing out the system? The newly approved government documents—ones the resistance had pre-prepared—stated that, as ruling monarch, I could object to a decision of the council, and if an agreement could not be reached, then the people would have the final vote. A scary thought because I didn't know the people yet, and I doubted whether enough of them would choose to abolish slavery and the importation of more bodies.

"Laney, are you sure you want to do this?" Leela asked, interrupting my thoughts. "It really needs to be your choice. It's not too late to change your mind."

Hollister and I glanced at each other, and then he squeezed my hand for assurance. "We've talked for hours and hours about it, and we truly think we can do good here," I said. It sounded crazy. Who was I to think I could be queen and reign over a city? I knew so little about politics or law or economics. But that was the place I found myself, all because a *body* hundreds of years ago wanted to enact revenge, creating the curse, so that a *body* would sit on the throne. "We'll miss you all so much," I added. "But I'm sure we'll be able to visit from time to time."

"And I can come visit y'all during school vacations!" Corey said with excitement. He'd become fascinated by every aspect of Antonia, eager to see everything and talk to everyone. I could imagine him becoming a regular light traveler. Leela on the other hand—I couldn't help remembering the excruciating pain she'd experienced when we were first struck.

"Are you worried about traveling home?" I asked her.

She shrugged. "A little. Now I know what to expect, so hopefully I can handle it better…and not pass out again."

Corey looked confused; we'd never told him. "What do you mean? What happened?"

But before we could answer him, Gigandet, Durham, and Phaedra appeared on the patio and walked toward us. The meeting had ended. Their faces were somber, and I braced myself for the worst news.

"They have agreed to freeing the bodies, as long as you follow through with being crowned," Gigandet announced.

I exhaled with relief. "Of course I will follow through. Why wouldn't I follow through?"

Durham took a deep breath, and then said, "Other than you becoming queen, we also had to make a big concession to come to a compromise about the bodies."

"What kind of compromise?" Hollister asked, his eyes narrowed with suspicion.

"The council has voted to destroy the travel center and close the portal. There will be no more travel between dimensions," Phaedra confessed.

"We didn't even know that was on anybody's agenda," Gigandet confessed apologetically. "They caught us off guard."

"That means…I won't be able to come back," Corey said, close to tears. Phaedra put an arm around his shoulder, comforting him like our mother would have.

"There's no way to change their minds?" Leela asked.

Durham shook his head. "They were very adamant that this is what their voters want, and that if we take it to a public vote, it will happen regardless. So, we decided to get something out of it—the release of the bodies. They believe the only group who will have issue with closing the portal will be the Strikers."

"I saw them protesting once," Leela said. "They're the ones fighting for public access to travel?"

Durham nodded. "They will not be happy with this decision."

"Why do they want to close the portal?" Corey asked, almost whined actually.

"They want to ensure that guns or any other corrupting material or people cannot enter Antonia from your dimension."

"If I come from such a corrupt place…" I rolled my eyes, "how can they accept me as their queen?"

Gigandet cleared his throat. "I'm going to be honest—they're only accepting you so their lives will be preserved," he said. "You, and any other bodies who choose to stay here, will have a lot of prejudice to overcome."

"So, that's an option?" Hollister asked. "The slaves can choose to stay here?"

"Potentially, yes," he said. "The council is allowing that option, but not expecting many, if any, of them to choose it. Durham will announce all of this after the coronation. That is, if you still want to go through with the coronation, if you still want to stay here knowing you could never go home again."

Durham gave Gigandet a hard look. Gigandet was willing to let me off the hook, but Durham wanted me on the throne to help carry out his plans. Corey turned his face away and sniffled, trying to hold back tears. I looked from him to Leela, who was maintaining a blank stare, not wanting to manipulate my decision in any way. I figured that although the medical student in her would want me to stay and end the sickness, the sister in her would have doubts—but she didn't show it.

"It's the only way for the bodies to be set free," Durham said, wanting to convince me, reminding me of the cost.

Leela finally reacted, saying, "Then you have to stay. It will help the greatest number of people—our people and their people." Hollister was nodding in agreement as she spoke. Their moral compasses were good, and I had always trusted them to make the best decisions.

So, I acquiesced. "Okay, I'll stay," I said as I stood. "I'm tired," I added as I excused myself. I needed to be alone. I normally didn't hide my tears, but in that moment, I didn't want their eyes on me while I cried, heartbroken that I would never again have a conversation with my dad or be wrapped in his big bear hugs, sad that I would never hold Annabelle or see the woman she would become.

I went to bed anxious that night. Antonia wasn't welcoming me as their queen—they were tolerating me—and I harbored an anger toward the people for not appreciating the sacrifices I was making for them. At the same time, I felt within my heart an intense pressure to win them over. Hollister didn't feel the same; his heart was harder toward the people. He didn't care if he pleased them—they had supported a system of kidnapping, bondage, forced labor, and in the case of my mother, murder. He had compassion, but held no qualms about doing the right thing regardless of public opinion.

We woke with the dawn, and I couldn't eat anything because my stomach was full of nerves. Leela helped me get dressed in a simple white satin gown, while she wore one of the red resistance uniforms. They wanted to make sure she was recognizable as the same woman from the broadcast. They wanted the people to see both of us in the same place at the same time, so they would never have any doubts about the two of us. She, Hollister, and Durham would stand on the palace steps, but there wouldn't be a crowd for the coronation, not like there had been for Gigandet and Elodie's forced wedding. Security didn't know how a crowd would respond, and not having enough soldiers in the royal guard—so many of them imprisoned—they decided not to open the meeting quarter. The ceremony would be broadcast to the living and working quarters, and we requested screens to be set up and available for viewing by all slaves as well. They deserved to witness the moment they would officially be set free.

"Do you feel like Hollister or I forced you to do this?" Leela asked as she fastened a necklace around my neck. "No matter what, you can still change your mind."

I shook my head. "The decision's been made. It's what's best. I just want to get on with it."

She wrapped her arms around my shoulders and squeezed me from behind. Suddenly, the horrible siren blared throughout the city. Leela jumped back. "What's that?" she asked with concern.

"That's what we have to hear every time there's a broadcast."

She grimaced. "You need to change that. Get them to play a beautiful melody or something," she joked. I forced a smile. I knew she was trying to lighten my mood. But this was no light thing—it was serious.

We rushed down the stairs to the great hall. The massive wood doors were being held open, and Gigandet and Durham were already on the veranda. Hollister was waiting for me though, dressed in an all-white suit of his own. He would not be crowned or given the title of king—at least not today—but he would be introduced as my husband and co-leader.

Gigandet's personal guard, Allen, ushered us outside and into our positions as the siren went silent. The current monarch stood behind a podium, a different one from the one Whirl had used. Gigandet didn't want any reminders of the man who'd done so much damage in just a few days.

The cameraman gave him a signal, and he began to speak. "Good morning. By now, I hope you have all had a chance to read the paper, to be informed about the true events and details from the past two weeks. I come before you this morning to renounce my claim to the throne and to pass it to one more worthy than I am. She is relinquishing her home and her family to do a great service for our people. You have been introduced to her in the paper, but let me present to you in person, Laney Sachtleben Glaske," he gestured to me, "as an official citizen of Antonia." It made me smile to hear my maiden name and Hollister's last name together, the way I'd been imagining it for years. Gigandet continued, "I also declare her husband, Hollister Glaske, an official citizen. They have both taken oaths of loyalty, and I trust they will work together with the council to govern Antonia with integrity."

Allen came forward with a clear glass box. It seemed like an emotional moment between him and Gigandet as his sovereign removed his crown and placed it in the box. Allen had made it clear to everyone that he would continue to serve Gigandet the rest of his days. We would be assigned our own personal security team, but Allen would not be a part of it. He would go with his king. When he returned to his place against the stone wall, another guard came forward—at first, I did not recognize him, but then realized it was Etienne. Hollister had told me Etienne had decided to remain in Antonia and serve us, but I didn't know in what capacity. However, it became clear as he stepped forward with a glass box of his own that he would be our Allen. Gigandet reached into the box and pulled out a stunning gold crown encrusted with clusters of multicolored jewels and set it on my head. He turned to the camera and said, "I present to you your queen."

From far away, in the living or working quarters, there was a faint sound—the people were cheering, at least some of them. My heart fluttered with hope. Perhaps it would be okay here. Perhaps they could accept me as their own. Hollister ascended two steps and offered me his arm, and we moved to the side, our backs against the palace wall, as Durham came forward to give his announcements. I held my breath, nervous about how they'd be received.

"Good morning, fellow citizens," he began from behind the podium. "For those who do not know me, I am Councilman Durham. I have longed for many years to see all of you have a representative government, and that day has finally come." There were more faint cheers. "The council members you elected had their first meeting last night, and I am here to tell you of two very important decisions we've made, decisions that will change the course of Antonia's future. Things will be different now in Antonia. Things will be better.

"First, the council had decided it is time for Antonians to depend on ourselves. All bodies will be released from service, and Antonians will be trained in their places. More information will follow regarding this process. We desire for the transition to be as smooth as possible." There weren't cheers anymore, but instead what seemed to be angry shouts. Phaedra and a few others had been stationed in the living and meeting quarters so they could report back to us on how things were *really* received, what the atmosphere was really like among the people. But they didn't have to report. The people were making their voices heard. "I know this is a hard announcement to hear, but we as a people have depended on other people for far too long. It is time for us Antonians to stand on our own."

He was making it about them when it wasn't about them. It was about us. I knew he was trying to calm the crowds, to convince them this was a good decision, but I really wanted him to confess that they'd all been wrong, that they never should have kidnapped and enslaved other human beings, that it was criminal. I wanted to push him aside and tell them that they weren't just *bodies*, that they were people, and that my mother had died because of them. I could tell from Hollister's clenched jaw he was feeling the same things. But, we both remained motionless and emotionless. *Change will take time*, I kept telling myself. I would have to earn their respect before they would listen to my voice.

"The second decision made by the council you elected is to end all light travel, to destroy the travel center's power grid and close the portal between dimensions. It will ensure our protection from outside influences, like the recent events we all experienced." The shouts of anger were quieter this time, barely audible, probably only coming from the small group of Strikers they had mentioned, the ones who wanted the freedom to travel. The other council members must have been right—this seemed to be something most Antonians desired. Yet it would forever separate me from my family. Every second the crown felt heavier upon my head; I feared they would not be an easy people for me to lead. At that exact moment Hollister gave my hand a squeeze, a reminder I wouldn't be doing it alone.

The ceremony was over, the announcements through, the broadcast ended. My new life had begun.

That evening, Hollister stood behind me with his arms wrapped around my waist, as we looked out from our balcony, watching the sun cast shadows over the city, the place that would become our home.

"What are you thinking?" he asked.

"I'm thinking…this life is going to be nothing like we ever imagined."

CHAPTER 25
(LEELA)

It was time for us to go home. All of us from my hometown, except for Laney and Hollister. . . and my mother. On my way to the science facility, I stopped in the fields to listen as Hollister spoke to the slaves. He had readily taken on the task of overseeing their transition.

"If you choose to go home, it is up to you to decide what story to tell," he said. "We will not control your narrative. It's already been controlled for far too long. Something to consider though—if you tell the truth about this place, at best you may be ridiculed, at worst you may be committed. There will be no way to prove Antonia exists. This will be the final passage. The travel center will be destroyed, and there will no longer be travel light between the dimensions. It is the only way to ensure nothing like this ever happens again." Hollister waited a moment before continuing. "If any of you choose to stay, you will assimilate into Antonian society and be granted Antonian citizenship."

To our surprise, there actually were ones who wanted to stay, ones who'd been there so long they didn't think there was anything to go home to. Some of them were interested in running the training programs, being able to teach the jobs and skills they'd been forced to perform for decades. Laura and James had come down from the mountains with the members of their community who wanted to go home or return to Antonia. I was grateful to see them one last time, wrapping Laura in an embrace even if she didn't want me to. "Will you be going home to California?" I asked her.

She shook her head with tears glistening in her eyes. "I've lived here almost thirty years. My son was born here…and he died here. I will die here too," she said.

I nodded in understanding. "And you, James?" I asked the man beside her.

"My home is where she is," he said, grabbing Laura's hand, his fingers intertwined with hers.

"We've been granted permission to build a house in the mountains," Laura said. "They want us to grow and manufacture the treatment in large quantities for those who've been infected. We gave some more to the AO on our way here, if you need to get some for Elodie."

As they walked away, Hollister approached. "Hey, I talked privately with everyone from home. They've all agreed to never mention Antonia and to pretend like they can't remember what happened to us."

"It's gonna be quite a town secret," I said. "You think the children can really keep quiet?" He shrugged. "Have they been reunited with their parents yet?" I asked.

For a couple of days the previous week I had stayed at the science facility, comforting the children from my hometown, and making them promises I wasn't sure I could keep, promises about them being reunited with their families. That was before we knew how the council would vote. After two nights with little sleep, Sheldon had sent me back to the palace, insisting I spend whatever time I had left in Antonia with my sister. Durham had assigned him to oversee the facility, so he'd assured me he would watch out for the children.

Hollister nodded. "Sheldon brought them out yesterday morning."

Sheldon. It was time to tell him goodbye as well, and I didn't want to. Ending the light travel was good for our people—they couldn't be kidnapped and enslaved again—but being separated forever from the ones I cared about was hard to accept. Sheldon and I had barely spoken since our descent from the mountains, since the loss of Curwen and the restructuring of Antonia. I berated myself for worrying and wondering if he would be sad to see me go, if he would miss me, even the smallest amount.

The gray concrete science building rose up out of the trees as I entered the clearing in the forest. Most of the scientists had been arrested for the crimes committed there; only a few of the medical staff remained to care for the patients, the ones injured on the mountain. Some of the members from the mountain community had actually attacked a group of Whirl's soldiers; they'd recognized them as guards who'd been cruel to them when they'd been enslaved. So other than Greer being injured, there were a few other casualties.

I entered his private room to find him sitting with the AO, deep in conversation and learning. The AO looked younger and more energized than I'd ever seen him, animated with excitement to have such a good pupil, such a good successor, someone to be the keeper of Antonia's history and pass it on to future generations. Gigandet had already awarded Greer for his loyalty and bravery, and then had released him from his guard duty so he could study to become the next AO.

"I won't be long," I said, apologizing for interrupting them. "I'll be going home tomorrow and wanted to say a final thank you and goodbye."

"You don't need to say anymore thank yous," Greer said. "I've told you before—I was just doing my job, obeying my sovereign."

He always had a way of making me feel little, like he wouldn't have protected me if he hadn't been ordered to. I took a deep breath. At least he was honest. "Will you obey your new sovereign?" I asked him. With the position of the Ancient Ones being reinstated, he would be an advisor to Laney.

"We'll see," he said. He smirked. "I've heard she can be difficult."

"Who told you that?" I asked.

Greer cut his eyes to the doorway behind me where Mara had appeared, carrying a tray of food. She may have started helping care for Greer as a distraction from the loss of Curwen, but a fondness seemed to be growing between them. The AO and I passed a knowing look as we observed them together, bickering and teasing and laughing. But Mara would barely acknowledge my presence. I accepted her coldness just as I had accepted Laura's. They weren't the only ones who blamed me for Curwen's death. I'd always carry it with me. I was grieved he couldn't be there to see that everything had, for the most part, worked out well. His death was the one thing that stopped me from wanting to celebrate the successes. I grabbed the supply of medicine for Elodie, hugged the AO, and waved as I closed the door behind me.

With each step down the dim hallway, I hoped to run into Sheldon, almost too nervous to intentionally seek him out, not sure how to say goodbye to him. When I entered the lobby, I paused to take in all the details, focusing on the fountain where I'd nearly been drowned to death, remembering the weight of Anderson's body on top of mine after Curwen had shot him, his blood mixing with the water. I traced the wall with my fingers until I found the small bullet hole from where I'd intentionally missed Anderson, not wanting to kill anyone.

"What are you doing?" a man's voice—Sheldon's voice—asked.

I spun around, startled, and found him standing in the entrance. Walking toward him and gesturing to the small bag in my hand, I said, "Just came to get more medicine for Elodie…and to tell everyone goodbye. We leave tomorrow."

"I know," he said. "But, you don't need to say goodbye to me."

"Okay…I'll just go then," I said in confusion and turned to leave. I had my answer. He wouldn't miss me.

He laughed softly and grabbed my wrist. "Wait. I didn't mean it like that."

"Then, what did you mean?"

"I'm coming too. With Gibson staying here, I'm going to take over his job at the campground owned by Haleh and her husband. At least, that's the plan, if they'll have me."

First shock and then relief washed over me. We didn't have to say goodbye. But… "But what about Phaedra and Durham?" I asked with concern. "They just lost one son. They can't lose another."

He shook his head slightly. "We've been discussing it for a few days. They're in agreement with my decision."

"Why *have* you made this decision?" I asked, nervous to hear the answer.

He smiled softly, an earnest expression in his green eyes. But as he was about to speak, one of the doctors entered the lobby, calling for his attention. "I'm sorry. I must go," Sheldon said. "This man is going to take over when I leave, and I have a lot to discuss with him before then. I'll see you tomorrow." He gave my hand a squeeze and then disappeared down another hallway with the doctor.

That evening Laney and I sat on the sofa in her room, and when she heard that Sheldon was going with us, she gave me a funny look. "Why is he leaving Antonia to go somewhere he's never been before, knowing he'll never be able to return?"

I shrugged. "I don't know. I asked him this afternoon, but he didn't get the chance to answer."

Her eyes narrowed. "Is there something between you two? Has something happened?"

"Nothing's happened," I said quickly.

"Yet," she added with an insinuating look.

I shrugged again, shaking my head. "I don't know," I said honestly. How did *I* feel? How did *he* feel? "We'll see in time."

"Well, I won't see," she said with tears in her eyes. "I'll be here. I won't get to see who any of you marry. I won't get to be an aunt to your children." She brushed the tears away. "It's okay. I know this was…is the right decision. It's just hard knowing the things I'll miss."

I put my arms around her. "I know. I can just imagine how pretty you and Hollister's babies are gonna be."

"We'll name the first girl after mama," she said with a smile. After a quiet moment, she stood and walked to the dresser. "I've written letters for dad and Corey and Annabelle." Opening a drawer, she pulled them out, and handed them to me. "There are two for Annabelle. One for her now, and one for you to give her when she's older, on her sixteenth birthday. Give Corey his when he turns eighteen."

"Speaking of Corey…do you think he's okay?" I asked. "After killing a man, I mean."

"I knew what you meant," she said. "He acts okay, like himself. But I'm sure we'll all need counseling at some point to deal with everything that's happened." He had been acting like himself. At that moment he was spending time with Hollister, their final hours together.

"I worry he's too obsessed with this place," I said. Even though I knew Corey loved Laney and Hollister and would miss them terribly—probably more than he realized—his behavior and comments had given me the impression he was more grieved about never being able to come back to Antonia. I felt the complete opposite, happy to never see this place again.

"You know that's just how he is," she said without worry. "He gets obsessed with something for a while, then he moves on to something else."

I hoped she was right because Corey's behavior the next morning made me doubt he would ever get over it. He was nothing but protests, angry that we wouldn't let him choose for himself. He wasn't going home without trying every argument. We reasoned with him until we could reason no more, and then we ignored him. I requested that a guard stay with him, so that he wouldn't run off and delay our departure. We would be the first to leave. Then groups of slaves would be sent home through the rest of the week.

Laney had asked if I was scared to travel back through the light because of the pain I'd experienced the first and only time I'd traveled. I'd barely slept in anticipation of it, mentally preparing myself. But any pain would be worth it to go home. We met in the field behind the palace, just as we had before. Sheldon was already there, talking with Durham, Phaedra, and Mara, who glared at me. Only then did it cross my mind that not only did she blame me for Curwen's death, but might also hold me responsible for Sheldon leaving. "Give this to my sister, and make sure she takes good care of you," I heard Phaedra telling him.

Corey stood beside me, his arms crossed. "This really isn't fair," he muttered.

"Nobody has ever taught you that life is fair," I said. "You are fourteen. You don't get to decide where you live, especially when it's a whole 'nother dimension."

"I could at least stay longer."

"Corey," Hollister said sharply. "I don't want my last words to you to be harsh. You're going home in a few minutes. Say no more about it." My brother looked like he might cry, and Hollister pulled him in for a bear hug. Laney gathered all four of us into an embrace. There were no words left to speak, and after a minute, we separated—Laney and Hollister walked back toward the palace with Durham, Phaedra, and Mara, leaving just the three of us in the middle of the green field.

"Are you both ready?" Sheldon asked us. I nodded, while my brother grunted. "We'll end up in a clearing near the cabin. I've got a map we can follow from there."

"We won't need a map," Corey said with attitude. "I can lead the way."

I grabbed both of their arms, with a tight grip on Corey's, afraid he would try to stay behind like I had. Almost as though he'd read my mind, Sheldon said with a smirk, "You're not letting go this time."

We all stared at our family members waving to us from the courtyard steps as Sheldon pressed the button on the transporter. I closed my eyes tight as soon as I saw the light shooting out of the sky, steeling my body to feel the pain. But there was nothing except a warm tingling on my skin, as Laney had described. As soon as it had begun, it was over. When I opened my eyes, it was night, a clear, starry night, and the air was cooler. Corey shook his arm free from my clutch. Sheldon didn't. He looked at me with concern. "How do you feel? Are you okay?" he asked.

I smiled and nodded. "It wasn't bad this time. I don't know why…"

"We don't have to know why," he said. "I'm just glad you're good."

Corey had already taken off. "Let's go, y'all!" he hollered back at us.

In the dark, my brother led the way with his flashlight bobbing through the woods. "Just follow the creek," he instructed. We didn't have far to go, and soon I saw a cabin with its porch light on. I smiled, imagining they knew we were coming because of Annabelle's visions. Before we even reached the front steps, the door was thrown open and Annabelle flew out. I knelt so she could fall into my arms, and she nuzzled her face in my neck as she'd done since she was a baby. "I like your hair this color," she whispered. I picked her up as I stood, and my father came near and wrapped us both in his strong, warm embrace. He pulled Corey in too.

When we finally pulled away, Sheldon approached and shook hands with my father. "It's good to see you again, Dan," he said.

"You too, son," my father said. "Thanks for bringing them back to me. Are you staying here, then?"

Sheldon nodded. "Yes. I'll call Haleh in the morning, introduce myself, and explain things to her."

We stayed at the cabin for two days, waiting to hear that our friends and neighbors had been returned to our hometown. Hollister had said they would be sent home shortly after our own departure, and Annabelle's vision let us know when it happened before the nightly news report did. We packed our bags and prepared to make the long hike home early the next morning, after Haleh arrived to pick up Sheldon.

When she pulled up out front, I peeked through the window; she really was Phaedra's identical twin. "Your aunt's here," I called to Sheldon. They were all sitting around the table finishing breakfast.

He came up beside me and looked out at her as she walked toward the cabin. "I've never had an aunt before."

"They're the best," I said with a smile. "Go out and meet her."

He met her on the steps. They hugged and talked for several minutes before he brought her inside. "I'm sorry to intrude," she said. "May I use your restroom?"

"Of course," my father said. "You're not intruding. You're welcome to what's left of breakfast also, if you'd like."

"Hey, Haleh," Corey said, "can you believe I went to Antonia?"

She gave him a stern look. "No, and you won't believe how mad I was when I found out." Corey just laughed. When Haleh disappeared down the hallway, Sheldon gestured for me to go outside with him.

"Is everything okay?" I asked as he shut the door behind us.

He nodded. "Yes. I just wanted to give you something."

His backpack was out in the yard with the rest of our stuff. I followed, wondering what he could possibly have to give me. Should I have gotten him something?

"Remember when we were at the black market and we saw Curwen's books there?" he asked. I nodded. "Remember how you pointed out your mother's favorite, and I said it was mine too?" I nodded again. "Well, I went back and bought it for you." He reached into his bag and pulled out the very old and worn copy of *Quo Vadis*.

I took the book firmly in my grasp for a moment, feeling its broken spine and tracing the engraved letters, but then I pressed it into his chest. "You should keep it. It's the first book Curwen let you read. It was his, and now it's yours."

Tears filled his eyes, and he tried to blink them away, but they came faster and harder until his body heaved with sobs. I held him and let him cry. His brother, his closest friend, had died, and he was only just beginning to let himself feel the pain. After a minute our breathing synced—in, out, in, out—and his shoulders relaxed. When he pulled away, he wouldn't look at me, embarrassed by his unrestrained emotion. "I'm sorry," he said. "This is not how I imagined this would go."

I cupped his face in my hands, wiping his tears away with my thumbs, forcing him to look at me. I smiled and said, "It's okay. If I've learned anything, it's that things rarely happen as we imagine they will."

Just then, the front door opened. "Is everyone ready?" my father asked.

Sheldon turned away quickly as everyone came outside, kneeling to put the book back in his bag and hide his face from the others. I squeezed his shoulder and stepped between him and them. "Yep," I said. "We're ready."

"Good," Haleh said. "We need to get back to the restaurant before the lunch rush. Good luck with everything, y'all, and call us if you need anything."

Sheldon tossed his bag in the backseat, shook hands with my father and Corey, and then gave me a hug. As he hopped into the passenger seat, I asked, "You'll come visit?"

He smiled broadly through the rolled-down window. "You couldn't keep me away."

We watched until they disappeared around the bend in the gravel driveway before picking up our bags and heading out—just the four of us. Our family was no longer whole, but we were going home.

9 780578 668048